Praise for

The Baron's Quest
"...simmers...a fantastic reading interlude."
—*Rendezvous*

A Warrior's Way
"Ms. Moore is a genius of the genre...5★s."
—*Affaire de Coeur*

"...a touching tale of a rugged, yet gentle knight who
awakens a staid Norman lady's heart to the wonders
of life..."
—*Romantic Times*

Praise for Deborah Simmons

"Simmons guarantees a page-turner..."
—*Romantic Times*

The Devil Earl
"GOLD 5★s."
—*Heartland Critiques*

Taming the Wolf
"What an adventure! Funny, challenging and
exciting...5★s."
—*Affaire de Coeur*

Dear Reader,

This month, we are delighted to bring you a new concept for Harlequin Historicals—our first in-line short story collection, *The Knights of Christmas*. Three of our award-winning authors, Suzanne Barclay, Margaret Moore and Deborah Simmons, have joined forces to create a Medieval Christmas anthology in this heartwarming collection. We hope you find these wonderful tales spread cheer, not just at this special season, but all year long.

Known for her moving and dramatic Westerns, award-winning author Susan Amarillas's new book, *Wild Card,* is the story of a lady gambler who is hiding in a remote Wyoming town, terrified that the local sheriff will discover she's wanted for murder in Texas.

Talented newcomer Lyn Stone is back with her second book, *The Arrangement,* a unique and touching story about a young female gossip columnist who sets out to expose a notorious composer and winds up first agreeing to marry him, *then* falling in love with him. And Kit Gardner's *The Untamed Heart,* a Western with a twist, has a refined English hero who happens to be an earl, and a feisty, ranch hand heroine who can do anything a man can do, only better.

Whatever your tastes in reading, we hope you enjoy all four books, available wherever Harlequin Historicals are sold. And the best of all seasons to all of our readers.

Sincerely,

Tracy Farrell
Senior Editor

Please address questions and book requests to:
Harlequin Reader Service
U.S.: 3010 Walden Ave., P.O. Box 1325, Buffalo, NY 14269
Canadian: P.O. Box 609, Fort Erie, Ont. L2A 5X3

THE KNIGHTS OF CHRISTMAS

Suzanne
BARCLAY

Margaret
MOORE

Deborah
SIMMONS

Harlequin Books

TORONTO • NEW YORK • LONDON
AMSTERDAM • PARIS • SYDNEY • HAMBURG
STOCKHOLM • ATHENS • TOKYO • MILAN
MADRID • WARSAW • BUDAPEST • AUCKLAND

ISBN 0-373-28987-1

KARA'S GIFT
Copyright © 1997 by Carol Suzanne Backus

THE TWELFTH DAY OF CHRISTMAS
Copyright © 1997 by Margaret Wilkins

A WISH FOR NOEL
Copyright © 1997 by Deborah Siegenthal

CONTENTS

KARA'S GIFT

Suzanne Barclay

Chapter One

Scottish Coast, October 1192

Icy rain fell in sheets from a leaden sky.

Duncan MacLellan didn't think he'd ever felt anything so wonderful. Standing in the prow of the rowboat, he tilted his face upward and sighed. "Ah, there's nothing like good, honest Scots rain to wash a man clean after all these years in the heathen desert."

"By God's toenail, it's so cold my arse is freezing to the seat," grumbled Angus MacDougal.

"Angus," Duncan chided.

His companion in arms snorted. "I'm sure God will understand the extremities that cause me to use his name in vain. Damn, if you aren't the only grown man I know who takes his faith so serious-like."

"'Tis what kept me alive these past three years among the Infidels." That and the determination to return to claim Janet Leslie for his bride, he reminded himself. By his own might and God's will, he was only days away from doing just that...at long last.

"Pity more of those who took up the cross weren't as honorable and unswerving in the loyalty to God as Duncan," Father Simon chimed in from his seat in the back of the boat. In contrast to the two brawny knights, he was a thin man, his bald pate still peeling from the desert sun. "Our holy enterprise might not have been such a dismal failure."

"We did not fail," Angus exclaimed. "King Richard negotiated a treaty with that foul Saladin, granting Christian pilgrims safe use of the coastal ports."

"The cost was too high on both sides," Duncan muttered. The memory of the terrible massacre at Acre, the slaughter of the Infidel hostages by England's Good King Richard still infuriated him. There was no excuse for such wanton savagery. Honorable men did not make war on unarmed folk.

"You've gone all queer about the mouth again, Duncan," Angus muttered. He frowned at the thick bandage visible beneath Duncan's mail. "Is your wound paining you again?"

"It aches a bit, nothing more." The slicing scimitar that had cleaved open his shoulder might have ended his life but for the timely aid of the nursing brethren of the Knights of the Order of St. John of Jerusalem.

"You should have stayed abed another week as the Hospitallers suggested," Angus said. "You're pasty as the sails of that cog what brought us home. And none too steady on your legs."

"I'm fine." Mentally Duncan crossed himself and pledged to repent the lie as soon as he reached Threave Castle. "If I weave a bit, 'tis the motion of the ship. Not the lingering effects of the fever. Seeing my Janet again, knowing we can finally wed will restore me as none of the brothers' potions could. Truth to tell, I was loath to tarry longer among strangers when I knew you two were leaving." Instinctively his hand strayed to the pouch hidden beneath his thigh-length tunic. Stitched into it was a fortune in large rubies. The Templars had handled that transaction, exchanging the heavy plunder Duncan had amassed for the more portable gems.

Angus grunted. "I hope your lady appreciates the risks you took to come home to her a wealthy man."

"She will." Duncan looked toward the land. A fine mist shrouded the port of Carlisle. He recalled the jumble of docks and squalid buildings only vaguely from the day over three years ago when he'd set sail. But he knew right well the road from there to Threave Castle some eighty leagues distant. Threave Castle and Janet. "More important, her father will give his blessing to our marriage."

"Three years is a long time for a woman to stay faithful. How do you know she's not found another?"

"Because we are promised to each other. Janet would not go back on her word any more than I would. Even her father must respect the vow, for 'twas sworn on a holy relic."

"Men do not always honor such things," Angus said.

"Niall Leslie will." Niall, laird of Threave and his father's third cousin, was a man of his word. "Even though he considers me worthless, Janet is his fourth and last daughter. He promised her mother before she died that Janet could choose her own husband. She chose me." The idea that someone as perfect as Janet wanted him still awed Duncan.

"Well, I hope you're right," Angus said, "else you've wasted three years of celibacy for naught."

"She said she'd wait for me. Could I do any less?"

"Aye, well, 'tis different for men than it is for women. Men have urges. Or were you blind to those dark-eyed lasses."

"Pagan women." Duncan's lip curled. Dark exotic creatures with sultry eyes and undulating hips. Many a Crusader had fallen prey to their seductive lures. Duncan had looked and lusted, but he'd not succumbed. He was made of sterner stuff, his self-control strong as tempered steel, thanks to the hard lessons beaten into him by Cousin Niall. Anxious as he was to see Janet, he was almost as anxious to watch Cousin Niall's face when he beheld the fortune Duncan had garnered.

Cousin Niall would not be calling him worthless scum or son of a harlot. Not when he beheld Duncan, wearing the Crusader's cross on his chest, his hands filled with jewels.

The prow of the boat came to a grating halt on the rocky coast. The sailors tumbled out and began to haul it up. As Duncan stepped ashore, his legs nearly buckled.

"Here now..." Angus grabbed hold of his arm to steady him. "You best take a room at the inn and rest up a bit till you've got your strength back."

Father Simon hurried over to prop up his other side. "I could delay my journey to the monastery if you like."

"Nay." Duncan straightened and gently pulled free of their well-meaning hands. He hated being weak, hated asking another for help. He'd been on his own, more or less, since his mother drank herself to death when he was ten and Cousin Niall had grudgingly taken him in.

"'Tis my Christian duty," Cousin Niall had proclaimed. But he'd made it very clear that Duncan was a most unwelcome burden. And a tainted one at that. That his favorite daughter had championed Duncan had made Cousin Niall all the more mean and spiteful...when she wasn't looking, of course.

"I'll be fine, Angus," Duncan said. "I've coin enough to buy a swift horse and a thick cloak to replace this rag."

"You know where I'll be," Father Simon said. "Should you be in need of help, send word to me."

"Or to me," Angus added.

Duncan nodded, knowing he'd do neither. Though they had been to hell and back together in the past three years, he couldn't let down his guard, even with them. He'd even hated being tended by the Hospitallers.

They parted company at the edge of town. A week or so, Duncan figured, and he'd be at Threave, basking in

Janet's gentle love and watching her father eat his nasty words.

The fever came on him two days later, sneaky as an Infidel warrior. At first, he thought the weather was growing warmer. So warm he threw back his cloak and let the damp air cool his body. His mind drifted, back to Janet and the day he'd left Threave. How beautiful she'd looked, neat and serene as a Madonna in a crisp blue gown that matched her eyes. Those eyes were red from weeping, but she'd done her grieving in private.

Bless Janet, his calm, sweet Janet, who never uttered a harsh word or a hasty one. They'd deal well together. They'd not shout and storm as his parents had. Nor would she disgrace him with her wild ways as his mother had after his father's death.

The land began to heave and buckle. He had trouble staying upright in the saddle. And it was hot. So hot he fancied he was camped at the gates of Jerusalem. Mayhap this was all a dream, and he was not back in Scotland.

Alarmed, he roused and glanced about. The terrain was rugged as the Highlands of his mother's birth, mountain peaks leaping from the rolling hills like giant beasts braying at the sky. Damn, but they were green. This must be Scotland, for no other place had such rich color. He saw the river then, rushing by but a few yards from the road. If he stopped for a moment to bathe his face, he'd feel better.

Duncan swung down from the saddle. His feet touched the ground, his legs buckled. This time there was no strong right arm to catch him. He snagged hold of his horse's stirrup, groaning as pain ripped through barely healed muscles. When the world stopped spinning, he crawled to the riverbank and splashed water over his burning face.

Cool. Cool as the chaste kiss he'd given Janet when he'd ridden off on Crusade. Over the frenzied rush of the river, he heard a low, feral growl.

Dogs, he thought idly.

Looking about, he spied a dozen dark shapes emerging

from the woods a hundred yards away. Cousin Niall's hounds come to greet him. He stretched a hand out and waited while the animals slowly worked their way toward him.

Not dogs, he saw as they drew closer.

Wolves!

Duncan tried to stand, but his feet slipped and he went down, striking his head. Darkness closed over him.

Wolves!

Kara Gleanedin stopped and turned in a circle.

The sun was just disappearing behind the ring of mountains that surrounded Edin Valley on all four sides. Steep and forbidding on the outside, the mountains gave way to lush, rolling slopes inside the long glen that had been her clan's home for generations. From her vantage point atop the pass that guarded it, she glanced down the valley.

Long shadows crept out from beneath the trees that covered the mountains. But the only thing moving on the grassy hillsides were the folk of Clan Gleanedin, laughing and playing as they stacked wood for the Samhuinn fires that would be lit three nights hence.

"What is it?" Eoin drew his long knife.

"Wolves."

"Inside Edin?" It wasn't unheard-of. Though the outside cliffs were too steep for men to climb, an occasional wolf was known to venture within to raid the tasty flocks of sheep that grazed on the slopes.

"I'm not sure." Kara looked into the small fire beside the hut where the guards sheltered in inclement weather. Her gift—the portents that sometimes came to her—could not be summoned at will. But the feeling was so strong.

There, in the leaping flames, she saw them again. A pack of dark-furred beasts slinking across the field toward the river. Their quarry...

Kara's eyes widened as the figure in the flames came clearer. A man lay on the bank of the river that flowed past the mouth of the valley. The sun glinted on his silver mail so he seemed to glow from within. His head was bare, black hair plastered to his skull. As she watched, he tried to rise, slipped and fell back, his fingers clutching the mud.

The wolves howled in glee, their faces...

Faces?

"Not wolves!" Kara exclaimed. "MacGorys in their wolf-skin capes." She ran from the fire and the images she'd seen there. Her coarse woolen skirts swirled about her bare legs as she raced to the spot where they'd tied their horses.

Eoin kept pace beside her. "You've had a vision?"

"Aye. There's a man on the flatlands beside the river. He's hurt or wounded." As she spoke, she swung onto her shaggy mount. "There's a pack of MacGorys circling him."

Eoin caught her reins. "It could be a trap."

"Mayhap." The MacGorys had tried most everything to conquer them, but the valley was protected from without by stout natural defenses. "Nay. He's not one of them."

"How do you know?"

"I just do." There was no logical explanation for her gift, except that all the women of her family had been special in some way. "Quick, gather the men."

"Wait!" Eoin called.

"There's no time." Kara wheeled her horse toward the pass. Behind her, the others scrambled to catch up.

Heart in her mouth, Kara charged through the natural tunnel that bored through the mountain, the only way into the valley. A hundred frantic paces later, she emerged into the twilight on a high cliff above the river. Looking below and to the left, she scanned the far bank.

Her eyes caught on a flash of silver and held.

"There! There he is!" Setting her bare heels into the mare's ribs, she sent them careening down to the river in a hail of small stones. The ford lay just ahead. She splashed across it just as the MacGorys began to run. Hide capes flapping about them like great black wings, they hurtled toward the figure prone on the riverbank.

Too late. She was going to be too late.

An arrow whirred over Kara's head, struck the lead MacGory in the throat and took him down. His fellow fiends turned, stared at Kara and her clansmen, then changed direction, coming toward them. Their obscene battle cry sent the birds screeching from the trees.

Eoin howled back a challenge of his own. "See to your stray, Kara," he called. "We'll carve up these—" The slur was lost in the pounding of hooves and the shouts of two score Gleanedins bent on revenge for the MacGorys' first raid six months ago and the maiming of their laird.

Kara muttered a hasty prayer for their safety, then raced the short distance to the fallen man. He was stretched out facedown in the mud, a dirk clutched in one fist.

Was this some trap? Or did he cower in fear of the wolves?

"You can get up now, the wolves are but a pack of stinking MacGorys, and Eoin's seeing to them." When he didn't respond, she gingerly nudged his hip with her bare foot. He didn't twitch a muscle. Unconscious, she decided.

"Damn, you're a big one." He must be well over six feet tall, and weigh sixteen stone, at least.

Mayhap he'd hit his head and conked himself out.

Kara hunkered down beside him, staring at the blue-black waves of hair clinging to his neck. Warily she felt beneath his jaw to see if he lived. The jolt of his pulse against her flesh made her own heart stumble. She jerked her hand back, fingers tingling. "What the devil?"

The man remained silent, motionless. Had she imagined the odd sensation? Kara shook her head. Never mind. She had to get him away from here, and she'd not do it alone.

"Hello. Are you awake in there?" She tapped his back. The metal links of his shirt felt cold and slippery to the touch. What an odd garment. She prodded him again, harder.

"Argh! Are you trying to kill me?" He rolled over, coming to rest on his back, an arm flung over his face.

"Nay, I but wanted to make certain you were unhurt."

"By poking me with hot pincers and leaving me in the desert to be eaten by wolves?"

"Wolves." Kara whipped her head around, spotted the MacGorys fleeing across the grassy field with Eoin and her clansmen in swift, loud pursuit. "You need not worry about the wolves, they've been routed. What is your name?"

"Duncan. Hot...damn me, but it's hot."

Hot? A brisk October wind whistled down the mountain slopes, icing Kara's skin beneath her simple skirt and tunic. "Are you sick?" she asked warily.

"Course not. Never sick."

"Wounded, then?"

"Antioch."

That must be a place, though not one around here. "Where on your body, Duncan."

"Shoulder."

She ran practiced hands over him and felt the thick bandage on the left one and pressed gently.

He groaned, a low, anguished sound.

"Does that hurt?"

"Nay. I will be fine. Just...just let me be."

"Men, never wanting to admit you're hurting," Kara scoffed, on familiar turf now. She touched his cheek. "Well, you are burning up with fever and like to die if you stay here. Nor have you the strength to rise without help."

He scrubbed a hand over his face. In the gathering dimness, it was all stark planes and shadowy hollows, wide forehead, sunken eyes, straight nose and strong chin. "Don't need help. Don't want help."

"Too bad, Duncan. We seldom get what we want."

"Kara!" a voice called. Aindreas, captain of the night guard, was just coming on duty. "Hob says the lads are hunting MacGorys and ye've a hurt man. Do you need help?"

"Aye, bring torches and blankets," she shouted back. "We'll need to rig a litter to carry him."

"Nay." Her patient struggled to sit. She pushed him down with one finger and kept him there till the men came. As the torches closed in to bathe the area with golden light, she got her first good look at Duncan.

"Gods!" Kara exclaimed.

"Do you know him?" Aindreas drew his long knife and waved it in the stranger's direction.

Only he was no stranger to her. "Put that away," Kara said sharply. "We need no protection from him."

"Who is he?"

"The man who will save us."

"Really?" Aindreas leaned closer, looking appropriately impressed. "The one you saw in the Beltane fires this May?"

"The very same." She sank down on her knees beside Duncan. "I am sorry I poked you."

He glared up at them, his scowl deepening. "Heathens."

Aindreas stiffened. "See here, now, no call to—"

"Pagan barbarians," Duncan muttered. "Got to get away." He surged to his feet with surprising strength for a man half-gone with fever.

"Duncan, let me help—"

He flung Kara's hand off. "No help." Wavering, he turned and started for his horse. "Got to get away." What he got was two steps before his legs gave way.

Aindreas caught him and lowered him to the ground.

"Filthy pagans," Duncan mumbled.

Aindreas glanced at Kara. "He's an odd way about him for a man what's come to save us."

"Nevertheless, he has. The vision said so, and my visions never lie." Kara rose with all the majesty she could muster, trying not to let on that Duncan's vehemence had shaken her. "He will stay, and he will help us."

Duncan was still protesting when Aindreas and the others carted him off.

It did not bode well for Kara's plans.

Chapter Two

"Untie me," Duncan ordered through clenched teeth.

"You are not well enough to be up and too stupid to realize it," his captor said cheerily. She stood gazing out of the arrow slit that served as a window for the tiny wall chamber where they'd brought him two nights ago.

Duncan recalled little of it, his memories a jumble of wolves and torchlight and desert heat. Nay, that had been a fever dream. But he was recovered. "My fever has broken."

"At dawn this morn," she replied without moving. "But you are still so weak you fell when you tried to rise."

"'Twas no reason to bind me to the bed," he snarled. "I will not do so again."

She turned and cocked her head in his direction. Bathed in the last rays of the setting sun, she resembled some pagan goddess. Her hair was wild and unruly, tumbling about her shoulders and down her back in a riot of dark curls. Where the sun struck them, her tresses glowed red as fine burgundy. Her face was more exotic than beautiful, golden cat's eyes slanting above high cheekbones, a straight nose, full mouth and a stubborn chin that warned of her willful nature.

Even her name was strange and pagan. Kara Guenna, she'd told him she was called. Not Mary or Margaret after

one of the saints. Or even a decent name like Jean or Janet.
Janet, good Lord, she was as different from his cool, neat
Janet as day from night. This Kara was not only dark and
exotic, but immodest. Her coarse skirts came only to her
calves, showing shapely legs.

Staring at her made Duncan's skin grow warm again with
a fever he knew too well. Desire. Deep inside him dwelt a
bad seed Cousin Niall had not beaten into submission.
Something in this wild girl called to the baser nature he'd
inherited from his mother. Gritting his teeth, Duncan pulled
on the ropes binding him to the bedposts. "Let me up."

"You will get up when I say."

A red mist obscured Duncan's vision and he ceased
struggling. "So, I'm a prisoner."

"You are my patient." Her voice was rich and low. Her
hips moved in seductive swirls as she walked toward him.

Damn. Duncan shut his eyes.

"See, this argument has tired you."

Ha. Duncan's eyes flew open at the precise moment she
stopped at his elbow. His nostrils filled with the scent of
her. Not the sour stink of sweat and horses. That he'd have
welcomed. Instead, she smelled of heather. Damn. He'd
dreamed of heather when he lay fevered in the Hospitallers
infirmary. Heather and home. It was almost obscene to
smell it now, underlaid with the sweet muskiness of this
pagan woman.

"I am not tired," Duncan snapped. "I am outraged to
think that you and your…your heathenish clan would way-
lay a Crusader knight returning from the Holy Lands."

"What is a Crusader?" She sat on the bed beside him.

Her scent overwhelmed him. Duncan groaned.

"Did I jostle your wound?" she asked.

Eyes squeezed shut, jaw clamped so tight his teeth ached,
Duncan nodded.

"I am sorry." She slid to the stool she'd occupied when
he'd awakened this morning. "What is a Crusader?"

"You've not heard of them?"

Wisps of curly hair flew about when she shook her head. She was so close he could see the freckles, sprinkled like cinnamon over her nose and cheeks, and the green flecks in her amber eyes. Witch's eyes, he thought. Which explained a great deal but didn't make him feel any easier about lying here.

"We Crusaders are knights who take the cross..."

"What cross? Where do you take it?"

"'Tis a figure of speech," he grumbled. "We lay our hand on the cross, pledge ourselves to the glory of God and go to drive the Infidels from the Holy Lands."

"Oh." Her face fell. "You are a priest?"

"At least you've heard of Christianity."

She straightened. "Despite your slurs, we are not pagans. We...we just happen to follow the old ways, too."

"You cannot be both pagan and Christian."

"Father Luthais doesn't mind, so why should you?"

"There is a priest here." Relief washed through Duncan. "Fetch him to me."

"Nay, I—"

"Fine, I will go to him." He tugged on the ropes.

"He does not dwell among us, but in the priory in Kindo. And cease struggling, you will chafe your poor wrists."

"Do not refer to me as poor." Duncan sucked in air as her fingers grazed his inner wrist, brushing him with fire. It leapt along his veins like lightning igniting a summer sky. Every nerve in his body sizzled, every muscle contracted. Especially those over which it seemed he had no control at all. Thank the heavens for the thick blankets, else she'd have known.

"Stubborn man. I want only to help you."

"Then let me go," he growled.

"And most ungrateful. Father Luthais says we should give thanks to those who do us good."

Lessons in civility from a little pagan. "I am grateful to you for saving me from..." He wasn't exactly certain what.

"MacGorys." She grinned. "Eoin and the lads killed four of the fiends and sent the others fleeing into the hills."

He tried to imagine Janet, who fainted at the sight of blood, speaking of a battle with such relish. "Well, my thanks for your timely arrival. And for tending me through the fever, but I am expected elsewhere and cannot tarry here wi—" He suddenly recalled the pouch with the gemstones. "Where are my things?" he cried, raising his head and glancing about.

"There." She pointed to the far corner, where his sword did indeed lean against the rough stone wall. "We are not robbers."

"That remains to be seen. There was a bag hanging from my belt. It contained my papers and a few coins."

The girl smiled and ran across the room, returning with the leather pouch. "Here is it."

"Loose my hands that I may see all is intact."

She scowled and clutched the purse to her heart. The action pulled her ugly brown gown tight across surprisingly full breasts. "We would not steal from you."

"Why? You've no compunction about tying me up."

She sighed. "Only to save you from harming yourself."

"I have been looking out for myself since I was ten, and I will be the judge of what is right for me."

Tears filled her eyes, magnifying their color. "You have no family," she whispered.

He didn't want her pity. "I have a cousin."

"Surely he—or she—took you in. We've orphans aplenty in Edin, thanks to the scurvy MacGorys, but we look after our own."

"Cousin Niall gave me a home," Duncan said stiffly.

"He was mean to you." She scampered over to the bed and plopped down again, enveloping him in a cloud of heather and woman. "Dinna worry. You have us, now." She stroked his cheek.

Duncan set his teeth against the sudden tightness in his

chest. 'Twas loathing, he told himself. "I do not want you."

"Oh."

She sat back, pain and confusion chasing across her expressive features. Did the girl hold nothing back?

"This is not at all the way it is supposed to be."

"What do you mean?"

Before she could reply, the door opened and the ugliest man Duncan had ever beheld ducked into the low-ceiled chamber. His face was seamed with wrinkles, his nose mashed to one side. Worst of all was the long scar running from his forehead to his right ear. 'Twas a wonder he'd not lost his eye.

"Fergie." The girl launched herself at the man, who enveloped her in a bear hug. "I missed you so." She cupped his cheeks with her hands and gazed adoringly at the battered landscape of his ruined features.

How could she hold that smile? Hardened as he was to battle scars, Duncan could barely stand to look at the man.

"And I you, lass." Fergie kissed the top of her head, then draped a mammoth arm over her shoulder and sauntered to the bed. "Eoin said as how you'd dragged in another stray," he exclaimed, his voice harsh as gravel in a cup.

"He name is Duncan MacLellan. Duncan, this is my uncle Fergie, laird of Clan Gleanedin."

"Why's he trussed up?"

Duncan had had enough of lying about while others stared at him. "Because she's a nasty, bossy little witch," he snapped.

Fergie threw back his gray head and roared with laughter. "That she is." He wiped tears from his eyes.

"I am not, and 'tis for his own good."

"That's what they all say when they want a man to do something he doesn't want to." Fergie winked.

Sensing an ally, Duncan focused his gaze on the man's eyes, for looking at the scars was both impolite and unsettling. "She's tied me up and forced noxious potions down my throat."

"Mmm. Cured you, though, didn't she?"

Duncan grunted.

"Sometimes it's handy having a witch about the place," the girl said airily.

Damn, was she truly a witch? "I've already thanked her for nursing me through the fever. But I really have to leave."

"He's an orphan, Fergie, with no place to go."

Duncan noted she called her formidable uncle by his first name, an honor Cousin Niall had denied his unwanted burden. "My cousin is expecting me." Another lie he'd have to confess. For a man who seldom sinned, he was amassing a large debt.

"His cousin resents him," Kara said.

Duncan started. "How do you know that?"

"I just do."

"Well." Fergie rubbed a gnarled hand over the scar on his forehead. "I'll admit another fighting man would be welcome."

"I won't fight for you," Duncan insisted.

"He will." Kara touched her uncle's hand. "He's the one," she murmured. "The one I saw in the Beltane fires."

"Really?" Fergie's eyes widened, raking Duncan from head to bare feet and back. "Are you sure, lass?"

Kara nodded. "He was wearing the metal shirt and carrying the long dirk." She pointed to the sword in the corner.

"See here," Duncan shouted. "I don't know who you think I am, but—"

"You're the one the gods have sent to save us," Kara said.

Blasphemy. "The hell I am." Duncan jerked on the ropes. "You people are all mad." He tugged again, barely feeling the hemp cut into his flesh. "Mad. Let me go or I'll—"

"Are you sure about this, lass?" Fergie asked again.

"Have my visions ever been wrong?"

Visions. Holy Mother, have mercy. Duncan's heart was pounding so loudly he could scarcely hear. "Filthy pagans."

"He doesn't seem to like us much," Fergie mused. "Hard to imagine him helping us."

"He will."

"I won't." Duncan seethed with rage and frustration.

"Leave it to me, Fergie." Rising on tiptoe, she kissed his scarred cheek. "Was the hunting successful?"

"Aye. We took two roebuck. Dod and the others are skinning them in the courtyard. I should see they don't make a hash of it, but if you need me to stay…"

"Nay. I'll fetch his supper, then we'll discuss things." She gave her uncle a dazzling smile. "Men are always more reasonable on a full stomach."

"Well…" Fergie scowled thoughtfully at Duncan, then shrugged. "You've never failed us yet." He chucked her under the chin, then sauntered out.

Kara turned that brilliant smile on Duncan. "There's fresh rabbit stew and boiled onions for supper. I'll fetch you some."

"I won't stay…even if you ply me with roasted peacocks and almond paste."

"I do not know what those things are, but you will stay."

"You cannot make me stay," Duncan snarled.

"I'll wager I can," said the little witch with a toss of her fiery curls. She walked from the room proud as a queen, her skirts swishing in time to the sway of her hips.

Despite his rage, the sight made an impression on the least discerning organ in Duncan's body. Cursing it, and females in general, he went to work on the ropes. Imprisonment had been Cousin Niall's favorite form of punishment, and Duncan had learned to rework knots at an early age.

He was determined he'd not be here when the witch returned.

Had she made a mistake? Was he not really the one?

Kara tapped a finger against her mouth.

He had not looked as large in her vision, nor as angry. In her vision, he'd smiled and laughed and looked on her with approval, not revulsion. But the clothes of silver metal and the long dirk were right. And the face...there was no way she could have mistaken it. Duncan had the rough-hewn features of a warrior and the eyes of a lonely child. Those troubled eyes called out to the healer in her. The rest of him, his big, muscular body, his ruggedly handsome face, awakened strong feelings of a different sort. Womanly feelings.

She'd never been drawn to a man before. Oh, she'd laughed and bantered with the men of the clan, and fluttered her lashes in fair imitation of her friend Brighde. But she'd never cared what any man thought of her.

Till now. She minded terribly that Duncan hated her.

Why did he? She'd risked her life to save his, nursed him through two days and nights, yet he sneered at her. Called her pagan and witch as though she were cursed.

Was he truly the one?

Kara stared at the leaping fire in the kitchen hearth. But no vision came.

"Here you are, then. There's more if he can eat it," added Black Rolly. He held out a tray set with a bowl of savory stew, brown bread and a cup of ale. The tray looked tiny in his big, warrior's hands. He'd smashed his leg the same night Fergie had nearly lost his eye. She'd stitched them both up, not daring to hope they'd live. But they were strong and adaptable. With his fighting days over, Rolly had taking up something he liked. Cooking.

"It smells wonderful, but don't be surprised if he can't finish it all. He's still recovering." In his present state of rage, he might refuse to eat at all. She had to do something to change that. How were they to win against the MacGorys if their appointed savior refused to play his part?

She took the tray, then hesitated. In his youth, Rolly had left Edin to ride in Border raids against the English. He'd even been to King William's court in Edinburgh and knew much of the outside world. "Rolly, do you know what a Cru...Crusader is?"

"Aye." He leaned his bad hip against the worktable. "They're knights who've sworn to free Jerusalem from the grip of the Infidels."

"Are they bad people, these Infidels?"

"Worse than the MacGorys. They dinna believe in God."

"Oh."

"And they cut out the hearts of those who do."

Kara gasped. "They must be fierce, indeed. He was wounded fighting them."

"Duncan?"

Kara nodded. "He's a strange man, full of pride and anger. For all he's weak as a new colt, he hates having us do for him. I fear I had to tie him up to keep him from injuring himself, which only made things worse. He thinks we are pagans."

"Some Crusaders have deep religious convictions." Rolly told her briefly about the training a knight went through, and the vow he made before God when he was knighted. "They pledge to protect the weak and vanquish the oppressors."

"That is good, we are being oppressed by the MacGorys. And we did save his life." Kara repeated that as she trudged up the narrow stairs. If the one thing didn't convince him to help, mayhap the other would.

She reached the second floor and found all was dark and shadowy. The torch at the near end of the corridor had burned out again. Poor Dod, Edin's steward, was growing forgetful. When she'd finished with Duncan, she'd set one of Dod's grandsons to replenishing the torches. Covertly, so Dod's pride wasn't hurt.

She nudged the door open with her hip, took a deep breath and pasted on a smile. ''Well, here we are....''

She stopped and gaped at the empty bed.

The savior of Edin Valley had slipped his bounds and fled.

Chapter Three

From his hiding place under the bed, Duncan listened with grim satisfaction to Kara Gleanedin's gasp of dismay. The wood floor was cold on his bare chest and legs, but at least they'd left on his braies when they stripped him. He watched her stomp one foot, the ragged hem of her skirts twitching in agitation. The ripe oath that followed made him scowl. That a woman should know, much less utter such foul phrases.

"Damn and blast." She stalked to the bed.

Had she seen him? Did she guess? He held his breath, wishing he'd had time to get to his sword, but her return had followed his escape by only moments.

Wood rattled on wood as she set a tray down on the stool where she'd sat vigil the past two nights. An unwelcome reminder of the debt he owed her. With one final curse, this time in Gaelic, she bolted from the room. He waited till her angry footfalls had faded away before he gingerly crawled out.

His shoulder throbbed, his legs were wobbly, his mind foggy, but he had no time to indulge such weaknesses. One hand on the rough, unpainted wall, he worked his way to his sword with the determination of a man pursuing the Holy Grail. Gripping the hilt made him feel better. He bent to retrieve the belt coiled neatly on the floor. The pouch was still attached to it.

Knowing he'd not rest easy till he saw the stones, Duncan took a few precious seconds to release the intricate metal clasp and open it. Inside were his few remaining silver coins. The silk lining of the pouch was intact. Then he saw that the stitches in one corner were made with black thread, not the red he'd closed it with when he'd hidden the gems behind the lining.

"Nay!"

He split the threads with the tip of his sword.

Empty!

He swore hoarsely, then tried to suck the words back.

Damn. Damn. Crushing the pouch in his fist, he glanced around the room. There was not much to see, an uncurtained bed with a chest at its foot, a table holding a fat candle and assorted small crocks. Crude woolen tapestries brightened the walls, but there was nothing concealed behind them. 'Twas a moment's work to ransack the chest. It contained a few sets of woman's clothes. Kara's he supposed, for her scent clung to them. But she'd been smart enough not to hide her stolen loot there.

Likely she had it on her person.

Or she'd given it to her uncle.

Duncan spun toward the door, his hand tightening on the sword hilt. With the Gleanedins out beating the brush for him, he'd search their castle. But he needed clothes. Preferably his own. Anger fired his blood, but his skin was cold and pebbled. Snatching a blanket from the bed, he slung it around his waist and over the wounded shoulder like a toga.

The hallway beyond the door was gloomy as a crypt, with only a single torch burning at the far end. He scanned the length with an invader's eye, noting the archway to his left where the stairwell came up, the pair of doors farther down the corridor. To search them, or escape while he could?

In the courtyard outside, he heard shouting and the excited trumpeting of horses. The sounds built to a wave of thunderous hoofbeats, then there was silence. They'd left.

Duncan grinned and headed for the next room.

Fergus Gleanedin, for this could only be his chamber, had few possessions, but what he had was well cared for. A polished claymore hung over the small hearth, where banked coals glowed. The bedside table held a candle and flask of fiery osquebae, the Scots breath of life.

Duncan took a moderate swallow, groaning as the liquid burned down his gullet and exploded into his belly. Ah, he'd missed that. It lent strength to his flagging muscles. False strength, but he'd take what he could get. Kneeling beside the trunk, he picked the lock with the tip of his dirk. Inside lay men's garments, homespun but well made. He set them aside and probed lower, prying into a pouch containing less silver than he had and another with more personal treasures. A bit of waxed thread attached to a steel fishing hook. A ring bearing a crudely fashioned crest. A hunk of amber on a fine gold chain. One side of the ornament was jagged, as though it had been split asunder. Likely the reason it was in here and not about Fergus's neck.

A private person by nature, Duncan found handling someone else's goods put a bad taste in his mouth. But they'd stolen from him. Resolved, he lifted out the last item, a tiny casket. Inside were a few feminine bits of frippery, a small silver brooch. A set of bone hair comb. And the other half of the amber, likewise suspended on a chain. Fergus's wife's necklet? Was she dead, and that was why the laird no longer wore his?

Duncan dropped the necklace. Unease crawled through his belly, and he knew it wasn't the whiskey.

"Enough of this sneaking about," he muttered, replacing each item carefully despite his urgent desire to be free of them. Just because they were a dishonorable pack of thieves was no reason for him to lower his standards. He'd go below, find Fergus and demand the return of his rubies.

Filled with new resolve, and another swig of whiskey, Duncan marched to the door, opened it and stepped into the hall. After the sunlit chamber, it seemed even darker.

"Have you finished pawing through Fergie's things?" drawled a familiar voice.

Duncan spun toward it, sword up, eyes narrowed.

A shadow moved, stepping into the spill of light from the room behind him. Kara, her chin up, her gaze scathing.

"Why aren't you out looking for me?"

"Because I knew you'd never left."

"How?"

"When I got to the bottom of the stairs, I recalled seeing your sword in the room. Only a fool would leave his sword behind, and you do not strike me as a fool. How did you get free?"

"I'm good with knots." He locked his knees to counter a sudden wave of dizziness. "Clever girl. Now what have you done with my jewels?"

"Jewels?" Her alarmed gaze dropped to his crotch. "I didn't know you were wounded there."

"Where? Oh." Duncan felt the heat crawl up his mostly bare chest. Suddenly he was aware of how close they stood, of the faint scent of heather swirling seductively in the air. "'Tis not proper for you to speak of such things."

"You're the one who brought it up."

The word set off an alarming reaction in the very nether parts they were discussing. Duncan shifted and cleared his throat. "Aye, well, 'tis not what I meant and you know it."

"I'm a witch, not a mind reader. Now my mother, Guenna, she always knew what a body was thinking. Very disconcerting."

Duncan blinked. "Stop trying to change the subject. I want my rubies, and I want them—"

"I've not a single clue what they are. Rubies," she added.

"Don't be daft. Everyone knows what rubies are."

"Well, I do not." Her chin was up again, her eyes flashing. "And I'll wager no one else does, either. We dinna see much of the outside world here."

"But—"

"Kara, lass, have you found him?" Fergus's voice echoed hollowly in the stairwell.

"Aye," Kara called, looking back over her shoulder. "He's up here—" The word ended with a squeak as Duncan snagged her and dragged her against him, one arm around her waist.

It was a mistake, for the lower swell of her breasts rested on his forearm and those sensuous hips he'd admired pressed into his. He tried to ignore those sweet curves, but his chilled body greedily savored the heat from hers. Before he could weaken, a herd of Gleanedins clattered up the stairs and crowded into the corridor, Fergus in the forefront.

"Stay back or I'll run her through," Duncan warned. He raised his sword, but kept it well clear of her slender neck, for his arm felt none too steady.

Fergus's battered face went purple. "If you cut her—"

"He won't harm me," Kara said with absolute calm.

"And what is to stop me?"

"Aye, what?" Fergus asked, backed by a sea of white faces.

"His honor. He's a Crusader knight, you know," she said. "Black Rolly says they are bound to show kindness and mercy to women and children. He'll not harm me."

Angered, Duncan spat, "Why should I show you mercy?"

"Well, aside from your knightly vows, I did save your life."

Foiled by the shackles of honor. "So you could imprison me and steal from me?" Duncan watched Fergus's face closely, but could detect no hint of guilt. One of the others, mayhap, but the crowd looked equally baffled.

"We've stolen nothing." Kara sounded earnest, and he

could feel the steady beat of her heart against his forearm. Either she was the coolest liar he'd yet met, or innocent.

"What is it you think we've taken?" Fergus asked.

"Rubies. You do know what they are?" Duncan snapped.

"Aye, and diamonds and pearls, too."

"What are they?" Kara demanded.

"Wee red stones...like glass, they look."

Kara wriggled a bit in his arms and looked up at Duncan. "You'd kill me for a few bits of red glass?"

Duncan shifted away from her. "They're very valuable."

"More valuable than a human life?" Kara asked.

An ugly murmur swept through the Gleanedins.

"Of course not. You're twisting my words."

"Explain it to me, then."

"Could we not remove to the hall and discuss this over a wee dram of whiskey?" Fergus asked silkily.

"He's already been into your whiskey," Kara snapped.

"Has he now?"

Duncan felt that betraying flush wash over him. "I, er..."

"No matter," Kara interjected. "It's back to bed with him. He's taking a chill standing about in naught but a blanket."

"Don't see why with you to warm him," someone called out.

Duncan set his teeth. "You will not talk about me as though I were some idiot child...."

"Then stop acting like one." Kara slipped out from under his arm as slick as a wet fish.

Duncan raised his sword and braced for the onslaught. The Gleanedins gazed back. They were a tough, hard-eyed lot, some bearing scars nearly as grisly as their laird's. They made no move toward him, but would have if Fergus had ordered it.

"For shame. You look like a pack of wild dogs sniffing each other out," Kara snapped. "Now be off about your business and let me tend to mine.'' Taking hold of Duncan's left hand, she gently tugged him toward his chamber. Or rather, hers.

Duncan wanted to resist, but his legs were wobbly, his brain fuzzy. "I won't leave till my property has been returned."

He was going to stay.

Kara's heart soared, but she did her best to hide her elation as she straightened the bottom sheet on the bed. Not only was it impolite to gloat, he was not exactly staying of his own free will. But he was staying...at least till he could find these silly red stones. "Into bed with you." She stood back.

His expression was thunderous. "Turn around."

"What?"

"I have to drop the blanket."

"I've already seen your drawers."

His tanned face turned even ruddier. "Well, I wasn't awake when you were doing the seeing, but I am now."

Outlanders were certainly prudish, Kara thought, but she obligingly faced the window till she heard the ropes supporting the mattress creak. She whirled about just as his long, lean legs disappeared under the covers. "I've sent for a bowl of hot stew."

"I'm not hungry." His belly growled in disagreement.

Kara bit the inside of her lip to keep from smiling. "Well, I am. I'll eat while you talk."

His scowl grew. "I don't want you standing about my bed."

Now was not the time to point out it was her bed. He'd probably leap up—wrapped in a blanket—and refuse the rest he so badly needed. "I thought you wanted to talk about these bits of red glass."

"Rubies."

"Whatever. Why are they so important to you?"

"They are worth several times their weight in gold. You do know what gold is?"

"Aye, and silver, too. We may be a bit isolated, but we're not completely ignorant of what goes on in the outlands." His skeptical look sharpened her tongue. "If you're a wealthy man, why do you not have a dozen men in your tail?"

"I'm not rich by birth. I, er, acquired the rubies in the Holy Land."

"While you were saving it for God?"

"Mmm." He frowned again. "You needn't make it sound as though I'm some loathsome mercenary."

That word she knew. "There's nothing wrong with selling your sword to earn your way."

"Exactly."

"But if these bits, er, rubies, were so valuable, why did you not hire men to help protect them?"

"I did not want to waste a sous on something I could do myself. Of course—" his eyes narrowed "—I did not realize I'd be set upon by a whole clan."

Kara snorted. "I should have left you for the Mac-Gorys."

"The men dressed like wolves?"

"They're a bad bunch, meaner and craftier than a pack of wolves. 'Tis said they delight in torturing a man till he begs for death." Her fists clenched at her sides. "They are responsible for Fergie's scars. He's the last of my line. I lost my parents when I was eleven, and he had the raising of me."

The stark mask dropped away, leaving his face soft and oddly compassionate. "I'm sorry. My father rode off to war when I was eight and never came back."

"And your mother?"

He stiffened. "Died a less noble death two years later."

"Oh." Kara wanted to know why he was so bitter, but his shuttered expression said the topic was closed.

"You're the logical one to have taken them."

"Them?" Kara blinked. "Oh, the rubies."

"Who undressed me?"

"Black Rolly did, but I was here the whole time," she quickly added. "He laid your things in the corner, there, and they've remained so ever since."

"You were with me the whole time?"

She nodded, momentarily baffled by his darkening expression. Then it hit her. "It does make a body feel twitchy knowing someone watched them while they slept. If it's any consolation, I spent most of the time helping you fight the fever."

The lines in his face smoothed. "I must seem ungrateful."

"A bit." She smiled faintly. "But I've never yet known a man who enjoyed being laid low."

A tap at the door heralded the arrival of a kitchen maid with a hot bowl of stew. Kara went to take it from her, mind awhirl with ways to maneuver Duncan into eating. When she turned toward the bed, he smiled ruefully.

"I'd be a fool to starve myself."

"And we agree you're no fool." Kara fairly danced to the bed, placing the tray on his lap with a flourish. "Do you mind if I stay to keep you company?"

"Nay, so long as I'm allowed to feed myself."

Kara plunked down on the stool and tried not to watch as he devoured the stew and bread. 'Twas obvious he was starving, yet he didn't stuff his mouth too full, or chew with it open. Finer manners than some of her clansmen displayed. After he'd wiped the bowl with the last of the bread, she rose and took the tray. "Will you sleep, now?"

He nodded, eyes already closing.

"Good, you need the rest to restore your strength. Swear you won't be so foolish as to leave till you're healed."

His lashes lifted, his expression hard again. "I'm not going till I've got my rubies back."

May you never find them, Kara thought, but that was

selfish. "Mayhap they fell out of your purse down by the river."

"Nay. They were stitched into it. Someone cut the threads and helped themselves to the treasure and stitched it back up."

"Mayhap you did it yourself while in the grip of the fever. You were not in your right mind when we found you. We could go out and look for these stones if we took enough men to guard against a MacGory attack."

"You said the river bordered your land. Do these MacGorys dare raid so close to your territory?"

"Aye, they are a lawless bunch, as fierce as the wolves whose hides they wear into battle. Rumor has it they were driven out of the Highlands and seek a place from which to raid and pillage. They've set their eyes on Edin Valley."

"Are you strong enough to defeat them?"

Kara shook her head. "Thus far Edin's natural defenses, the mountains and the pass, have kept them at bay, but one day that will not be enough. They grow stronger, bolder and more numerous, while we grow fewer and weaker. Too many of our men have fallen in battle." She bit her lip to still its trembling. "I fear we will soon be a clan of women."

Duncan grunted. "Can you not buy men to protect you?"

"With what? We are a poor clan, living simply off the land that has been our home for generations. But we will not give up without a fight. If you were to advise us..."

"Me?" He scowled. "I am through fighting other people's wars. Besides, what could one man do against so many?"

"I do not know for certain, but you figure somehow in Edin's future. I saw a vision in the Beltane fires this spring, and—"

"Vision." He glared at her contemptuously. "'Tis blasphemy to even think such things."

"Why?"

"Because it is. All things are in God's hands."

"I agree," Kara said quickly. "Father Luthais and I have discussed it often. He said such things are mentioned in the Bible and read me the stories of Saint Peter and—"

"Exactly. Saints have visions. Ill kempt lasses do not."

"Ill kempt?" Kara looked down. "My skirt and bodice are made of the finest wool our women can weave." She spotted a small stain where her knee had ground into the mud while she tended his wound. Covering it with her hand, she went on. "My clothes are clean, as are my hands and face. How am I ill kempt?"

"I did not mean you were dirty, only untidy. Your hair flies about in a most unseemly manner instead of being confined to a braid and covered. And...and you are tanned where a woman's skin should be pale. Why, even your nose is freckled from the sun."

Kara self-consciously wiped at the offending spots. "Fergie teases me about them, but they don't wash off."

"Ladies of quality bleach them or cover them with flour."

"Really?" The inference that she was not quality stung nearly as much as being called unkempt. "It sounds messy."

"But ladylike." He closed the subject by shutting his eyes.

Kara tried not to feel hurt or rejected. Duncan MacLellan was not at all the gallant savior she'd imagined. Still if they were to survive, the Gleanedins needed a champion. They needed Duncan. Somehow she had to convince him to help. "Tomorrow or the next day, we could ride out and I'll show you Edin Valley."

He stirred. "I'd welcome a chance to stretch my muscles."

It was a start, she thought as he drifted off to sleep. There was no need to sit with him, for he was on the mend. Still she lingered, her eyes caressing his handsome face and strong chest as her hands longed to. How wonderful it had felt to be held by him. If only he would hold her again, in peace, not anger. If he stayed, it might happen.

Inexperienced though she was, Kara was not ignorant about what happened between men and women. She'd felt desire stir in him despite his anger. Passion was a powerful weapon, so Brighde had told her. One she might wield to keep him in Edin.

Chapter Four

The sun was just peeping up over the mountains the next morning when Duncan and Kara rode out of Edin Tower.

"Impressive, is it not?" Kara asked.

Looking back, Duncan eyed the tower. Situated in the center of a large loch, it rose from the shimmering water in a dark, smooth column of seemingly solid stone. The only way to reach it was across the narrow causeway they'd just traversed. When the drawbridge was raised, an attacking army would be forced to fashion boats or swim the loch to get at the keep. 'Twould be suicide to try, for there was not a spit of soil next to the tower on which to land, and no openings on the ground floor through which to crawl. "Most impressive," he agreed. "To take it, a commander would need to build a bridge and—"

"Not the tower, the valley."

Duncan followed the sweep of her hand, eyes widening as he beheld the majestic land around them. 'Twas lush and green, rolling hills bounded on all sides by the jagged mountain peaks he'd glimpsed from the outside. A strip of water meandered down the keel of the valley, reflecting back the brilliant blue of the sky. In the distance, smoke drifted upward from a cluster of tiny whitewashed huts. "It's so...peaceful," he whispered.

"Edin," Kara said proudly.

Duncan wondered if it was blasphemy, then decided it could not be, for surely God's hand had fashioned this place. "I've never beheld a place so beautiful and unspoiled."

"Come," Kara said, grinning. "I'll show you some of my favorite places."

"We should not stray far from the keep without an escort."

Kara laughed, the sound as dazzling as the day. "I have wandered these hills alone from the time I could walk. We'll come to no harm as long as we stay in the valley. Though I think you'd be more comfortable without all that metal."

"I'm used to wearing it," Duncan muttered. Despite her objections, he'd donned his padded gambeson and over it a full suit of chain mail, shirt and breeches. His helmet and shield were strapped behind the saddle within easy reach. "While on Crusade, we often slept in our mail."

"That sounds most uncomfortable." She giggled. "Especially for your bedmates."

Duncan scowled. "'Tis not seemly to speak of such things."

"I was only teasing. Are you always so serious?"

"Life is a serious business, mistress."

"Aye." She sobered, eyes focused on some distant pain. Her parents' deaths, mayhap, or Fergus's maiming. Then she blinked the sadness away and grinned. "Which is why a laugh from time to time is needed to keep the spirits up."

Duncan grunted. "Are you going to show me the river that I may search for my treasure?"

"You're a hard case, Duncan MacLellan, but aye, I'll show you what you want, providing you can beat me to yon clump of trees." She raced off, leaving him to follow.

Duncan tried to keep his borrowed horse to a sedate canter, but the challenging glance Kara threw over her shoulder made him reckless enough to give chase. She rode with careless abandon, and though he was the better rider, she was lighter and drew rein in the shelter of the grove a second before he did.

Sliding from the saddle, Kara bent to drink from the stream.

Duncan followed more slowly, scrutinizing the area for trouble before kneeling to sample the water. It was cool and sweet as nectar.

"'Tis the best water in the world, is it not?" She looked fresh and unspoiled as the woods around them, her face glowing with vitality, her eyes warm as the sun dappling the leaves.

"Aye," Duncan said, his voice oddly strained. He should look away, but the droplets of water on her lips held him in thrall. What would it be like to lick them away?

She leaned forward, her mouth brushing over his before he could retreat. Cool and soft, her lips clung to his, sending liquid heat shuddering through him. This was wrong. But it felt so right. She tasted of mountain water and shy innocence, her kiss untutored yet more rousing than a courtesan's. He couldn't stop his mouth from molding to hers, his tongue from sliding past her lips to explore the honeyed recess within.

Gasping, she drew back. "Why did you do that?"

"You kissed me," Duncan snapped, angered by this unprecedented loss of control. Damn, his pulse was racing, his body throbbing with a need the like of which he'd not felt...ever.

"'Twas a forfeit...for losing the race." She regarded him with wonder. "But no one's ever kissed me like that."

"Humph." Duncan wanted to stomp back to the horse and ride away. Anything to regain his sanity. But if he stood she'd get an even greater surprise. Shifting slightly to ease the pressure in his loins, he contemplated dumping water down his braies.

"That was most...thrilling."

"It was a mistake of the worst sort and won't happen again."

Her smile faded. "Why?"

"Because I am promised elsewhere."

"You have a wife?"

A betrothed. Duncan squelched the words. Janet was not yet his and might never be if he didn't find the rubies. These Gleanedins might hold him for ransom if they knew he was nearly contracted to the daughter of a wealthy noble. He'd rather die than have Cousin Niall buy his freedom. "Nay, I cannot afford a wife." That was true…unless he recovered his treasure.

Her smile was dazzling. "The man who weds me will not need wealth. I am Fergie's heir. My husband will rule this valley."

"Providing he can keep the MacGorys at bay."

Her eyes moved to his sword. "You could, once you're well."

"Nay. I could not." Having gotten his rioting body back under control, Duncan stood. "I told you—"

"That you do not fight another's war." She leapt to her feet, grinning again. "So I will have to make this your war. Come, we'll ride to the pass so you can gauge our defenses."

"I am not interested in your defenses. I want my property ret—" Once again, Duncan found himself standing still while the little whirlwind rode off. He followed. Not to see their puny defenses, but to look for his rubies.

There were fifteen small crofts on the way to the pass, Kara told him as they stopped at the first one. The farm was neat and orderly, if not very prosperous looking. A few hardy kale plants grew in the garden plot beside the hut where the family lived. The pen behind it held a pair of shaggy sheep.

"They spend the spring and summer grazing in the high pastures," Kara explained as they dismounted before the croft. "Come autumn, the shepherds drive them down to winter over where we can watch them and feed them."

Duncan thought of the huge herds of cattle and sheep

owned by Cousin Niall's villeins. "You've land enough to support vast numbers of sheep and cattle. Why do you keep so few?"

"The MacGorys have depleted most of the game in the lands outside the valley where we used to hunt. We were forced to slaughter the sheep to feed our people."

"Did Fergus not return from hunting yesterday? How did he get into the valley without encountering the Mac-Gorys?"

"Er, well—"

The door to the hut opened and a red-haired lass ran out, a babe in her arms. Three more bairns hurtled after her, the oldest a lad of seven or so. Their hands and faces were clean, their clothes much mended. Squealing in delight, they charged Kara.

She laughed and knelt to hug all three rowdy bairns. From somewhere, she produced apples and handed them around. As the youngsters raced off with their treats, she stood and embraced their mother. "Una, this is Duncan MacLellan."

"'Tis pleased we are to have ye here," said the mother, curtsying to Duncan. "We've need of a strong warrior to stop those MacGorys from murdering any more of our men." Her eyes misted, and she held the babe a bit tighter. "Thanks to them, my Thom never got to see the last bairn he gave me."

Kara patted her shoulder. "I know it can't ease your loss, but I've brought you a sack of oats and some roast venison."

Una's chin came up. "We need no charity."

"You are not getting any more than your due," Kara said briskly. "Fergie took two deer, and we divided the meat just as always. I've brought your share myself since I had a strong man to help with the hefting." She looked over at Duncan. "Please unstrap that pack behind Tessa's saddle and bring it here."

Miffed at being relegated to the role of serf, Duncan

nonetheless swallowed his irritation. Una had clearly had
enough unpleasantness. He freed the bundle and laid it on
the ground. Kara opened it, revealing not only the oats and
a hunk of meat wrapped in oiled cloth, but cheese and a
thick, woven blanket, as well. He recognized it as the one
from his bed…Kara's, actually.

"I thought you might be able to use this," Kara said as
she stood and held out the blanket.

Una touched the wool reverently. "Oh, I couldn't."

"'Tis an extra one, and the nights are getting colder."

"Aye, they are." A single tear oozed down Una's cheek.
"It'll be a long winter, hard winter without Thom."

Kara wrapped the blanket about Una's thin shoulders and
hugged her. "You could move into the tower."

"Nay." Una knuckled the tear away. "The farm was
important to Thom. He would want me to stay and make
a go of it for our wee lads. I'm bringing them to the fete
tonight," she added.

Kara went still, then began refolding her pack with the
same zeal she'd applied to winning the horse race. "Duncan, could you tie this down for me?"

As he accepted the bundle, he made certain his hand
closed over her wrist, trapping her. "What fete?"

Beneath his fingers, her pulse leapt then hammered like
a hide drum. "Nothing of interest to you." She slipped free
and hugged Una. "We must be going. Duncan's inspecting
our defenses."

Una gave him an adoring look. "God go with ye."

"He seems to be ignoring me this far," Duncan muttered. He held his tongue till they were away from the farm,
then growled, "Did you not hear me say I can't stay and
help?"

"I heard, milord, but I do hope to change your mind."

"By holding my treasure hostage?"

She regarded him levelly. "I do not have these rubies."

"Someone does."

"You've already searched my possessions and Fergie's. Would you like to go through the rest of the tower, too?"

Duncan winced, thinking of the way he'd violated Fergus's store of personal mementos. "You'd not offer if you thought I'd find something. You've likely hidden them on your person."

"Would you like to search my person?"

Aye. "Nay. You'd not offer if—"

"Damn, but you are stubborn."

"I'd not have survived three years in the East otherwise. And 'tis not proper for a lady to swear."

"You do not think I'm a lady, so it matters not." She tossed her unruly auburn curls and kneed Tessa into a brisk canter. Her back was poker straight, her slender shoulders squared beneath that ugly brown gown. Her fragility was deceptive, hiding a will of pure steel. Frankly he didn't know what to make of her. And if there was one thing that intrigued him, it was a puzzle.

Duncan hurried after her. A familiar task. As he pulled alongside, he glanced at the empty pack bouncing behind her rounded rump. "Why did you give Una your own blanket?"

"Because she needed it more than I."

"The oats were from your own larder, too, weren't they?"

"What if they are?" She didn't look at him.

"Does Fergus know you took them?"

"If I say nay, will you run and tattle to him?"

"Certainly not. I merely wondered if—"

"If I'd stolen them." She glared at him. "I didn't ask Fergie's permission, but he'd have granted it quick enough. Before the winter's out he'll likely go hungry himself so the rest of Clan Gleanedin can eat."

Duncan's belly cramped in sympathy. The Crusaders' supplies had often run low, and he well remembered the fine lords squabbling among themselves for a hunk of bread. "There are not many lords who'd share with their villeins."

"Villeins!" Kara reined in so quickly Tessa danced on the narrow road. "These are not serfs, they are my people. I would sacrifice anything—anything—to keep them safe and fed." Her face glowed with militant passion. Those flashing eyes and pink cheeks scrambled Duncan's insides.

"I understand," he said hastily.

"I doubt it." Her eyes narrowed. "Black Rolly told me all about knightly vows and Crusader pledges, but I must say I am vastly disappointed in you. You are more interested in your damn rubies than in righting wrongs and protecting the weak."

Duncan bristled. "I am not."

Her chin stuck out to challenge his. "Prove it, then. Stay and make certain no more Gleanedin wives are widowed by the MacGorys, no more wee bairns orphaned before they're born."

Trapped. Duncan raised one brow. "Do you play chess?" When she frowned and shook her head, he smiled faintly. "You'd be very good at it, I think."

"Are you poking fun at my ignorance again?"

"Far from it." Duncan sighed and looked around. The air bore a nip of autumn, yet was sweet and fresh. A hawk wheeled overhead in the azure sky. A symbol of the freedom Kara enjoyed. "You were incredibly fortunate to grow up in a place like this."

"'Tis why I want to keep it safe."

Duncan nodded. "I understand that. I went on Crusade to free the Holy Lands and prove myself."

"Did you succeed?"

"Partly." He told her about the treaty Richard had wrung from Saladin. "Less than we'd hoped for, but something. And my share of the plunder we took made me a rich man."

"That was what you needed to prove? To have wealth?"

"Not the wealth itself, but what it would allow me to do."

"What?"

Duncan shrugged. "It matters not. Without the rubies, I stand no chance of gaining what I've wanted all my life."

"I do not have them," Kara said simply, and he believed her. "But if I did..." She lowered her head, then met his gaze again. "I do not know that I'd give them to you if it meant you'd leave."

"Why is my staying so important?"

"I told you...I had a vision in the Beltane fires this spring. You vanquished the MacGorys and saved the valley."

Duncan snorted. "Foolish nonsense. A hope fed by desperation. Doubtless you saw a knight—"

"I saw you." Her features tightened. "But I do not expect you to believe in me. 'Tis enough that I believe."

"But—"

The ringing of a bell cut off his words.

"MacGorys!" Kara cried, and plunged down the road in the direction of the pass with Duncan close behind.

A huge pile of rocks sixty feet high blocked the exit from the valley. Kara wheeled around a huge boulder and sprinted along the narrow switchback trail that led up the face of the mountain. Two men waited for them on the plateau at the top. They wore conical helmets and the Scottish leine croich, a thigh-length quilted coat. It offered less protection than Duncan's mail, but made them quicker, more agile fighters.

"Is it MacGorys, Eoin?" Kara asked.

"Aye." The man was thickly built, his weathered face folded into a fierce scowl. "They're sneaking up on a party of travelers riding along the river road. Bloody fools."

"Merchants?" Kara asked.

"Nay, priests by the look. Bloody fools," Eoin repeated.

Duncan frowned. "Surely they'd not attack a priest."

Eoin looked him up and down, then sniffed. "MacGorys are a wee bit short on chivalry. They'd kill their own mothers."

"Have they attacked?" Kara asked.

"Not yet, but we saw those heathen MacGorys crawling about in the long grass." Eoin spun around as a motley herd charged up the trail. "Ah, here come the rest of the lads."

Some of the lads were bent and gray, others not yet old enough to sprout a beard. There were even a few women.

"Where are your fighters?" Duncan exclaimed.

"We're all that's left," replied a toothless old man. "But we're still strong enough to give those MacGorys a drubbing."

Kara was frowning, her eyes filled with pain, but she straightened her spine and looked at Eoin. "Let us see what those fiends are about."

"Wait," Duncan called, but he was left in the dust as the warriors of Gleanedin disappeared into a tunnel to his right. Swearing under his breath, Duncan went after them. The darkness pressed all around him, his eyes ached from trying to pierce the shroud. Then his mount rounded a bend and he saw a square of light beckoning.

When he emerged, he found himself on a high cliff. The Gleanedins were gathered at its edge, studying the broad plain that lay between the mountains and the distant Lowther Hills. The river flowed past the cliff, bordered on the far side by a thick stand of trees. From this vantage point, Duncan saw immediately the natural defenses of which Kara had boasted.

There was only one place shallow enough to ford the river, only one tiny trail leading up the sheer face of the cliffs. Both lay in the shadow of this plateau. A few bowmen could easily pick off any attackers brave enough, or stupid enough, to attempt an assault on Edin Valley.

"Eoin, is there a guard posted here at all times?" Duncan asked. At Eoin's nod, he went on to ask about numbers, rotations and means of summoning reinforcements.

Eoin's answers were clipped, but the frost left his voice as he warmed to the subject and to Duncan. "We twice beat back the MacGorys. The third time, they fashioned big hide shields and came at us bunched together so our arrows bounced off them." He grinned wolfishly. "But we gave them such a hot welcome they've not been back." He pointed to a wedge of scorched earth that flowed down the mountain and bisected the trail. "Poured grease down yon slope, we did, and set it afire."

Duncan laughed, causing heads to turn. His eyes locked on Kara's curious ones. "Eoin was telling me about the hot feet you gave the MacGorys last time they came calling."

Grinning, she walked over. "That was Fergie's idea. He was hurt too bad to fight, but not to think."

"The MacGorys are massing," someone called, and they all raced back to the edge of the plateau.

"What can we do?" Kara whispered, her eyes, like everyone else's, fastened on the dozen or so men in long, cowled robes.

Seemingly unaware of the danger lurking in the long grass, the priestly column slowly advanced along the road. They rode single file, a pack animal bringing up the rear of the line. Less than a mile and they'd be abreast of the waiting MacGorys.

Duncan's fists balled in frustration. The distance was too great for them to hear a shouted warning. Even if they did, they could not hope to outrun their attackers.

"We have to help the priests," Eoin said grimly. Murmurs of agreement greeted his statement.

"'Twould be suicide," Duncan argued. The Gleanedins were no match for the strong, well-armed warriors he'd glimpsed running into position a few moments ago.

"Even so, we must try."

"Mayhap some of us could divert the MacGorys while the rest ride and warn the priests," Kara said.

Eoin nodded. "Aye, that might work."

Duncan scanned the area again. The hair on his nape prickled, and his gut knotted. Something about this troubled him. "I have a better idea," he murmured.

Chapter Five

Kara stared at Duncan, aghast. "What do you mean, we should do nothing? Do you want the priests to die?"

"They are not priests," Duncan repeated.

Kara looked at the scowling Eoin, then at the men riding down the plain. They were closer now and she could see their bare feet swinging against their mounts' ribs. "They wear homespun robes, tied at the waist with rope, I think. And look there, is that not a crucifix about that one's neck?"

"It may be, but they are not priests," Duncan growled. "And if you try to help them, the MacGorys will wipe you out."

"You belittle our fighting skills?" Eoin snapped.

"Quite the contrary, I applaud your bravery, but 'twould be spent in a lost cause."

"We cannot just sit here and watch the priests die."

"Why would you care? You do not worship God."

"What do beliefs matter when there are lives at stake?" Kara exclaimed, amid shouts of agreement.

Duncan glared right back at her. "I am trying to save lives—yours. Only you are too impetuous to listen—"

"Ah," Kara said, brightening. "You have a plan. Are you going to sneak down and—?"

"I am not going to lift a finger."

"Oh, you...you—" Angry and disappointed at her craven hero, Kara punched him in the chest. It was like hitting solid rock. "We will go without you."

He caught her arm and tugged her back against him. "You are not going anywhere." His grip was painless but inescapable. "That's better," he said when she stopped struggling. His thumb whisked over her reddened knuckles. "You'll have more than a few bruises if you don't listen."

"I'll listen," Kara snapped. "Then I'm going down—"

"Think a moment, all of you," Duncan said angrily. "What would a dozen priests be doing here? Kara herself told me that Father Luthais comes only a few times a year."

"Mayhap they come in force to convert the heathen Gleanedins," Eoin said.

"More likely, 'tis a trap," Duncan countered. "Think. The day is warm, yet they wear thick cloaks and cover their heads. Why?"

"Mayhap God's servants are immune to the heat."

"I spent three years crusading with some of the most devote priests and monks. They do hunger, thirst and sweat as we do, and some are none too quiet about it."

"If you are wrong, twelve priests die," Eoin grumbled.

"I am not wrong."

Kara felt the steady beat of his heart against her back and wondered how he could be so cool, so certain. "But—"

Duncan released her and stepped away. "Shall I go down alone and prove I'm right?"

"Nay." Kara caught his arm, steadied by the strength of his muscles. "I could not bear it if we were wrong."

"'Twould not please me, either." He smiled faintly, giving her a glimpse of the softness he hid.

"What do you suggest we do?" she asked.

"Wait."

Kara grinned. "We Gleanedins are not very good at waiting, but we will do as you suggest." There was a bit of grumbling from the youths, who hungered for battle, but everyone settled down on the rim of the plateau. As the minutes dragged by and the others watched the procession draw closer, she studied Duncan's rugged face.

He was concerned but calm, the tick of a muscle in his cheek the only evidence he was not completely relaxed. Suddenly he shifted, hand falling to the hilt of his sword.

The column had reached the concealed MacGorys.

Kara held her breath, going up on tiptoe to see.

A scream ripped across the plain, startling the birds from the trees below. They took flight in a shrieking plume as the MacGorys leapt from hiding and raced toward the cowled men.

"God have mercy." Kara grabbed hold of Duncan's arm, twisting her face away from the grisly sight. His hand cradled the back of her head, holding her close to his chest. The links of his mail pinched, but no less than her conscience.

"Shh. It's over," he murmured, stroking her hair.

"So quick?" Kara turned and beheld an incredible sight. The MacGorys and their would-be victims milled about on the road, shaking their spears and screaming curses at those on the cliff.

"They're furious we didn't take the bait," Duncan said.

Kara's relief was so great she sagged against him. "Bloody hell, what if you hadn't been here to stop us?"

"But I was...and don't swear."

Kara leaned back, staring intently into his dark eyes. "Aye, you were here, and you saved us. Just as I knew you would."

He jerked as though she'd scorched him, then let go of her. "Do not read more into it than there was."

"I am not. The facts speak for themselves." Kara's heart was beating so fast she clasped her hands over it. "You saved us, just as the Beltane fires predicted."

The savior of Edin Valley scowled. "Fine. Now mayhap you will return my rubies, and I'll be on my way."

"I do not have them," Kara said softly, her mind already

aping ahead. "And the MacGorys are not vanquished, merely thwarted for the moment. An enraged wolf is a dangerous adversary, Duncan. We need you more than ever."

"And I need my rubies." He turned and stalked away.

Kara gave chase. "Where are you going?" she asked.

"To search Edin Tower from top to bottom."

As she watched him go, Kara hoped that the cursed rubies were either buried in the muddy riverbank where they'd found Duncan or that the thief had them well hidden.

Duncan came down to dinner that night in a foul mood. He'd spent the day exploring every corner of the old tower. The folk of Edin had given him leave to paw through their pitiful belongings. They'd emptied their pouches, pockets and even their boots. When that search yielded nothing, he'd gone looking for safe holes and hidden chambers. His shoulders were bruised from butting them against walls, his fingers scraped from grubbing for secret trip mechanisms.

"So, how was the hunting?" Fergus asked, stepping from the shadows at the bottom of the stairs.

"Futile." Duncan had learned to judge men's honesty by the way their gaze met his. Fergus's was guileless. Besides, he'd been hunting at the far end of the valley when Duncan arrived.

"Kara thinks 'tis possible these gems were lost along the river when you were felled by the fever."

"They were stitched into the lining of my leather pouch. The thread had been cut, the stones taken and the stitches reset."

"Hmm." Fergus scratched at his beard. "Could your traveling companions aboard ship have taken them?"

"How did you know I came by ship?"

"How else would you cross the sea?" Fergus questioned sagely.

"I still had the stones when I camped my first night out of Carlisle. I could feel them through the lining."

"Well, 'tis certainly a mystery, but I'm glad you're con-

vinced we didn't take them." He threw a companionable
arm across Duncan's shoulder and steered him toward the
great hall.

Duncan shrugged out of his grasp. "I am not convinced.
Someone here took the rubies and my letter."

"Letter? This is the first I've heard of a letter."

"'Twas a short note." Janet had slipped it to him when
he left Threave. In it, she pledged her undying love and
swore she'd wed him when he returned, whether he'd made
his fortune or not, although his code of honor prohibited
him from doing that.

"Well, it would be lost on the likes of us, for no Glean
edin can read or cipher." Fergus threw open the big double
doors and motioned for Duncan to precede him into the
hall.

No sooner did Duncan step over the threshold than a
great cheer went up, and he was mobbed by grinning,
shouting people. Men pounded him on the back, women
kissed his cheeks and thrust their runny-nosed bairns at
him.

"What the hell?" Duncan muttered.

Kara appeared to take his elbow, her smile radiant. "'Tis
our way of saying thank you for saving us today."

"By smothering me?" he asked.

"You're a fraud, Duncan MacLellan," Kara chided.
"You're touched but too stubborn to admit it." She stood
on tiptoe and kissed him. Not on the cheek, but full on the
mouth.

Odd how the feel of her soft lips could harden the rest
of his body. And she knew it, too, for when she moved
away, she slanted him a teasing grin. "Come, sir knight, a
feast awaits." She held out her hand, and he took it, following her through the cheering throng like a man in a
daze. Kara Gleanedin was a very dangerous woman.

There was no high table, no dais like the one from which
Cousin Niall looked down on his retainers. But the table to
which Kara led him had been spread with a flaxen cloth.

and laid with matching crockery instead of the wooden bowls and cups.

"Thank you. This is very fine, indeed," Duncan said, surprised to find that he meant it, he who had eaten off silver plates with the kings of two nations. More surprising was the catch in his voice.

"You are kind to say so." There was an edge to Kara's tone, a twinkle in her eye that said she knew he was used to finer.

Duncan looked out over the sea of Gleanedins, dressed in their mended homespun, but what he saw was their shining faces, their genuine smiles. "'Tis a banquet fit for a prince."

"It'll be a cold feast if ye don't cease talking and start eating," grumbled the big man who stood at the side door that led to the kitchens.

Everyone laughed, then turned to seek their places at the rough-hewn trestle tables and benches. The servants streamed in, passing among them with heavily laden platters. Steam rising from them filled the air with the rich scent of roasted meat.

"I thought you were short of food," Duncan murmured as he helped Kara step over the bench.

"In addition to thanking you for your quick thinking, we celebrate Samhuinn tonight."

"The feast of the dead?" Duncan said, appalled.

"We prefer to think of it as the winter solstice. The day we bring our flocks to their winter folds and give thanks to all gods for the harvest. Still, I'm surprised you know of it."

"My mother practiced the old ways."

"You do not approve."

Another memory flickered through his mind. A bonfire at dusk, people dancing around it, eating, drinking and laughing. His parents, holding hands as they gazed into the fire. "I was taught to think such things unholy."

"By that dreadful cousin of yours?"

"Cousin Niall is a godly man." If a bit overzealous.

Kara snorted. "Too much of a good thing can be bad."

"I do not agree." But he was beginning to question.

"I've saved the best bits for you." The huge man who'd been by the door set a platter down on the table.

"Duncan, this is Black Rolly MacHugh."

Duncan nodded. "You're not a Gleanedin, then?"

"In spirit only." He began heaping slices of roasted venison into Duncan's bowl. "I was wed to Kara's aunt."

Duncan assumed she'd died in a MacGory raid, but when Rolly had moved on to serve Fergus, Kara leaned over and confided that Annie Gleanedin MacHugh had died in childbed several years ago.

"Black Rolly stayed on here. He was with Fergie when the MacGorys attacked and took a blow to the hip. Now his leg's stiff and nearly useless. So much suffering," she said sadly, looking out over the crowded hall.

It was tiny compared with the great hall at Threave, the vaulted ceiling so low the battle banners hanging from it nearly brushed the heads of the diners. Poor and mean, Cousin Niall would have called it, for the rough-hewn timbers were soot streaked from the smoke of countless fires. But colorful woolen hangings brightened the stone walls, and the rushes underfoot smelled of fresh herbs.

To Duncan, the greatest difference was the people.

"Your clansmen have endured much," he said. "But their trials have neither broken nor embittered them." Indeed, the folk of Edin bounded about like a brood of boisterous pups. They laughed and teased each other. They praised Black Rolly's feast and devoured it with disarming relish. "Never have I seen people take so much enjoyment from a simple thing as eating."

"Life can be harsh and short," Kara explained. "We've learned to wring as much pleasure as possible from each moment that comes our way. The good times should be savored like sweet mead as a buffer against the troubles sure to come."

Duncan's throat tightened. Heathens, he'd called them, yet their ideals were far more Christian than those of many a seemingly pious knight he'd met on Crusade.

"What troubles you?" She laid a hand on his arm.

The casual gesture jangled every nerve in his body, made him suddenly conscious of her leg pressed against his beneath the table, the subtle scent of her hair, the sheen of her skin in the torchlight. He knew exactly what caused his heightened awareness of Kara. A passion he should be ignoring. Unfortunately, he didn't want to. He wanted to sweep her from the hall, to take her away someplace dark and private. Someplace where he could act on the impulses that had plagued him from the first time he'd laid eyes on her.

"Duncan?" she asked softly.

"Hmm." He struggled to bring his mind back to the business at hand. Food. Eating. "The meat is good."

She chuckled. "Then why are you scowling at it?"

"I…" He stared into her upturned face, his mind veering down paths it had no right to explore.

"I know," she whispered. "It is the same for me."

"It cannot be."

"Why?"

Because I am promised to another. The statement was not strictly true. In all honor, he was pledged to Janet, but he felt things for Kara of Edin that went beyond honor.

God help them both.

"There is no shame in what we feel," Kara said softly. "'Tis a special gift that comes to very few."

"Lust," he said curtly.

"Mmm." She cocked her head. "Aye, there's a fire between us that I've not known before, but there's more."

Duncan wrenched his gaze away from the passion smoldering in her eyes, darkening them. "There can be nothing between us. We are too different…our hopes, our beliefs."

"Our methods are different, I grant, yet we both value the same things—honor, duty and peace." She reached un-

der the table, lacing her slender fingers with his large, callused ones.

Duncan sucked in a sharp breath, the ordinary gesture
rife with possibilities he dared not explore. Or did he?

If he could not go back to Threave, what was to prevent
him from staying here? The notion was as tempting as Kara
herself.

Chapter Six

When the last bite of beef and last swig of mead had been consumed, Fergie rose and gestured for silence.

"We've partaken of the bounty, now let us honor those who went before us. Those whose sweat and blood kept Edin Valley free for us generation after generation."

Kara's stomach knotted. Would this be the last generation to inhabit the valley? She saw her fear mirrored in the gloomy faces around her. Beside her, Duncan stirred restlessly, but he didn't meet her gaze. Why would he not help them? What was it that kept him from making a commitment to her and her people? He'd said he was promised elsewhere, yet claimed to be unwed.

"Let us go forth and pay homage to our ancestors," Fergie said, his voice clear yet solemn as the occasion.

The folk of Edin rose, quietly trooped out of the hall and across the bailey. Singly and in pairs, they marched over the drawbridge to attend a ritual nearly as old as the hills.

"Where are we going?" Duncan asked, walking beside her.

"To light the Samhuinn fires."

He flinched, and she could feel him drawing away, shattering the link that had bound them since the meal began.

"You do not have to come," she said.

"How can you practice such heathen rites and still claim to worship God?" he asked incredulously.

"Father Luthais attended last year," she said defensively. "He said it was good to remember those who've gone before us."

"Father Padric had me whipped for crying at my mother's grave. He said it was not seemly to shed tears for a harlot."

Kara was so shocked she stumbled. "How horrible."

Duncan took her arm to steady her. "One reason I went on Crusade was to atone for her mistakes."

Kara stared at his profile, stark in the torchlight, appalled to see he really believed that. "Tell me of her."

"She was the daughter of a neighboring laird. My father was promised to another, but ran off with her instead. Grandfather claimed she was a witch who'd ensorcelled Da."

"And this Cousin Niall vilified her after she was dead."

Duncan nodded, his throat working. "Da was killed in a Border skirmish when I was eight. A few months later, a man came to live in our tower. When he left, another took his place. And so it went on for two years till she died."

"Your mama was doubtless lonely." *And so were you.* "'Tis hard for a woman to keep a place up without a man about. Just ask Una or any of the other widows."

Duncan nodded, but she knew he wasn't convinced. She held tight to his hand as the procession wound its way across the valley and up through the trees to the hilltop. Slowly they approached the circle of ancient stones where the ceremonial fires had been lit from earliest times. Piled in the center were branches of rowan, for luck, and oak for strength.

When all were assembled, Morag, the bent crone who was the keeper of the flame, stepped forward. Holding a torch in one hand, she began to chant in the lost tongue of the Celts.

"What is she saying?" Duncan asked stiffly.

"She's calling on those who have left us, telling them we come to honor them, to praise them…"

"And to protect the living from harm," Duncan added.

Kara smiled. "You've been to a Samhuinn before."

"Aye. Long ago with my parents. I thought it exciting. We danced around the fire, calling the names of the dead." He grimaced. "Pagan nonsense."

"You need not stay."

Duncan hesitated, fifteen years of Niall's dictates warring against the lure of an old, pleasant memory. As the fire crackled through the dry wood, he stared deep into the flames. The scent of wood smoke and the low musical litany of old words swept him back. He remembered sitting on his father's lap, watching the fire, listening to the seanachaidh, the clan storyteller, weave tales of times gone by. In turn, the other folk told their own stories, adding the thread of a loved one's life to the tapestry.

His father had spoken of his mother, a woman of rare courage, keen wit and dazzling humor. "I've been lucky to snare such a lass for my own," he'd added, gazing deep into his wife's eyes. "She's the only woman I'll ever love."

"Nor could I love another," his mother had whispered. "If aught should happen to ye, I'd curl up and die myself."

"Duncan?" Someone shook him. He started, surprised to find the fire blazing high and Kara watching him.

"You had a vision, didn't you?" she murmured, the firelight playing over her exotic features.

"I did not."

"You saw something in the fire," she insisted.

"I was thinking about my parents. Naught more."

She smiled slowly, softly. "And what do you think a vision is, Duncan MacLellan? A blast of unholy light and a whiff of black smoke?"

"I did not have a vision."

"Call it what you like, you saw—or remembered—something that eased your soul."

Duncan looked away, but he could not escape the fact that she was right. He remembered what he'd forgotten in the grief of losing his mother and being sent to Threave. He remembered how much his parents had loved one another. Small wonder his mother had never wed again. Small wonder she'd died a scant two years after losing her beloved husband.

Duncan remembered something else, too. He remembered the last words she'd spoken to him.

"I wish I could live to see the man ye'll become, my love," she'd whispered. "I know ye'll be as great and good a man as yer father was. But I cannot bear to be without him, and so I must leave ye. I stayed till ye were old enough to find yer way."

He hadn't understood then. Now he did. She'd hung on, a hollow husk, till her son was old enough to care for himself.

"It makes all the difference, doesn't it?" Kara asked.

Duncan looked at her, touched by the compassion glowing in her eyes. "Aye, it does," he admitted. "But it was not a vision."

"Whatever you say." She grinned cheekily. "Are you not going to ask what I saw in the Samhuinn fires?"

"I'm afraid to."

"The two of us...dancing to the pipes."

Right on cue, the pipers stepped into the firelight and began to blow. The shrill wail of the pipes filled the dark night, and Duncan's heart soared along with the notes. The music eased a void in his soul, one he wasn't even aware existed.

"It has been a long time since I danced." He bowed and held out his hand. "But you're a braw lassie."

"That I am." She took his hand and together they joined the couples spinning about the forest glade.

Her head came only to his breastbone; her waist was so slender his hands met around it, yet she led and he followed. At first. The music stirred memories of earlier times, and he somehow knew just where to step, when to turn.

"Fie, sir," Kara said, laughing up at him. "Your feet are as nimble as your tongue."

Duncan laughed. It felt so good, he did it again, drawing Kara closer. Her breasts brushed against his chest, intensifying the desire he'd tried to suppress. His blood heated to match the wild cadence of the pipes. He wanted to carry her off into the night, yet perversely, he wanted this moment never to end. Lifting her off her feet, he spun in a circle. Their eyes linked in silent communication. 'Twas like gazing into a golden mirror and seeing the other half of himself reflected there. Inside him, the knot of pain he'd borne since his mother's death splintered. As it broke free, it loosed something sweet and wonderful. "Kara," he whispered.

"Aye." Her smile was welcome as the sun after a long, dark night, her laughter pure magic. She tossed her head, curtaining them in silky auburn hair, cutting off the rest of the world. "We belong together," she murmured, arms twining about his neck.

Duncan hesitated, honor warring with something more vital, more overwhelming. Love. He loved her as he'd never expected to love any woman. Now he knew how his parents had felt. Hungry. Desperate. Yet, oddly at peace. The realization that he would do anything to be with Kara was frightening yet wonderful. Aye, holding her in his arms, gazing deep into her fire-bright eyes and knowing she wanted him without reservation, without censure, made him feel ten feet tall. But...he was not free.

Duty gnawed at the fabric of his happiness.

"Kara," he began.

She silenced him with a quick kiss. "Do not worry about tomorrow. Let us savor the time we have together."

He wanted to. "There are things I must tell you...."

"You will, and I will listen. But not tonight." Her mouth closed over his again, but this time 'twas no fleeting thing.

She kissed him with all the pent-up fury of a summer storm, unleashing the torrent that had raged inside him all evening.

Groaning, Duncan molded their bodies together, hard to soft. His hands raced down her supple spine as he took the kiss deeper. With an answering moan, she arched into his embrace, straining to get even closer. Good. She felt so good, so right. The primitive need to make her his shuddered through him and left him shaking. "Kara," he murmured, wrenching his mouth from the heaven of hers. "I want you so badly it's tearing me apart."

"And I you." She framed his face with her hands, her touch gentling the savagery of his desire. "But not here." Tossing back her hair, she unveiled the firelit glade. Many other couples embraced under the guise of dancing, but a few knowing eyes and sly smiles were cast their way.

Duncan lowered Kara to the ground and loosened his grip on her, though it nearly killed him. "I am sorry to shame you."

"I am not ashamed of loving you."

"But..."

"Ah, there you are." Fergus elbowed his way through the crowd, his expression bland.

Duncan hoped the darkness hid his flushed face.

"Black Rolly and I are going back to the tower," Fergus said. "We'll leave you bairns to the dancing."

"What is wrong, Fergie?" Kara asked. Letting go of Duncan, she went to her uncle and tucked her arm through his.

"Naught," the old man said.

She tisked and asked if his chest pained him again. Fergus shrugged and tried to sidestep. The interchange went on for several moments, Kara bullying for answers, the old man dodging her questions with light banter. Their love for each other was evident in each word.

Duncan's chest tightened as he watched the interplay between the two. 'Twas jealousy, pure and simple. More than anything, he wanted to be loved like that, deeply and un-equivocally.

"I trust ye'll keep my lass safe," Fergus said.

"I'd lay down my life for her," Duncan replied honestly.

A wry grin lifted Fergus's lips and set his eyes atwin-kling. "I'm sure ye'll throw yerself into it soul and body. Judging by the way ye were keeping her warm when I came up."

"Fergie," Kara chided. "You're making Duncan squirm."

"And here I thought 'twas you making him do that." Fergus roared over his own joke, then walked off with Black Rolly.

Duncan exhaled and dragged a hand through his hair. "Mayhap we should go back with him."

"Whatever for?" Kara asked, frowning.

"Well..." Duncan looked at the toes of his boots. "Feel-ing as I do about you, I don't think I can be trusted—"

"I trust you."

"You should not, for I do not trust myself," he snapped.

Kara grinned. "Let us just enjoy the music and dancing and see where the night leads."

Into trouble. Duncan knew that, but he wanted so much to be with her. To talk with her, look at her, listen to her laugh. Surely if they stayed in the light, with the crowd...

"Oh!" Kara turned toward the woods, eyes wide with alarm.

Duncan drew his sword and shoved her behind him, poised to repel an attack. "Is it MacGorys?"

"Nay. I..." Her hesitation spoke volumes.

"A vision of some sort?" he asked curtly.

"More like a feeling." She shivered and chafed at her arms. "I've been worried about Brighde all evening. And just now I had a feeling she needed me."

"Who is this Brighde?"

"My best friend in the whole world. We were inseparable till she wed Donald. Poor Donald.'' A shadow passed over her face.

"He is dead?"

"Killed by the MacGorys in the same battle that took Una's Thom. 'Twas in the spring. Brighde had just realized she was carrying their babe.'' She shook her head, eyes filling with tears. "Another bairn who'll never know his da."

Duncan instinctively reached out and put his arm around her. She turned into his embrace as naturally as though he'd spent a lifetime offering her comfort. She nuzzled his chest, and his heart fluttered. "Would you feel better if you saw her?"

She nodded. "But she lives at the far end of the valley."

"'Tis a fine night for a ride."

The road was a silvery ribbon stretching along the valley floor, the fields and hills glowing under a coat of frost.

Kara shivered and pulled her cloak closer about her body, chilled more by apprehension than the nippy night. Brighde was fine. Her babe was not due for another fortnight, and she was surrounded by servants in the tidy tower Donald had inherited from his family.

"I fancy I taste snow in the air," Duncan said. He cantered along beside her, his cloak thrown back over his shoulder.

"Why aren't you freezing?"

"Many a night sweltering in the desert I dreamed of this. The cold, clear air of home." He breathed deep, then exhaled, his breath congealing into a white cloud.

"You look like a dragon, my love."

His eyes blazed at the endearment. "Best be wary, then, dearling, for dragons are known to devour young maidens."

She shivered deliciously, the memory of the heat generated by their kisses driving out the late autumn chill. "I can think of no better way to perish."

"Nor can I," he said slowly. "Unfortunately."

Kara snorted in exasperation. There it was again, that mysterious something coming between them. If he'd been wed to another, she'd have fought her love for him, but he wasn't. He was hers, promised to her in the bright flames at Beltane. "Things will happen as they were meant to."

"I wish I could be as certain as you."

"Call it fate or God's will, you would not have been sent to us if we were not destined for each other."

"The Lord giveth and the Lord taketh away," he grumbled.

She heard the thunder of the waterfall and brightened. "Look, there is Stratheas, Brighde's tower."

Duncan reined in and studied the small tower set high in the glen at the apex of the valley. "How do we get up there?" he asked over the rush of the water spilling one hundred fifty feet from the mountaintop to the loch at the base of the tower.

"There's a wee trail over there." As they rode up it, Kara told him how Donald's great-grandfather had come to build here. "He was the cousin of my great-grandfather— everyone in the valley is related somehow—and a loner who wanted a place to himself."

"Well, he certainly found it here."

They were scarcely halfway up the trail when they met a single rider coming down.

"Thank God ye've come," cried old Ned.

"'Tis Brighde, isn't it?" Kara asked.

"Aye. Her time's come and the babe's caught. Diedre just bade me saddle up and ride for help."

Without waiting to hear more, Kara crowded past him on the narrow trail and galloped toward the tower. Duncan was right behind her, sliding from his saddle before she'd halted and lifting her down.

"Do you need anything?" he asked.

"Pray for Brighde." She squeezed his hand before dashing into the keep. Taking the steps at a reckless clip, she

burst into the master chamber. A wave of hot air nearly
drove her back. It stank of fear and helplessness
"Brighde?"

"Kara!" Brighde called.

"Aye. I'm here." She crossed the dark chamber, shoving
past a ring of stricken women. One look at the woman in
the bed, and her own heart quailed.

Brighde's face was ashen, her lips bitten bloody. Her
dull, sunken eyes were filled with pain and a hopelessness
that was more damaging than poison for it sapped the will

"Well, your lad seems eager to join us," Kara said.

"I...I don't know," Brighde's said listlessly. "It's taking so long...I fear..."

"None of that," Kara said briskly. She sent the maids
hopping for hot water, fresh toweling and a few things she
didn't even need. Anything to inject life into this death
chamber.

Dame Wilma, the midwife, pulled her aside and whispered, "The babe's caught wrong wise. Coming out feet
first." She made a sign to ward off evil. "Best to let them
slip away."

"What?" Kara exclaimed so forcefully everyone in the
room stopped and cringed. Furious, she pushed the bulky
woman from the room. "Get you gone."

"Gladly." Wilma puffed up till it seemed her massive
bosom might explode. "I'll be no part to—"

Kara shoved her face into Wilma's sweaty one. This was
one case where the old ways and superstitions were wrong.
"You will leave and quietly. If I hear one word against
Brighde or her bairn, I'll...I'll get Morag to cast a spell on
you."

Wilma squeaked in fright and fled down the dark corridor, chins jiggling, skirts flying up behind her.

A dark figure roused from the shadows at the end of the
hallway. "Kara, is aught wrong?" Duncan asked.

Kara sagged against the open door. Everything. Her

friend was suffering, mayhap dying, and she felt so inadequate. "I—"

"Shh. Tell me." His arm slipped around her waist.

"The babe is stuck backward." She rested her forehead on his chest, drawing strength from his solid presence.

"Can you not turn it?"

Kara's head snapped up. "Of course," she said softly. "I once saw Black Rolly save a mare and her foal by doing that, but I do not know if I can—"

A guttural groan from inside the room decided the issue. For Brighde's sake, she had to try.

The maids shrieked and one of them ran from the room when Kara told them what she wanted to do.

In the end, she had to rely on Duncan. Loath as he was to enter the birthing room, he came when she called him. He held Brighde steady while Kara worked to turn the slippery babe. The task was messy and arduous, but after several attempts, Kara managed to slip the babe back around.

They roused Brighde with a dram of whiskey and let nature take its course. A few moments later, the wee squalling lad landed in Kara's outstretched hands. She dried him quickly and set him on Brighde's stomach.

"Is it...is it all right?" Brighde asked.

"He's perfect." Kara looked over at Duncan, who lurked uncertainly in the doorway. "They both are. Brighde, I would introduce you to Duncan MacLellan, the man whose timely suggestion saved you and your wee Donald."

"You were heaven-sent to help us," Brighde said softly. For once, Duncan didn't dispute the point. Mayhap he was coming to believe, Kara thought.

Chapter Seven

Duncan stared out a narrow slit in a chamber high in Stratheas's tower. The room was small and simply furnished, yet he'd chosen it over the larger one below, leaving that for Kara.

Was she sleeping, his brave, sweet Kara?

Idly he watched the snow drift down from a leaden sky. It was just past midnight, and below him, the keep slept. He was tired, too, but unable to sleep. Several hours had passed since the birth of the new laird of Stratheas, yet he was still in awe of the experience. He'd been a soldier all his life, had seen many a man die, a share of them by his own hand. 'Twas invigorating to have helped one into this world.

They'd done it together, he and Kara.

The pain Brighde had endured had humbled him, yet now, with the horror fading, he thought of Kara. Imagined her swollen with a child. His child. Impossible.

Nay, not impossible.

The rubies were gone, either lost along the river or stolen. Without them he could not, in all honor, return for Janet. If she was even still waiting for him. Three years was a long time. Mayhap Janet assumed him dead and herself free to wed another. Or was it selfish yearning to hope she'd found someone else? As he had.

Damn, if he only knew...

A slight sound outside the door had him swinging around, his hand falling to the knife in his belt. In the next breath, he relaxed and straightened. Knowing exactly who was outside, he strode over and opened the door.

Kara stood in a spill of light from the candle she held, a mix of yearning and trepidation on her face.

"You shouldn't be here," Duncan said.

"I know." Her lips smiled, yet her eyes were wary, vulnerable. "But I couldn't stay away."

Duncan took her hand and drew her inside. "You're cold."

"I stood too long at the foot of the stairs, debating with myself. Warm me."

He opened his arms and she stepped into them. Exhaling softly, he folded her close. Her body was like ice, leaching heat from his. He gave it gladly. "You're so cold you are shivering."

"'Tis fear, mostly."

"Fear of what?" He tipped his head back and read her expression. "Not fear of me?"

"I was afraid you'd send me away."

"I should." Even as he spoke, he hugged her tighter, balanced on the knife edge between duty and love. The plunge from grace would hurt, but not as much as letting go of her.

"You cannot." She looped her hands around his neck and tugged his head down till her eyes filled his vision. They were the color of molten gold, wide, beguiling and yearning.

Her need undid him, magnifying his own.

"You are right, Kara, love. I cannot let you go." He lifted her so their mouths met, groaning as she wrapped herself around him and kissed him back with a ferocity that stole his sanity. The taste of her, the scent of her clouded his senses when he needed a clear head. A cool head. Struggling for control, he left her lips and sought the hollow of her ear. "Easy. Give me a chance to catch my breath, to slow down."

"I do not want slow. I want you."

"You'll have me." He drew back, staring into her passion-flushed features. "But this is your first time."

"It does not matter. I'm not afraid."

"It matters to me." Duncan grinned at his imperious love. She might not be afraid, but she was vulnerable and infinitely precious. He was not taking her standing up in the doorway like some paid strumpet. "I want to savor you…like a plum tart."

"You do?" Her wonder was all the incentive he needed to curb his own rioting passion.

"Aye." Swinging her into his arms, he kicked the door closed and crossed to the simple bed. He tugged back the woolen coverlet, then gently laid her down on the sheets. Her hair flowed like a red banner over the bleached linen. The blue bed robe was a perfect foil for her pale skin. "You are so beautiful, like a dream I've held in my heart always."

"Oh, Duncan. I feel as though I've waited a lifetime for you, too." Kara shivered as she watched him remove his boots, then pull off his tunic. As his head emerged, his eyes locked on hers, glittering with sensual promise. Anticipation drew her nerves so taut her clothes felt scratchy and a size too small.

"Hurry." She tugged at her robe.

Duncan knelt beside the bed and captured her hands. "Nay. We will not rush this." He stilled her protests with a kiss. He tasted of wine and a passion she met eagerly. Groaning, he took the kiss deeper, his lips moving over hers with devastating thoroughness. His tongue coaxed and seduced, tempting her to follow his lead. By the time he raised his head, Kara was clinging to him, her nails buried in his bare shoulders.

"Duncan," she whispered, gasping for air. "I do not

think I can wait. I...I have never felt so desperate for anything as I am to be with you.''

"And I you, my love." He stretched out beside her on the bed and dropped stinging kisses on her mouth. "You try a man's control." He nibbled her ear. "The fire that burns between us—'' his tongue slid down her neck, leaving a trail of tingling flesh in its wake ''—makes ashes of my good intentions.''

Shivering, Kara let her head drop back to give him greater access. Her arms twined about his neck, her body blindly seeking the warmth of his. Even through their clothes, she gloried in the strength of him, the solid muscles of his chest brushing her breasts, the fullness of his arousal filling the hollow cradle between her hips. "Duncan." She twisted against him, struggling to ease the pressure building inside her.

"Aye, love, I feel it, too." His mouth slanted over hers, hungry, demanding.

Kara kissed him back with all the longing pent up inside her. This was what she'd been missing all these years. But she wanted, needed more. Impatient, she tugged at the belt of her robe. Instantly he was there, helping. Cool air rushed over her heated flesh, countered by the brush of big, callused hands as they swept down her spine, drawing her close. The hair on his chest abraded her breasts, making them swell and peak.

"You are so soft." He filled his hands with her breasts. "So responsive," he murmured, drinking the gasps of pleasure from her lips as his thumbs teased her nipples into aching nubs. His mouth raced over her collarbone and beyond, nipping and laving. She started when his tongue stroked one sensitive breast, gasped when his mouth closed over the peak. Hot. Wet. Wonderful.

"Duncan," she cried, clutching his head to keep him there.

He obliged by drawing down on her, suckling greedily. With his hands and mouth, he roused her to heights she'd not known existed. Desire came in waves, like the churning torrents in the loch below the keep. Nowhere did it burn more fiercely than in the juncture between her thighs.

"Please," she whimpered. Her hips began to rock against his, instinctively seeking relief.

"Aye, I'd please you, love." He gently explored her most intimate secrets, his long fingers slipping inside, finding the focus of her yearning.

She cried his name, feeling vividly alive, her body straining to the rhythm set by his clever fingers. She'd not realized such sweet torture existed, had not known she could want so keenly her whole body flamed.

Duncan shifted suddenly, tearing free of his clothes and rising above her, face taut with passion, fierce with love. His hands trembled as he parted her thighs. Then he hesitated. "I do not want to hurt you."

"You won't." She lifted her arms in silent welcome and drew him down. A soft moan escaped her and her eyes closed as his body brushed hers. The moan became a groan of pleasure as she accepted the solid strength of him to fill the aching void inside her. The pain was fleeting, buried in a wash of pure wonder. He stretched her to the limits, yet he completed her, body and soul. She wanted to tell him, but when she opened her eyes, one look at the tenderness shining in his, and she knew no words were needed.

"Now we are one," Duncan whispered, moved to tears. Cradling her bottom in his hands, he set about loving her as though she were the only woman in the world. For him, she was. With each thrust of his hips, they soared higher. Her little whimpers of delight made him burn hotter and hotter till he thought he'd burst into flames.

"Oh, Duncan," Kara cried, and he felt the first tremors of her release begin deep, deep inside her.

Gasping her name, Duncan buried himself in the heart of the explosion that shattered her, consumed by the feel of her body tightening around his, demanding his ultimate surrender. He gave and gave, pouring himself into her, heart and soul.

Moments later, he found the strength to roll to his side, yet he kept her with him, their bodies still joined.

"I never knew it could be like this," Kara whispered.

Duncan stroked her satiny back. "Nor did I." But one worry intruded. "Are you...are you all right?"

She stretched like a lazy cat, her breasts brushing against his chest. "More than all right. And you?" There was pure siren in the look she slanted him through her lashes.

"I have never been happier in my life."

"Nor I." Kara's eyes roamed possessively over his wide, bronzed shoulders. The dark swirls of hair on his chest fascinated her. She ran her fingers through the pelt, stroking and kneading the hard muscles beneath. Idly she traced a line from his breastbone to the belly button below his narrow waist. In response, she felt him stir inside her.

He grabbed her hand. "You should sleep." The kiss he placed on her fingers robbed his words of their sting.

"I'm not at all tired." She gently rocked her hips.

Duncan gasped as his body answered the call of hers. "Kara...you are new to this and—"

"I'd be willing to practice." She rubbed her breasts against his chest, shivering as the nipples peaked. "See. Not tired."

"What am I going to do with you?"

"Love me."

"I do," he answered, and proceeded to prove it so tenderly, so sweetly, that she cried with the wonder of it.

Duncan kissed away her tears and tucked her close so they slept heart to heart, but long after Kara had fallen asleep, he remained awake. Worrying.

Not about Janet or proving himself to Cousin Niall. Those things no longer mattered, though he wished he knew if Janet was well and happy.

He worried about all that must be done to make Edin Valley strong enough to repel the MacGorys. He worried about making a home for Kara, about making her as happy as she made him.

The snow had stopped falling by early afternoon when Kara and Duncan rode away from Stratheas, but the few inches on the ground made the trail down the mountain slippery and treacherous. Shivering, Kara pulled her cloak closer, glad of the thick woolen hose Brighde had lent her to pull on under her skirt.

"Stay close behind me and go slowly," Duncan admonished.

Kara nodded, smiling to herself. She'd traveled these hills from the time she could ride, often in far worse weather, but since last night, Duncan had turned protective as a hen with only one chick. Because he loved her. A thrill shot through her, and she shifted in the saddle, the faint ache in her muscles a subtle reminder of their lovemaking. Magical as the night had been, Duncan had been quiet this morn, and she feared he regretted what they'd done.

When they reached the bottom of the mountain, Kara pulled her mount alongside his. The grim set of his jaw would have warned some away, but not her. "Are you sorry?" she baldly asked.

"About what?" He scanned the mountains, his expression fierce and wary, one hand on his sword.

"That we, er, coupled."

Duncan whipped his head around, eyes blazing with a different sort of light. "We made love, Kara," he said softly. "And I am not sorry." He exhaled a plume of dragon smoke. "Except for the timing. I should not have touched you till we were wed."

Wed. Her heart soared, then fell again. "Do not feel you must wed me because we...we..."

"I am not. I am wedding you because I do not think I could live without you."

"Oh," Kara breathed. "Why did you tell me now, when

I can not show you how much you mean to me without risking frosted, er, parts," she added, giggling.

"For just that reason," he said gruffly. "There will be no more of that till we're properly married."

"You are a prude, sir knight."

"It is a matter of honor. 'Twas dishonorable of me to sleep with you before—"

"There was very little sleeping, as I recall."

"Kara!"

"Well, there wasn't." She nibbled on her lower lip. "I am sorry you find me too bold, but I was raised to be open and plain speaking. I love you, I desire you, and I cannot hide it."

"Nor do I want you to." His smile was as dazzling as the sun on the fresh snow. "Your honesty is one of the things I like best about you, my love. I am only trying to do the right thing."

"Loving me is the right thing?"

"Aye, though we must not sleep together again till we are wed," he added, his sternness ruined by the tenderness shining in his dark eyes.

"I do not see why," she grumbled. "Many couples handfast or wed themselves according to the old way." She glanced at him.

He shook his head. "When will Father Luthais come?"

"Not till after nollaig, Christmas."

"We'll wed then, if Fergus gives his blessing."

Kara sighed and resigned herself to six weeks of purgatory. They rode in silence for few moments till she worked up the courage to ask the question that had nibbled at the back of her mind since waking. "Will you stay in Edin, then?"

"Aye." He fixed that scowl on her. "Though I've naught to offer you but my heart and a strong sword arm to protect you."

And a marvelous body. But she decided against mentioning that. "The first, I'll treasure always, for I've given mine to you. The second, we'll need if we're to drive off the MacGorys. But what of the promises you mentioned earlier?''

His scowl deepened. "''Tis a blot on my soul that I cannot keep those promises...not without the rubies." He told her, then, about Janet and his vow to make his fortune so they could wed.

"She'd not have you unless you were wealthy?"

"Her father, Cousin Niall, would not agree to the match unless I could provide a home such as she deserved. I needed the coin to refurbish the small keep Da left me. Janet is used to fine things, to a walled keep and servants to order about."

And I am not? Kara thought fiercely, then her sense of humor came to the rescue. Nay, she was not. Nor did she want to be. "She may have found someone who could give her these things." Janet sounded shallow and selfish enough to do just that.

"If so, 'twas because Cousin Niall pressed her to do so. I'd not put it past him. Though he promised Janet could choose her own husband, he has always hated me. Still..."

"You do regret loving me."

"Nay. Never that," he said so forcefully she had to believe. Then he sighed and scrubbed a hand over his stubbled chin. "I am not certain of much except my love for you. Meeting you, loving you, has made me realize what I felt for Janet was friendship and gratitude. She, alone, made me welcome at Threave. Small and fragile as she was, she championed me, taking my part against her father. I admired her courage, and I desperately needed someone to fill the emptiness left by Mama's death. Janet became my companion, my confident, my anchor in a troubled world. She was the sister I never had. Only I didn't know..."

He looked so miserable Kara ached for him. "I understand. When I was little, I wanted to wed Eoin." She grinned as he started. "He is fifteen years older than I, but many lasses wed older men, or so I told him when I proposed."

Duncan chuckled and shook his head. "Poor man."

"Fergie refused permission, because I was only ten. When Eoin wed Annie, it broke my heart—for all of three days. Fergie gave me a new pony, and I swore off men...till you, love."

"Fergie is a wise man."

"Wise, aye, but..." She sobered. "His heart pains him from time to time, and I fear..." She could not say the words. "We need someone to lead us."

Duncan nodded. "I will fight in his place, if it comes to that. But I wonder if we couldn't find a peaceful solution."

"Make peace with the MacGorys? They're savages."

"We said the same about Saladin's people," he said slowly. "But we were evenly matched. A treaty seemed the only way to avoid wiping each other out. The MacGorys cannot conquer you, nor will they want to winter in the hills. Mayhap—" He broke off and stood in the stirrups. "What is that?"

Two dark splotches stood out against the snowy hillside a quarter mile or so across the valley floor. Everything around them was pristine white.

"Stay here," Duncan said over his shoulder as he rode off.

Kara followed without a qualm. When she saw what awaited them, she was sorry. Two bodies sprawled facedown in the snow, like dolls tossed aside by a careless child. "Are they...dead?"

"Aye," Duncan muttered. He stood, giving her a clear view of the face pillowed in the snow.

"Orna," Kara slid from the saddle. Shock held her immobile. "Poor thing. The other must be her husband, Cuddie. They live in a croft beyond those trees and were inseparable from the day they wed fifty years ago. They must have gotten caught in the snowstorm. But what were the old fools doing out in the first place?"

Duncan crossed to her, his expression hard. "They were not killed by the storm."

"What?" She tried to move past him, but he held her fast.

"They were...murdered."

"No one would harm them. They were old, feeble and as poor as everyone else in the valley." She started forward.

He caught her. "Do not look. They were tortured."

Kara felt her gorge rise. "Who...who would do such a thing?" She looked up at Duncan for answers, but his eyes were flickering over the landscape, so filled with fury she scarcely recognized them. "You know who it was?"

"MacGorys...the bastards."

"Inside Edin Valley? That's impossible."

Duncan opened his hand and showed her a bunch of thick black hairs. "Wolf fur. Cuddie ripped it from his killer. He and his wife did not die easily or quickly. The MacGorys must have wanted information about the valley."

"Oh, my God. How many of them do you think there were?"

"Only two." He led her past the bodies, their faces mercifully covered by their cloaks. "See those tracks?" At her nod, he went on. "Two men afoot, heavy men by the depth of their prints. They came from the north, back toward Stratheas and are traveling south down the valley."

"Toward Edin Tower." Fergie. Black Rolly.

"Or the pass. They have not been able to take it or to trick you into coming out. So—"

Kara's blood turned to ice. "But why only two men?"

"They may be scouts. Whatever, we've got to find them and stop them from taking the information back to their leader." He scowled. "Hard to believe they came over the mountain."

Kara swallowed. "There's another way into the valley. A wee, twisting tunnel through the mountains that comes out below Stratheas. There is a slab of stone blocking it, and no one knows of it save Fergie, Black Rolly and me. I—I would have told you, only there's been no time.''

"I understand. But now two MacGorys may know. I want you to ride back to Stratheas, gather a party of warriors and tell them how to find the mouth of this tunnel. If the stone is displaced, they're to reset it. Either way, they must wedge something into the base so it cannot be opened.''

"Where are you going?''

"After the MacGorys. We've wasted too much time already. Go to Stratheas and stay there. Do not go down to the tunnel.''

"But...''

Duncan grabbed her upper arms and hauled her up against him. "Kara, if you love me, you will do exactly as I say. How can I keep my mind on finding the MacGorys if I'm worried about you?''

Kara nodded. "I will not go to the tunnel,'' she said. But neither was she letting Duncan face the MacGorys alone. She'd give his orders to the captain of Stratheas's guard and return.

Chapter Eight

Duncan emptied his mind of everything but finding the MacGorys. Thanks to hours spent in the woods as a boy, he was an experienced tracker. He rode slowly along the base of the mountain, one eye on the footprints in the snow, the other on the land ahead, alert for an ambush.

A half hour after leaving Kara, he cautiously rounded a bend in the trail and spotted a small croft nestled into a grove of trees up ahead. His gut clenched when he circled and found the tracks led straight to the hut but not away. Driven by the images of more dead innocents, he left his horse well back in the trees and threaded his way through the pines. Coming up at the front of the windowless croft, he debated the wisdom of rushing the door or—

The door popped open and a girl ran out, a bundle clutched to her chest, her eyes wild with fear. Behind her hurtled a man straight from a child's nightmare. Huge and dark, half his face obscured by a beard as black as his scraggly hair. He had arms and legs as thick as tree trunks, and a wolf's skin slung across his body. A MacGory!

"Run!" the MacGory shouted. "There's naught I like better than a good hunt. Whets my appetite, it does." His laugh as he lumbered after the girl was more terrifying than drawn steel.

Duncan drew his sword and measured the distance across

the clearing. Too far, he'd never reach the MacGory before he caught the girl. And once he did, the fiend would not hesitate to use her as a shield to force Duncan's surrender. The lass darted through the trees like a hare driven before a mad fox, shifting this way and that. Suddenly she changed direction, heading straight for Duncan.

"Come on," he silently urged. "A few more steps." They were close enough so he could hear her labored sobs under the panting of her pursuer. Now!

Duncan stuck out his left hand, grabbed the lass's arm as she stumbled by and swung her behind him. In the same smooth movement, he stepped onto the path and met her charging pursuer with a length of tempered steel.

"Argh!" the man cried. He tried to stop, stumbled and pitched forward onto Duncan's sword. His eyes rounded in shock. Blood bubbled between his lips as he reached for the blade protruding from the middle of his chest.

"Damn." A dead man would tell no tales. Duncan pulled his blade free and shoved the man down. Kneeling beside him, he pressed the dripping blade to the man's throat. "Who are you?"

"Egan...MacGory. Who...?"

"What are you doing in the valley?"

Egan shook his head, eyes already glazing over. He died before he could answer any more questions.

Damn. Spinning on his heels, Duncan regarded the girl cowering against a rough-barked oak. "Where is the other one?"

She shuddered and clutched her bundle more closely. It whimpered piteously, one tiny hand coming out to grasp at the air. "Dinna kill us," the girl murmured.

"I'll not hurt you," Duncan said as gently as he could with his nerves shouting for speed. She couldn't be more than ten and so frightened she'd tell him nothing if he pressed. "I'm Kara Gleanedin's betrothed. I've been trailing some bad men. Where is the one who was with this wretch?"

"Hut," she whispered. Her eyes went black with panic. "Mama. Poor Mama, she told me to take wee Peter and run while she…"

Duncan nodded. Removing his cloak, he slung it around the shivering girl. "Stay here. I'll go and see to your mama." He cleaned his blade on the MacGory's tunic, then trotted off toward the hut. As he cautiously approached the open doorway, he heard a woman's cries and a guttural grunting that curdled his stomach.

His teeth clenched so tightly they hurt, Duncan slipped into the hut, shoved the bastard off his victim and onto the floor. Once more, his blade flirted with dirty MacGory flesh.

"What the hell," the fiend snarled. He was older than Egan, his face scarred and weathered. "Who are ye?"

"Divine retribution."

"There's no clan of that name hereabouts."

"Who are you? How many in your party?" Duncan asked.

"Sim MacGory's my name." His flinty eyes shifted toward the square of light coming in through the doorway.

"Egan's not coming. He's dead."

"Bastard!" Sim bucked, then lay still when the blade nicked his throat. "He was my son."

"I'm not surprised. Where is the rest of your clan?"

The MacGory pressed his lips shut. It would not be easy to pry secrets from this hardened old reprobate. Duncan had never had a taste for torture, no matter how foul the prisoner, but his time in the East had taught him that fear could be a greater loosener of tongues than the lash or thumbscrews.

"See that pouch at my waist?" Duncan asked softly.

The MacGory grunted. "Ye going to pay me?"

"Such fine, pale leather is much prized where I've been. This one was fashioned from the skin of a man who stole from me." Duncan smiled grimly as the man's eyes wid-

ned. "Aye. I made him stitch it up for me before I finished
im."

"His...his own skin?" The MacGory's throat worked
gainst the sword. "Jesu..."

"Tell me what I want to know, and I'll see you are dead
efore I carve you up."

"Ivor would kill me if I betrayed him."

"I'll find out...one way or the other. 'Tis immaterial to
ne how long it takes, but by the time I'm done, you'll be
orry you didn't speak more quickly."

The MacGory spilled his secrets like the craven brute he
vas, eager to prey on the weak, yet weak himself. A dozen
MacGorys had been given the task of searching the hills
utside the valley for some way in. After weeks of pains-
akingly combing every foot of the countryside, he and
Egan had stumbled upon the tunnel. Uncertain where it led,
hey were exploring when they came upon the old couple
gathering the last of the acorns.

"They said this was Edin Valley, right enough, and told
is how far 'twas to the pass at the south end."

Duncan nodded. If these two had found the tunnel, others
might. His mind seethed with plans and counterplans. First
he needed to secure his prisoner. Duncan risked a quick
glance at the woman. She'd pulled her skirts down and
huddled against the far wall. "How are you called, lass?"

"Ma-Mairi."

"I'm Duncan MacLellan."

"Kara's knight?" Some of her wariness fled.

"Aye. I need to be off, but I can't leave this vermin
oaming free. Can you get me a stout rope to bind him
vith?"

She nodded and scrabbled in a dark corner, coming up
vith a narrow loop of hemp. Her thin face was pinched
vith pain, but her hands were steady as she tied Sim's
vrists and ankles. "What will ye do with him, Duncan?"

"I'll—"

The thud of hooves and babble of excited voices her-

alded the arrival of several people in the yard. A big man
burst into the hut. His head swung back and forth like a
bear at a baiting, then he snarled something at Duncan.

"Nay, John!" Mairi leapt on the newcomer, sobbing.
"'Tis Kara's Duncan. He saved me from yon bastard."

Duncan rose slowly. Just as he gained his feet, a body
streaked through the doorway and slammed into his.

"Duncan!" Kara cried. "When I saw the dead man, I
feared—"

"Shh." He stroked her back and held her close, thanking
God she hadn't been with him when he'd come here. "You
were supposed to stay at Stratheas."

"I couldn't." She looked up at him, lashes spiky with
tears, her eyes brimming with love.

"See if you can calm Mairi, will you? I'd best be off to
talk with Fergie about what needs doing."

"You've learned something?" At his nod, she wiped the
tears from her cheeks. "Tell me."

Duncan hesitated. "War is men's business, Kara."

"Surviving is everyone's business." She looked around
at the others who had crowded into the hut. The women
were comforting Mairi and her bairns. The men had
dragged the MacGory out into the yard and were questioning him none too gently. Lowering her voice, she added,
"Fergie is not as strong as he was."

"Eoin, then. I'd speak with him."

"When we are wed, the men of Clan Gleanedin will
follow you, but till then, I am Fergie's heir."

Duncan glared at her. "I'll tell you what I know, but you
are not riding out to fight. No matter what."

"Fight? What of your notion to sign a treaty with
them?"

Duncan looked across the hut to Mairi. The dimness
couldn't hide her cut lip or the bruises on her throat. Worse
was the lingering horror in her face and that of her small
daughter. "The MacGorys have less honor than the Infi-

dels. Nor do I think men who torture old people and rape children are the sort to keep their word," he muttered.

"I'm glad you see that, but how are we to stop them?"

"I'm not certain, yet."

"But you have a plan."

"An idea." It was sneaky and devious, unworthy of a Crusader knight, but he realized that some things went beyond honor. He only hoped God would understand what he was about to do.

Next morning, Kara stood atop the pass and watched the sun rise above the mountains. Its long, golden fingers stretched across the plain, dancing on the ripples in the river. The snow had melted, but a heavy frost the previous night left the grass sparkling as though sprinkled with fairy dust. High above, a hawk wheeled and banked in search of a stray mouse. On the riverbank, another, more subtle type of hunt was underway.

"Have they taken the bait?" Fergie muttered.

Kara whirled. "You're supposed to be resting."

"And how would a man do that, with the life of his clan at stake?" His face was gray, but his eyes crackled with vitality.

"Duncan will not let us down." Her gaze went to the men working on the far side of the river.

'Twas easy to spot Duncan, his dark head rising above her red-maned clansmen. Stripped to the waist despite the chill, they busily cleared the brush and trees from the bank. Another party of men used the green timber to fashion a palisade. Once up, it would prevent anyone from approaching the water and make it doubly difficult to sneak up on the pass.

At least Duncan hoped the MacGorys were canny enough to figure that out. He wanted to push them into making a move, into taking a chance on attacking the seemingly vulnerable work party.

"Do you think they'll come?" she asked.

"Aye. Our men look like a bunch of dumb, frightened sheep. Why ye cannot even see anyone standing guard to sound the alarm. What wolf could resist such easy prey?"

"Indeed." Kara looked over her shoulder at the spiny ridge of the mountains. Nothing stirred on the cliff face, yet behind every boulder hid a bowman. All part of Duncan's plan. What if it didn't work? What if the MacGorys came in such numbers that they overwhelmed the men working in the open?

"Easy, lass, ye're shaking like a leaf in a storm."

"I'm afraid." She chafed the gooseflesh on her arms, her gaze swinging back to Duncan.

"Ye love him, do ye not?"

"With all my heart."

"And what of yon knight? He was that eager to be away when we first took him in, but he fits in right well now."

"He's had a hard life, Fergie, orphaned at ten, raised by a cousin who despised him. He's found happiness here with us. When this business with the MacGorys is settled, he plans to ask if we may wed," she added shyly.

"Ah." Fergie lifted her off her feet and hugged her. "I hoped 'twould come to that." Setting her down, he wiped his eyes on his tunic sleeve.

"What is it?"

"I'm happy for ye, that's all. I'll not rest easy till I know my wee lass is settled with a good man." But he avoided looking at her, which wasn't like Fergie at all.

"Does your chest pain you?"

"Nay."

Unease prickled her skin. "Fergie, what is it?"

"Naught," he said quickly. Too quickly. Suddenly he straightened. Shielding his eyes, he stared over the plain toward the hills where the MacGorys camped. "Did ye see a flash yonder?"

Before Kara could answer, the guard atop the cliffs gave the raven call, bringing the men on the riverbank to instant attention. 'Twas a mark of their respect that they immediately looked to Duncan. He signaled with another raven call, then went back to work. One by one, the others bent to their tasks.

Kara glanced from her loved ones to the sea of tall brush. The MacGorys were taking extra pains, the only sign of their passage a twitch here and there in the long grass. The moments stretched out till her nerves screamed. "How can they bear the waiting? My skin's fairly crawling."

"Aye, that's the worst." Fergie's scarred hand gripped the pommel of his claymore. "I should be with them."

"Nay, Fergie—"

The raven called again.

Scarcely had the sound faded than the MacGorys rose from cover. They were barely fifty feet from the river, shrieking like banshees, weapons glinting ominously in the sun.

"Hurry, Duncan," Kara whispered as her clansmen dropped their tools to pick up the swords and shields concealed nearby.

Seeing their victims intended to fight, the MacGorys howled even louder and closed in for what they assumed would be an easy kill. They were thirty feet from their target when a wedge of flaming arrows arched out from the cliff tops. Clearing the water, they struck the grass in the MacGory's path.

"Ye shoot like women," a MacGory shouted. But their jeers turned to cries of horror, for the night before Duncan had doused the bracken with grease, and it burst into flame.

The wall of fire chased the MacGorys back. Before they could regroup and work around it, a second flight of arrows ignited the brush behind them, enclosing them in a circle of fire. Singly and in pairs, the MacGorys burst free, only to be met by the warriors of Edin Valley.

"Come, lass." Fergie took her hand and led Kara away from the brink of the cliff. "'Tis not a fit sight for ye."

"But what if Duncan needs my help?"

"Ye can help the most by seeing that when this battle's

done he has a hot bath to wash off the soot, a whiskey to clear the smoke from his throat and a hot meal.''

Once Kara would have scoffed at being kept from the action, but she had not the stomach for fighting and bloodshed. Duncan had done his part to save them. She must do hers. At the bottom of the trail, the women of Gleanedin waited anxiously for news. Fergie gave them the glad tidings, and Kara set the women to work. Half of them started for the tower to begin preparations for a victory fete. The others stayed to tend the wounded...while praying there would not be many.

"We've won," Kara said, clinging to Fergie's hand. "I can scarcely believe we'll finally be free of them."

"Aye." Fergie ruffled her hair. "Thanks to Duncan."

Chapter Nine

That night, Edin Tower's great hall shimmered with the sights and sounds of triumph. It was etched into every smiling face, woven into every tale and toast as the victorious warriors of Gleanedin retold the events of the day. One name was on everyone's lips.

"Duncan! Duncan!" They chanted.

Seated in the place of honor between Fergie and Kara, Duncan felt his face heat. "'Twas no one man's doing," he protested, unused to being the focus of so much praise.

"Ye'll not convince us of that." Fergie stood and lifted his hands for silence. "Thanks to Duncan, we can once again hunt and fish the lands outside the valley. We can travel to market and trade for what we cannot raise ourselves." He turned toward Duncan, tears in his eyes. "Whatever we have, is yers."

Duncan rose stiffly, his barely healed body protesting today's vigorous activity. "The idea may have been mine, but 'twas the blood and bravery of every man here that won the day."

A roar of approval greeted his words. As he resumed his seat, Kara leaned close.

"I love you," she whispered.

"And I you." Duncan shifted, following Fergie's progress about the room as he laughed and chatted with his clansmen. It would be tomorrow, at the earliest, before he could get her uncle alone and ask for Kara's hand. Not nearly soon enough.

"Why do you scowl so darkly, my love? Does your shoulder pain you?" Her fingers brushed his arm. Desire shot through him. Only years of training kept Duncan seated when he wanted to drag her from the hall to some dark corner. He focused his attention on her concerned face. "Nay. Though I've more bruises and scrapes than I can count—" he kissed the tip of her nose "—I've never been happier in my life."

"'Twould be perfect if we could sneak away and—"

"There'll be none of that." He softened his words with a kiss, her mouth so sweet he lingered till they were both breathless. "Never doubt I want you, but I'd do this right."

"If we declared ourselves wed before my clansmen—"

"I want more than a handfasting for a year and a day. I want you to wife...forever."

"Forever." She sealed the vow with a kiss so tender it nearly melted his iron will.

He wrenched his mouth away and gasped in a steadying breath. "I should check on the guard at the pass."

"Do you think some of the MacGorys escaped?"

"None left the battlefield alive, and their camp was deserted when we found it. It is possible they had a few guards there, who ran off when we came searching, but I doubt it. That doesn't mean we can relax our vigilance. Others may come and try to take the valley. What we need are more men."

"We've not the coin to hire them."

"Not mercenaries, men with ties to our clan."

"Our clan." Kara laced her fingers with his. "It gladdens my heart to hear you speak of them thus."

"Not half as much as it does mine." He glanced about, drinking in the sights and sounds of boisterous Gleanedins. "I never thought to find a place where I was so well come." A tiny niggle of regret lingered. Someday, some way, he must find out how Janet fared.

A cry went up from the other end of the hall.

Instantly a dozen men leapt up and drew their swords.

"'Tis Fergie!" someone shouted.

"Kara! Kara, come quick!"

Duncan lifted her over the bench and cleared a path for her.

Fergie lay on his back, his eyes closed, one hand clutching the front of his tunic.

"Oh, God." Kara sank to the floor beside Fergie.

Duncan followed her down, watching her face contort with anguish, her hands tremble as she examined her uncle.

"He...he lives," she whispered. "Help me get him to bed."

A dozen men crowded close to help. Duncan waved them back. Together he and Eoin carried the laird to his chamber. They stood uselessly by while Kara and the women bustled about making Fergie comfortable. The scent of herbs filled the room yet couldn't hide the stink of fear.

Squeezing his eyes shut, Duncan began to pray for a miracle.

The hours dragged by with little change in Fergie's condition. Eyes closed, he lay unmoving in the center of the big bed where he'd been born, his face gray as his shock of bushy hair. The heavy silence in the room was broken only by the shallow rasp of his breathing and the crackle of the fire.

Seated in a chair beside the bed, Kara watched his chest rise and fall, willing his heart to keep beating. She'd sent the women to bed, but Duncan had refused to leave.

He straddled a low stool, his back against the wall, his eyes shut. How uncomfortable he looked. How exhausted he must be to sleep in such a cramped position. Come morn, his muscles would pain him something fierce.

"Duncan," she whispered.

His eyes flew open, thè stool thumped as the legs settled to ground. "What?" He glanced at Fergie, then at her.

"He's just the same," she whispered. "Go on to bed."

"Nay, I'll stay and—"

"There's naught to do but wait to see if the foxglove infusion will strengthen his heart. If you sleep now, you can spell me on the morrow."

Duncan frowned but rose, moving so stiffly she knew he must be in pain. "Wake me if there's any change." He grazed her cheek with his knuckles. "I'm so sorry, love. Just when it seemed peace was within our grasp—"

"He'll recover," she said quickly. "He has before."

"Aye," Duncan replied, but his face mirrored her own fears. "I'll come down again at first light and see how he does."

Kara nodded. If she was any judge, Duncan was exhausted enough to sleep the sun around. "Morag and the others are just outside. They'll come if I call."

The room seemed oddly cold and empty with Duncan gone. Shivering, Kara wrapped the extra blanket about her shoulders and turned toward the bed.

"Kara?" Fergie asked hoarsely.

"Aye." Kara grasped his icy hand in hers. "How do you feel?"

"Like I'd been kicked in the chest by a horse. Is there any whiskey about?"

"No whiskey." She picked up the cup containing the decoction of foxglove. For generations, the healers of the valley had valued it as a remedy against all forms of heart troubles. "Take a wee sip of this, then some water."

Fergie made a face but did as he was told. Which worried Kara more than his labored breathing.

"Lay back and rest."

He lowered his head to the pillow. "Have to tell ye."

"Tomorrow."

"Now." His eyes were ghosted with the knowledge that

he might not see tomorrow. "Have to tell ye where I put them."

"What?"

"The red stones."

Kara froze, heart thudding with dread. "Duncan's gems?"

"Aye." He licked his lips. "Black Rolly read the paper."

"Duncan's letter? The one in his pouch?"

"From a lass...Janet. He'd vowed to win a fortune and return to...to wed her." Fergie closed his eyes. "Couldn't let him...leave."

"Oh, Fergie. You stole his treasure? How could you?"

"I did it for ye...for the valley."

"But...but to steal what was his, to make him stay under false pretenses." Blood beat against her ears. Or was it the death of a dream she heard in the thunderous wash?

"He loves ye." Fergie's hand tightened on hers. "He loves our people. He's happy here as he never could be with that lass."

"Aye, he is." The knowledge that he loved her people made the pain all the more unbearable. "But I have to tell him."

"Why?" Fergie tried to rise.

She pushed him back down with frightening ease. "Never mind, Fergie. We'll speak of it no more."

"I did it for ye."

"I know," she said softly. Could she honestly say she wished he hadn't done it? If Fergie hadn't taken the stones, Duncan wouldn't have stayed, wouldn't have fallen in love with her. The pain was stifling, for she knew what she must do. Duncan was a man who valued honor above all things. She could not base their lives on a lie. Even if it meant losing him.

Duncan stared at the pile of red stones Kara had poured into his palm. They gleamed like droplets of blood. His life's blood, draining slowly away as the truth sank in.

His fortune had been returned.

"I'd told Black Rolly you were the man sent to save us. Wanting to know more about you, he searched your pouch while I was busy tending your wound. When he read Janet's letter—"

"Fergie said no Gleanedin could read."

"Rolly is a MacHugh. He studied with the priests before coming here. Fearing you would leave, he took the letter and the gems and showed them to Fergie the moment he returned. Fergie hid them in the hollow hilt of his dagger."

Duncan stared blindly at the top of her bent head. "I wish to God he'd never given them back."

Her head snapped up, face glowing with hope. "Duncan?"

"Kara." He fisted the rubies and dragged her into her arms, needing the feel of her in his arms, unable to watch as his words drained away her happiness. "I want to stay with you. Believe I want that more than I have ever wanted anything. But I have to go. You know that."

She buried her face in his chest. "Aye." The shudders that rippled from her body into his tore him apart.

Could a man die of grief?

"I swear I'll come back to you. If I reach Threave and find Janet has wed another, I'll be free of my vow and—"

"Shh." She stilled his lips with the tips of her fingers. "Please do not promise what you may not be able to fulfill."

"I won't. But I wish...God I wish you'd thrown them away."

"Do you?" Her startling amber eyes focused on his. "I wanted to, but I could not begin our life with a lie. Even if you never found out that Fergie had taken the rubies and I had kept them from you, I would have known."

He nodded. "It is seldom easy to do the honorable

thing." He touched her cheek. "If Janet has found another, I'll return."

The land around Threave Castle was much as he remembered, Duncan thought as he slowly rode toward the great pile of stone glaring down from its lofty hilltop. Below it stretched the broad fields belonging to the laird, fallow, now, and blanketed by a thin cover of snow, but neat and well tended. As were the crofters' huts clustered at the bottom of the hill. Sporting a fresh coat of whitewash, new thatch bristling from the roofs, even they were monuments to Cousin Niall's passion for order.

He shivered, already bracing for the moment when he'd ride through the gates and face them, the man who'd made his youth hell, and the woman whose friendship had kept him sane.

All too soon he was passing under the sharp teeth of the portcullis. His mount's hooves rang hollowly on the cobbled courtyard. As he drew rein before the imposing tower, a fresh-faced lad of twenty or so ran out to take his horse.

"Is Cousin Niall in residence?" Duncan asked.

The lad blinked then started. "Why, 'tis Duncan, home from the Crusades. Do ye remember me...Wila's Harry?"

"I do, but you were a good deal shorter when I left."

"There've been a lot of changes these past three years."

"Any weddings?" he asked hopefully.

"A few."

"Duncan. Duncan, is that really you?" A woman walked sedately toward him. She was dressed in the height of fashion, the long sleeves of her formfitting blue surcoat swept the ground. A fortune in gems decorated the throat and hem, winking in the pale sunlight. Her hair was properly concealed by a long veil, held in place by a gold circlet. Everything about her was proper and controlled, including her small, welcoming smile.

"Janet?" Duncan asked.

"Aye." A dimple dared to disturb the perfection of her

face. Her eyes were as warm and accepting as he remembered.

"It has been a long time," he said. This was hard, so hard.

"Three years. Oh, Duncan, I was afraid you'd been killed."

He opened his arms and she threw herself into his embrace as she used to when they were growing up. She was taller than Kara, her curves more lush, but the press of them left him unmoved. Damn, how was he going to wed her when Kara filled his mind and his heart?

"Duncan." She leaned back, hands on his chest. "You're taller and...broader...than I remembered."

"Fighting builds muscles."

She shivered. "Don't speak of it. Every night I prayed for God to bring you back safely to us."

"I...I feared you'd given up and wed someone else," he teased, but his chest was so tight he could scarcely breathe. Please. Please let her have found someone.

"Nay. We made a pact, you and I. Oh, Duncan, I'm so very, very glad you've come home."

"I, too." But as he looked around at the stark walls of Threave, he felt anything but at home. A crowd had gathered, many of them glaring at him as they used to.

Ingrate. Son of a whore. Fortune hunter. The words crept through the throng, icy as a killing frost.

I don't want to be here, Duncan silently cried.

"Duncan, did you make your fortune?" Janet whispered.

"Aye," he said dully. "I vowed I'd not return without it. And I'd not break that oath."

"Of course." She smiled up at him as though he'd granted her fondest wish. "Oh, Duncan, I am so happy. Father will be livid." She chuckled. "I've prayed for this day. I've longed for your return. We must talk in private. Make plans—"

"Laird Niall wants ye in the hall," growled the captain of Threave's guard, a great brute of a man who'd taken pleasure in whipping Duncan whenever he stepped out of line.

"I'd speak with my betrothed in private," Janet said.

Mangus's lip curled. "Himself said now."

Janet sighed. "Very well."

On leaden feet, Duncan followed Janet across the courtyard up the stairs to the entryway and through it to the great hall. Dinner was in progress, the servants passing platters of food to the orderly rows of diners. The rushes crunched beneath his heel, giving off the sweet scent of rosemary. Whitewash brightened the walls, colorful tapestries softened their austerity. Dozens of flambeaux in rings on the walls illuminated the scene, but the people were cold and stiff.

When he was younger, the orderly way of life at Threave had seemed to him the epitome of grace and civility. A goal to be sought, a way to wipe out the stain of his mother's impropriety. Now it seemed stark, cold and oppressive.

"So, you have returned." The voice was not loud. Niall Leslie never shouted. But it carried the length of the hall, stilling all talk and turning heads toward the threshold, where Duncan stood with Janet.

Duncan straightened his shoulders and advanced toward the figure seated at the table on the raised dais. Dimly he was conscious of the censorious folk he passed and of Janet's sweaty hand clenched tight in his. Mostly he felt a sense of loss.

"Duncan," Cousin Niall inclined his head of close-cropped gray hair. "Have you gained that which you sought, or do you crawl back here a failure like your—"

Duncan tossed the sack of rubies onto the table. The grim satisfaction he felt when Niall beheld the treasure inside paled beside the grinding ache in his heart.

"Hmm." Cousin Niall leaned back in his chair. Fingering his pointy chin, he regarded Duncan and his daughter

as he might two bugs that had invaded his tidy bed. He had
the face of a hawk, eyes as cold as a witch's soul. "So,
there's to be a wedding?"

Duncan drew in a steadying breath, then exhaled
"Aye." *May God help us both.*

Chapter Ten

The first winter storm struck on Christmas Eve day, but it didn't deter the folk of Edin from bringing in the Yule log. Trailing snow, faces red from the cold, they paraded the log around the great hall to the raucous lilt of the pipes then placed it in the hearth with due ceremony.

Surrounded by her merry kin, Kara felt as close to happy as she got these days. The familiar sights, sounds and smells of the festive season were a balm to her aching heart. It had been a relief, actually, to turn her thoughts away from her private pain and attend to the myriad of tasks. She must carry on without Duncan. What choice did she have?

"The hall looks that grand," Fergie commented.

Kara grinned, eyes sweeping from the garlands strung along the beams of the ceiling. Interwoven with the ivy were sprigs of holly to keep the fairies away, and sprays of yew decorated the center of every table. "That it does."

"We've much to be thankful for."

"Aye." She hugged his waist, pleased by the strength of his lean muscles. "Most of all, I'm grateful you're well."

"Well, I'm glad the MacGorys are not about. If only..."

"Do not say it, Fergie," she whispered. "Duncan would have come back ere now if he were free."

"'Twould have been better if he'd never come."

"If he hadn't, the MacGorys would be living at Edin Tower."

Fergie grunted. "That's true enough, but—"

"None of that. We'll not be ruining the best season of the year with useless regrets." Kara whirled him about and gently shoved him toward a bench. "The lads are about to sing."

When they were seated, the gillean Nollaig, the Christmas lads, chosen for their sweet voices, stepped forward. Clad in long white shirts of bleached wool, tall white hats on their heads, they began to chant the traditional songs.

They finished with the first song, and the leader bent to the cradle by the hearth and lifted out Brighde's wee Donald Duncan, the babe chosen to play the part of the Cristean. Wrapping the little Christ in the skin of a male lamb, the lads carried him sunwise three times around the hall. As they went, the gillean sang the Christmas hail.

A shout rang from the ceiling as wee Donnie was returned to the cradle, and the tower folk rushed forward to lay small offerings around the Cristean. A crock of honey, tiny buns dotted with currants, a carved wooden horse and woolen booties. All the while, he cooed and waved his hands as though blessing them.

Cups were raised to the triumphs of the past year and prayers offered to thank the gods, both old and new. The feast that followed went on joyously all through the day. It stopped snowing at dusk, and the gillean marched out, followed by a goodly number of merrymakers, to visit the nearby crofts.

That first day set the tone for the week of festive celebrations. Kara was in the thick of things, overseeing the preparation of special meals, organizing games for the children. She danced till her feet hurt, smiled till her cheeks ached. But before she closed her eyes each night, she'd stare deep into the small fire in her corner hearth, seeking a vision that never came. Duncan must have wed his Jane.

she reasoned, else he'd have come back to her as he promised.

Heartbroken, she'd bury her face in her pillow and cry herself to sleep. But there was no escape there, either, for she dreamed of Duncan. Rich, vivid dreams of their night together. Dreams so real she awoke sweaty, aroused and disappointed to find 'twas not his arms wrapped around her but the twisted bed linens.

By New Year's Eve day, she was weary and hollow eyed. Still she joined the folk of Edin as they left the tower, bearing torches on eight-foot poles. Around the loch they paraded, in an ancient ceremony intended to drive out evil and insure prosperity. The sound of the pipes rose in the air, mixing with icy bits of snow. When the hourglass showed midnight had come, they piled up the torches, formed a circle around them and watched till the fire had died out before retiring to their beds.

Facing another dream-filled night, Kara volunteered to stay up and make certain the fire in the great hall did not go out. Likewise, candles would be kept burning in the windows to insure that evil would be kept from the tower in the coming year.

Eoin, Fergie and Black Rolly sat with her for a time. She forgot her own sorrows as she listened to their tales of long ago, and even laughed when Fergie told about the Hogmanay he was chosen to play the part of the bull. Dressed in a hide, including the horns and hooves, he led the procession from croft to croft. At every farm, they climbed to the flat edge of the thatched roof and enacted their little drama.

Fergie shook his horns and bellowed; the other lads chanted and struck him with sticks to keep him under control, while the pipers played. The noise was horrific, but once the ritual was complete, the farmers would come out of their huts to pass around cakes and ale.

"We visited nigh every croft in the valley, so they tell us. By the time we reached the last one, we'd had so much ale we none of us were too nimble. Still we climbed onto the roof. Promptly lost our balance and fell backward. Right through the thatch, we went, and straight down into the hearth. They couldn't get the stink of burned cowhide out of the place for a year.''

Everyone roared with laughter, and that tale blended into the next. But eventually, the others drifted off to seek their beds, leaving Kara alone with her thoughts.

She too found it easier to look backward than forward. As she stared into the sacred blaze of the Chulluinn fire, she searched over every moment she'd spent with Duncan. Nay, she did not regret loving him. In the flickering flames, she saw them dancing as they had Samhuinn eve, and the magic lifted her soul. Warmed by the fire and her memories, she drifted.

''Kara?''

She started, surprised to find Eoin standing over her. More surprised to find pale light glowing behind the oiled hides that covered the hall's narrow windows. ''The fire…''

''Still burns brightly,'' he assured her. ''I came to tell you we've had a signal. Riders sighted coming down the valley.''

Her heart lurched. ''How many?''

''Three score, mayhap more.''

''Oh.'' Her shoulders slumped, then fear intruded. ''Invaders?''

''Nay. The lads would have sounded the alarm if the pass had been attacked. The men ride slowly, openly, like invited guests.''

''Father Luthais, then, though he usually comes alone.''

''I thought ye'd like to wash the sleep from yer eyes and don a skirt that doesn't look as though ye slept in it.''

Kara cuffed his arm and dashed upstairs. On her bed lay the deep green tunic and matching skirt she'd planned to wear for this most special of days. She donned them in a trice, mind leaping ahead to seeing Father Luthais again. He was dear little gnome of a man.

Back down the stairs she went, arriving breathless in the hall just as a knock sounded on the stout wooden door. The other folk of Edin dropped what they were doing and froze, waiting to see who would cross the threshold, for 'twas believed that the first foot to enter the hall was a portent for the coming year.

Fergie walked slowly to the door and opened it.

Snow swirled into the room, bringing with it the tang of clean, crisp air and a big man wrapped in a thick cloak. Its hood obscured his features, but he was too tall for Father Luthais.

"Damn, but 'tis cold," exclaimed the man in a muffled voice. He shook like a dog shedding water, then flung aside the cloak.

"Duncan!" Kara cried. "It's you."

"Aye." The red, chapped skin about his eyes crinkled as he smiled. "A bit frozen, but none the worse for—"

"Duncan!" Kara launched herself at him with such force she drove him back into the men who stood behind him.

"Easy, love." He laughed and hugged her so tightly she couldn't breathe. "You'll bruise the gift I brought you."

"You are all the gift I want." She buried her face in the cold folds of his neck. "What of Janet?"

"Later. I'll tell you all of it later." He stroked her back, then set her on the ground. "First, I have to see to our men."

"Our men?" Kara echoed. Looking behind him, she saw a throng of dark-clad men file into the room. "Who—?"

"MacLellans," Duncan said proudly. "Eight and twenty stout lads come to see if life in Edin Valley will suit them. If you'll give us leave to settle here, that is."

"Us?" Kara repeated. "You mean, you've come to stay?"

"If you'll have me," he said with the first note of uncertainty she'd yet heard.

"If!" Kara's mouth rounded. "Oh..."

"Course she will." Fergie waded through the crowd of

wide-eyed Gleanedins. "We'll summon Father Luthais from Kindo—"

"I'm already here." The wee priest stepped around two of Duncan's clansmen and grinned at Kara. "I was that surprised when yon knight turned up at the church door yestereve. But when I heard what he wanted, I was only too happy to trek through the snow for the pleasure of seeing Kara wed."

The wedding was held that afternoon, in the great hall decked with ivy, holly and mistletoe. It was a mix of pagan and Christian, as was only proper, Duncan had said, for the joining of a redheaded witch and a Crusader knight.

The bride wore a garland of holly and a tunic of finest wool in a brilliant gold that matched her eyes. A gift from her groom. He was resplendent in forest green and a smile so wide it put dimples in his cheeks. Father Luthais conducted the ceremony in the great hall, for there was no kirk.

"Come spring, we'll build one," Duncan said, raising a cup to toast his new-made wife.

"Hmm. Well…" Kara glanced uncertainly at the old ones, Morag and those who still kept to the ancient ways. "I don't know."

"'Twill be a joining of the old and new. A tribute to God for leading me here to you." Duncan's arm tightened around Kara, the fire in his eyes warming her clear to her toes. There'd been no chance for them to be alone together, but soon…

"An excellent idea," Father Luthais said.

"I dunno," Morag muttered.

"We could put it on the side of the hill," Duncan said softly. "Leaving free the crest where the sacred fires burn at Beltane and Samhuinn. That way the people may have both."

Morag sniffed. "Ye're a right canny lad, fer an outlander." Drawing her robe about her withered body, she limped off toward the hearth. "We'll see, come spring," she added.

"'Tis a sound idea," Fergie said. Eyes twinkling, he glanced at the crowded trestle tables, where Duncan's broad-shouldered MacLellans broke bread with the Gleanedins. "They're a likely looking bunch."

"Our lassies seem to think so," Kara said, noting the women buzzing about them like flies to honey. "Come spring, we may be needing that kirk for a host of weddings."

"And baptisms," Father Luthais added. "Mayhap I'd best hang about for a fortnight or two...in case I'm needed."

"Ye're more than welcome." Fergie threw an arm about the priest's shoulders. "Come sample the mead."

As the two men wandered off through the crowd, Kara felt Duncan tug her back toward the door.

"What?" she whispered.

"Come away with me."

"But you've not had your supper."

"I'm not hungry...for food."

Suddenly, neither was she.

Hand in hand, they slipped from the hall and across the entryway to the stairwell. Barely had they gained the steps, when a shout warned their escape had been noted.

"Run," Duncan cried.

Lifting her skirts, Kara dashed up the stairs with Duncan pounding after her. Propelled by the clatter of their pursuers, they reached the upper hall, hurtled down it and into Kara's room. Duncan kicked the door shut behind them and shoved the bar into its bracket.

"Let us in." The latch rattled.

"Not on your life," Duncan called. "Take them downstairs and get them drunk, Fergie," he added, laughing.

There were a few grumbles about being cheated of the bedding ceremony, but finally her uncle coaxed the crowd away.

Kara collapsed on the bed, laughing and gasping for air. "I thought sure they'd catch us."

"Never." Duncan sprawled beside her, his breathing ragged. "They had not half the incentive I have."

She met his gaze, her senses ignited by the fire glowing there. Her heart skipped a beat, then slammed into the next. "I can scarcely believe you are here."

"I'm real." He took her hand and placed it over his own racing heart. "I'm here. I'm yours."

"How? What of Janet?"

"Later…later I'll tell you all, but I've hungered so long for this moment. If I don't hold you, touch you, I'll die." He lowered his head and claimed her mouth.

She'd expected his kiss to mirror the savage hunger in his eyes, but he was gentle, coaxing, the trembling in his body the only hint of the forces warring inside him. "Duncan," she whispered against his lips, then she turned aggressor.

Duncan groaned as Kara took control of the kiss. Their mouths mated in a prelude to the erotic joining to come. She tasted of sweet wine and a passion that tore at his control. One sip, and he was nearly mindless with desire. Slow. Dimly he realized he wanted to go slowly, make this moment special. Wrenching his lips from hers, he trailed them down her neck while his fingers worked the laces at the back of her gown.

"Aye." She began tugging at his belt.

"Easy." He caught her hands, kissed them, then laid them palm down on the coverlet. "I've waited weeks for this, and so have you. We'll be taking our time…"

"Savoring each other?" she asked archly.

Duncan groaned, his good intentions nearly burned away by the flames dancing in her eyes. "Aye."

And so they did, undressing each other by turns, pausing to kiss each bit of flesh unveiled. She moaned softly when he cupped her breasts, the nipples peaking at his touch. He took one in his mouth, making her arch off the bed as he suckled. They rolled together across the bed, legs twining, hands clutching.

"Duncan, please...I can wait no longer," Kara gasped.

"Nor I." He rose above her, parting her thighs with hands that shook. His gaze was steady, though, eyes locked on hers, dark with desire, shimmering with so much more. "I love you," he murmured. "So very, very much."

Kara tried to answer, but he drove into her, filling her, completing her. "Duncan!" she cried. Tears welled, blurring the face suspended over her. "I love you so."

"Shh. No tears." He gathered her against him and held her as though he'd never let her go. "I felt dead without you, and now..."

"'Tis like being reborn." She wrapped her arms around his neck, her body tightening on his.

Duncan groaned, the floodgate of desire suddenly opening, sweeping him away. He thrust into her, glorying as she matched his rhythm. They made love with the fierce, driving urgency fueled by weeks of separation, weeks of fear they'd never be together again. 'Twas a celebration, a feast for the senses, for the heart and soul.

"Duncan. Oh, Duncan," Kara sobbed as her love for him crested, sweeping through her, all heat and light. Dimly she was aware of him shouting her name, of his big body shuddering as he poured himself into her.

Gradually awareness returned. She was buried under his dead weight. Wonderful as it was, she couldn't breathe. "Duncan?"

"Mmm." He turned onto his side, yet kept her close, their bodies still blissfully joined, his face pillowed by her breasts.

"What of Janet?"

"Mmm. She's taken the veil."

"What? Tell me the whole of it."

He raised his head and grinned. "'Tis amusing, really. Soon after I left on Crusade, Janet realized what she felt for me was brotherly love. Her heart belonged to Christ.

Cousin Niall didn't want her to take the veil, and used our pledge to keep her from the convent. When I showed up, he was nearly glad to see me. Janet and I spent a few days pretending we wanted to wed, each afraid to hurt the other. Sensing she was troubled, I pressed till she told me what was wrong. Imagine our delight to discover we neither of us wanted the other.'' He laughed.

"Wretch. Why did you not come to me right away?"

"I had to settle things on the land I'd inherited from my sire. I'd left the small tower in the care of a cousin. I signed it over to him in exchange for the sheep and cattle we brought with us. There's even some fine breeding stock to stud.''

"Is it the cattle, or the MacLellans you refer to?"

Duncan laughed. "Just don't be casting your golden eyes on any of the lads. You're a married woman, now."

"Aye." She wriggled closer.

"When they heard I'd a valley of beautiful lasses all to myself, I had my pick of men. Those who came are strong fighters, second and third sons looking to make a place for themselves.''

"Judging by their reception, I don't think they'll have trouble finding wives and land." Kara toyed with the hair on his chest. "Thank you for my gown. I only wish I had something to give you. But I didn't know you were coming.''

"You've given me the greatest gift of all," Duncan assured her, his hands stroking her bare back. "Your love and understanding. Your faith and your trust in me. You cannot know how much they mean to me."

"Aye. I think I do." Kara smiled softly, basking in his love. Slowly her hand trailed over her belly. As she'd drifted down from the heights of their loving, she'd felt her body quicken. 'Twas just possible that in nine months' time, she'd be giving him more tangible proof of her love.

"You are all the gift I need," Duncan repeated.

For now. She kissed him, sighing as he hugged her back. "Love is the greatest gift, Duncan, and I will love you forever."

*   *   *   *   *

Author Note

There's something about Christmas that seems to bring out
the best in all of us, whether it's donating your time at the
local shelter or baking cookies for a friend. To me, nothing
better encapsulates this time of giving and sharing better
than O'Henry's *The Gift of the Magi,* which served as the
inspiration for my own Christmas offering to you.

Kara's Gift is actually a prequel to my 1996 release,
Lion's Legacy. A single sentence in that book tells how the
MacLellans came to inhabit Edin Valley. "The wee stone
kirk had been built by a crusader knight who wandered
wounded into the valley in the hills." Duncan MacLellan
is that crusader, a deeply religious man betrothed to another. Kara Gleanedin is the lovely witch who wins his
heart under false pretenses and must then choose between
love and honor.

If you enjoy this tale of love and sacrifice, I hope you'll
look for my next historical, set in Medieval England.
Knight's Rebellion is the sixth story about the Sommerville
family, and features the daughter of Gareth and Arianna
from my 1993 release, Knight's Lady.

The heroine of Knight's Rebellion, Lady Alys Sommerville, stops to help a wounded man and is forced to join a
band of rebels. In self-defense, she pretends to be a nun,
but the disguise doesn't prevent her from falling in love

with the rebel leader. Trust doesn't come easily to battle weary Gowain de Crecy, but Alys's purity of spirit soon wins his heart, only to nearly lose it again when she reveals she is a wealthy, titled lady. Even if he can forgive her deception, will their love survive the threat of his powerful, vengeful enemies?

I love hearing from readers and can be reached at P.O. Box 92054, Rochester, NY 14692. To receive a Sommerville Family Tree, please include a large SASE.

THE TWELFTH DAY
OF CHRISTMAS

Margaret Moore

Chapter One

Warwickshire, All Saints' Day 1226

The base of the wine goblet struck the table with a loud clang. Several men-at-arms lingering in the large, well-appointed hall after breaking the fast momentarily turned to look toward the high table.

"*What* did you say?" Sir Wilfrid Wutherton demanded, glaring at his niece, who was seated beside him.

Seeing that their choleric lord's anger was directed at Giselle, the soldiers quickly returned to their conversations, many of them with amused smiles. All knew that while Sir Wilfrid Wutherton could be fierce, when it came to his ward, the anger was surely more show than substance.

Considering what Giselle was asking, she was much less sanguine about her uncle's reaction. She put on her most winning, feminine smile and tried to ignore everyone else. This was as good a chance as she was likely to get to make her wishes known to her uncle, who rarely stayed inside the hall if the weather was at all promising for a hunt. And very rarely was he ever actually alone, a state not unusual considering the size of his estate and his castle, or his wealth or his rank—or the fact that her uncle was the most gregarious and kindhearted of men.

She had counted on his goodness when she planned to talk to him about her future betrothal. "I do not expect to choose my husband, Uncle," she said sweetly. "I only ask to be able to refuse your choice, if he doesn't appear to suit."

Sir Wilfrid leaned toward her, his heavy gray brows lowering. "Surely you didn't get this incredible notion from Lady Katherine?" he growled.

"No, Uncle, not at all," Giselle hastened to confess. Indeed, Lady Katherine had drummed into the heads of all the noblewomen fostered under her care that it was a woman's place to accept the dictates of the heads of their families, whether father, uncle, brother or cousin. Over the years, it had dawned on Giselle that those dictates apparently included a complete separation from friends and family upon marriage. Even her closest friend, Cecily Debarry, had seemingly been imprisoned after her marriage. Since the wedding, Giselle had had no communication of any kind from her, which had to mean that Bernard Louvain, her husband, kept an even stricter rein upon his wife than Lady Katherine had. Although the one time he had visited before their wedding he had been quite pleasant, Giselle had grown certain that his manner had been all for show. Surely nothing but a husband's selfish orders would keep Cecily from visiting.

"Haven't I always been a dutiful niece to you, Uncle?" she pleaded softly. "I went to Lady Katherine and stayed without complaint. I've done everything expected of me, and more. I've never asked you for anything. Since I'm the one who's going to have to be married to the man, whoever he may be, I don't think my request is so very strange."

Sir Wilfrid blinked and her hopes grew, but only until he spoke again. "You should have said something sooner," he muttered, leaning back and picking up his goblet again. "I've already found you a husband."

Giselle swallowed hard and anxiously searched his face. "You...you have?"

"Yes. It was arranged the last month you were with Lady Katherine."

Giselle drew in a deep breath and regarded her uncle as steadily as she could. "Why didn't you tell me?"

Her uncle didn't respond, instead taking another drink.

"Why didn't you tell me," she pressed, "unless the betrothal is not final? Perhaps the proposed groom has some reservations?"

"No, of course not!" Sir Wilfrid declared. "With your dowry, he'd be a fool not to want you."

Ah, yes. Her dowry. Her inheritance, to be paid upon her marriage. She knew full well that it was a sizable sum, if not the exact amount. "I'm grateful you don't think he's a fool," she replied, struggling to keep her voice calm although she felt anything but calm in the face of the knowledge that her future had apparently already been decided. "Might I know the gentleman's name?"

"Sir Myles Buxton."

It meant nothing to Giselle, but that wasn't so surprising. She could count on the fingers of one hand the number of young men's names she would recognize. Lady Katherine went out of her way to shelter her charges from anything that might be even remotely construed as gossip, and that generally meant news of any kind.

Then she thought of another question. "Is he very old?"

"He is five years your senior."

Not old, thanks to the saints for that.

"Is he in need of money, then?"

"Of course not, girl!" her uncle barked. "Do you think I'm in my dotage, or that our family isn't one a man would wish to be allied to?"

"I'm sorry, Uncle," she said contritely. "I'm just trying to discover why you have not yet confirmed the betrothal, if I was not to be consulted."

"He has to sign the contract, that's all."

Giselle grasped at those words like mistletoe clinging to an apple tree and she looked at her uncle appealingly, drawing her final weapon. "I'm sure you've made a fine choice, Uncle," she said, "but if it's not completely official, I don't think it is too much to ask to be able to refuse. After all, legally, I would be within my rights."

Her uncle started, knocking over his goblet, and stared at her, oblivious to the bloodred wine staining the white cloth spread over the trestle table. "How in the name of Saint Agatha did you learn—!" He halted, then shook his head. "No, you can't refuse him!"

"That's not what Lady Katherine's priest told us," Giselle replied, recalling the poor young man she had insisted tell her the law regarding marital consent. "He said a lady could refuse her family's selection."

"God's teeth!" Sir Wilfrid snarled, shifting in his massive oaken chair as a servant appeared to blot up the wine as best he could. "So, you want to reject Sir Myles Buxton? You haven't even met the man!"

Giselle thought quickly. She was gaining ground and she didn't want to lose any. "When could I meet him?"

"He's coming at Christmas—to sign the contract."

"Then this is what I propose," Giselle said, making her tone as reasonable as possible. "Allow me to arrange the Christmas festivities—"

Her uncle started to object, but she kept going.

"To prove to you that I am a mature woman capable of making good decisions. If I have proved myself over the twelve days of Christmas, and I decide that Sir Myles does not suit me, you will agree to break the betrothal."

Sir Wilfrid scratched his thick beard thoughtfully. "You think you will be able to organize the feasting, the accommodation for our guests, the entertainment and the decorations for the hall?"

For a moment, Giselle hesitated—but only for a moment. She knew she was capable of seeing to all the preparations for Christmas. She was up to that challenge, and any other when it came to guaranteeing even so small a measure of freedom. "Yes, Uncle, I do."

"Then, Giselle," Sir Wilfrid replied, "I agree."

With a triumphant smile, Giselle rose and curtsied to her uncle. "Everything will go smoothly," she said eagerly. "You will see. Now if you will excuse me, I must talk to the seneschal at once." She hurried toward the corridor leading to the pantry.

Sir Wilfrid watched his pretty, headstrong niece leave and smiled indulgently, even though giving in to her request was setting something of a dangerous precedent.

Or rather, it might be if any other man had been the proposed groom. Refuse Sir Myles Buxton? No young woman in her right mind would do such a thing.

Not even Giselle.

Weeks later, Giselle stood in the entrance to the kitchen and tried to concentrate on what Iestyn, the cook, was saying. Unfortunately for him, the change in the weather from chill and damp to cold and icy was causing Giselle to think more about the delayed arrival of guests and necessary foodstuffs than his litany of complaints about the servants, the freshness of the fish, the dearth of salt, and whatever else seemed to occur to him.

Yesterday it had suddenly turned cold after several days of rain, so that the stones in the courtyard were slick with ice. The muddy roads were treacherous, and more than one cart had already gotten stuck, delaying the delivery of additional food. Several guests had arrived either early, fearing such weather, or were apparently likewise late, throwing off all her careful calculations regarding accommodations. The early arrivals had depleted the stores she had already laid in, too.

The kitchen itself was like something out of one of Father Paul's descriptions of hell. Although the upper louvers were open and the day frigid, the room was still as hot as a midsummer's day.

The flurry of activity about her had a certain demonic quality, too. Several boys scurried about carrying small

casks of flour and wine, and baskets of fruit and dried fish.
Two young lads turned the spits that held haunches of beef
and mutton, their faces a study in concentration lest they
turn too fast or too slow, or upset the pan beneath that
caught the drippings. Another pair of boys industriously
pounded spices with mortar and pestle, their arms moving
rhythmically as they chatted quietly.

Three stout, strong women, attired in the new aprons
given them for Christmas, were busily kneading dough for
pastries or bread or meat pies, whatever Iestyn decreed. The
kitchen cat hissed at one of the ever-present hounds waiting
for the scraps that might fall from the long, heavy tables
that ran the length of the enormous room.

All in all, it was hustle and bustle with an undercurrent
of happy excitement—for it was Christmas Eve, and when
their work was done, everyone would enjoy finer bread than
usual, richer food and definitely better wine. They would
have their own sport in the kitchen, with music and dancing
and games, to which their masters would turn a blind and
forgiving eye, as long as they were able to work the next
morning.

Giselle agreed that Iestyn was suffering and reminded
him that wagons bearing the necessary items were supposed
to arrive that very morning. As for the servants, well, surely
it was nothing more than good spirits, and once the twelve
days of Christmas were over, things would return to normal. In the meantime, she begged him to be patient.

Iestyn, satisfied with her response, wiped his broad,
sweaty brow with the back of his hand. "The turbot, then,
my lady, it shall be for today, since it's the freshest fish to
be had," he said, a vestige of the Welsh of his childhood
in his deep voice. "And all of it, is it?"

"Yes," Giselle replied with a smile. "We wouldn't want
anyone to think my uncle is destitute."

Iestyn's response was a roaring laugh that shook his rotund belly as if it were a jelly, and that confirmed to Giselle
that his good humor was restored. "Destitute!" he cried,

trying to catch his breath. "Sir Wilfrid! Oh, that's a fine one, my lady! You ought to be a jester, you ought!"

"My lady!"

Giselle looked outside and saw her maidservant, Mary, hurrying toward the kitchen as quickly as she could across the icy yard. "My lady, come quick! To the gate!"

Giselle nodded a swift farewell to Iestyn and went out into the freezing air. At first it was refreshing, after the heat of the kitchen, but only for a moment. "What is it?" she demanded as she joined her servant, who had already turned and was now heading away from the kitchen toward the gate, which was on the other side of the hall.

"The yule log, my lady. It's stuck in the gate!"

Giselle and Mary rounded the corner of the hall and Giselle halted as the scene at the gate came into view. The great yule log, nearly a yard in diameter, had slipped off the long wagon being used to bring it to the castle and was now wedged in the entrance between the outer portcullis and the inner gate.

With a groan of dismay, Giselle gathered up the skirt of her thick brown woolen work dress and ran forward, forgetting the ice underfoot, until she slipped. She felt herself falling and struggled, arms flung out, to remain upright. She did not succeed and landed rather heavily on her rump. Unhurt but embarrassed, she got up quickly and surveyed the damage to her garments. Her cloak bore muddy witness to her accident and, judging by the openmouthed stare of the cart's driver standing beside the horse's head, as well as those of the other servants hurrying about their tasks, she must have made a pretty spectacle.

Giselle took a deep breath and told herself to be calm. A fall was not so very humiliating and the wedged log but a moment's trouble. It need not mean that her uncle would not allow her the right of refusal.

Suddenly a voice boomed from behind the motionless wagon. "What fool is responsible for this?"

Giselle's teeth clenched and she quickened her pace, albeit with caution and very great dignity.

"I said, what fool is in charge?" the man's voice demanded again, and this time, she caught sight of the arrogant speaker, for he climbed onto the log and stood scanning the yard like some out-of-place ship's captain, his arms akimbo. "Can't he see this is blocking the way?" he demanded.

With considerable regret Giselle realized that he was probably one of her uncle's guests, for he was well dressed, with an embroidered tunic of dark wool, fur-lined cloak and fine leather boots. Therefore, she would have to be polite.

The nobleman nimbly made his way along the enormous log until he reached the front of the wagon, then leapt into the courtyard. She noticed that he did not slip, but landed as easily as a cat.

She also noticed he was handsome, with wavy brown hair, strong, square jaw and very fine nose. Even off his makeshift deck, he had a distinctly commanding air about him that was very difficult to ignore.

"Excuse me, sir," she said, momentarily ignoring Old John, the wagon's driver. "I believe you wish to speak to me?"

He started, and his face reddened, but she thought that more likely from exertion than shame for his manners. He did not look to be easily embarrassed. "*You* are in charge?" he asked. "I trust Sir Wilfrid is not ill?"

"My uncle is in his solar. If you would care to join him, please do so. In the meantime, I will set some men to clearing—"

"You are his niece?" The man's smile grew broader as his impertinent gaze flicked over her.

Suddenly she experienced a definitely sinking feeling, as if the proud captain before her had suddenly run their ship aground.

Oh, Uncle, what have you done? Giselle wanted to moan. How could he have selected for her husband this pompous, arrogant nobleman who was handsome, yes, and young, yes, but surely as conceited a fellow as it had ever been Giselle's misfortune to meet.

"If Sir Wilfrid is my uncle, I think one could safely assume I am his niece, sir," she said, attempting to keep sarcasm from her tone.

"Then you must be Lady Giselle." He made a sweeping, graceful, yet completely virile, bow. "I am Sir Myles Buxton, my lady. A most happy meeting. The reports of you that I have had have not done justice to your beauty," he said, his deep voice intimate as he came toward her, despite the increasing noise from the crowd waiting impatiently behind the log cart.

It was all Giselle could do to keep the skeptical look from her face, for she was very aware that she was looking far from her best. Her scarf was askew, her cloak a muddy disaster, and she was sweating. Beauty? Perhaps sometimes, but this was not one of those times! Obviously this man was as hypocritical as Bernard Louvain.

She reminded herself that whatever else he was, Sir Myles was her uncle's guest and made a curtsy. "Welcome to Wutherton Castle," she lied prettily. "Now if you will excuse me, I had better see to having—"

Before she could finish, Sir Myles nodded, turned on his heel and ordered three of the castle servants lingering nearby—watching the commotion, no doubt—to put their shoulders to the log. Before she could remind him that she was in charge, he stripped off his cloak and tunic and tossed them onto the wagon, revealing a very fine white shirt—and a chest and pair of shoulders of which no man need be ashamed—before joining the servants at their task.

For an instant, she was impressed, both by his physique and his willingness to help, until he looked at her and grinned, as if to say that he was a marvelous fellow, was he not?

If he hadn't been the man her uncle had picked out for her to marry, she might have been more willing to agree.

As it was, his apparent vanity annoyed her. "Since you seem to have this matter under control, Sir Myles, I will attend to your accommodation. I understand you have brought ten soldiers for your guard—"

"Twenty," he said, before signaling the men to begin shoving the log back into place on the wagon.

Twenty! She had been told ten and had planned for that number. An additional ten—where would they sleep? What about the food? This was terrible, worse than the unexpected cold!

Because Sir Myles was occupied, she felt free to glare at him for a moment before approaching Old John, who was struggling to keep the large draft horse steady as the log began to shift. "When the log is back on the wagon," she said, "bring it directly to the hall."

Sir Myles straightened. "Your every desire is my command, my lady."

She smiled amiably and said, "Oh, you need not trouble yourself, sir. Old John knows exactly what to do."

A warning shout from one of the servants reminded Myles of his chore, for the log was beginning to slip off the wagon again. To be sure, such a task was beneath him, but helping a lady always went a long way toward encouraging her good regard, as Lady Giselle's response had proved.

He was kept busy pushing the log back into place, so if she bade him a farewell—and surely she had—he didn't hear her. When the log was once again on the wagon and two servants quickly moved to lash it down securely, she was already walking toward the hall.

He noted that she was going rather slowly, thereby demonstrating that she was reluctant to leave his presence, and when he saw the muddy mark on the back of her cloak, he thought he had found the reason for her somewhat unexpected curtness toward the man she had to know was intended to be her husband.

She was embarrassed by being seen in such unusual circumstances and in less than perfect attire.

Ah, the vanity of women! Myles thought complaisantly as he retrieved his garments, happy to leave the delivery of the log to the old man. He put his tunic back on and continued to watch her retreating slender, and quite graceful, form.

Astonishingly Sir Wilfrid's report of his niece's beauty had not been exaggerated, as one would expect during marriage negotiations. If anything, the man had been too modest on her behalf. Even in her drab brown gown, crooked scarf and mud-stained cloak, she was lovely, with heart-shaped face, snapping green eyes, delicately pointed chin and a mouth…a frowning mouth, if he were being honest.

And she had been somewhat sarcastic, too, for a maiden. Now that he considered her reaction, he suddenly realized that she didn't seem very impressed with him.

Surely he was wrong. Surely it had to be the embarrassing circumstances of their meeting, and the wish to get out of the cold that had made her seem unfriendly.

The draft horse lurched into motion, the wagon wheels creaked, and the yule log began its journey once again.

Well, what did her initial response matter, Myles thought as he waited for his soldiers to enter the castle. The contract was as good as signed, the woman was pretty and her dowry would surely make up for whatever slight defects he might notice in her character. All in all, this was as good a match as any man could reasonably hope for.

Or any woman, either. Sir Myles Buxton was the most sought after male matrimonial prize in England, and he knew it.

Chapter Two

As Myles strolled into the great hall of Sir Wilfrid's castle later that day to join the feast, his gaze took in the perfect proportions of the large room. A variety of tapestries covered the walls, each bright with a myriad of colors depicting scenes of hunts and battles and Christmases past. Flambeaux and candles provided ample illumination to admire the handiwork, as well as the clean whiteness of the linen spread upon the many trestle tables.

Pine boughs, holly and mistletoe had been strewn upon the cloths, their scents mingling with the beeswax of the candles, the smoke from the flambeaux and hearth, and the more pungent odor of fresh herbs sprinkled over the clean rushes. In keeping with the season, sprays of holly and ivy hung from the tapestry hooks, along with more pine branches, and bits of greenery lay upon the sills of the tall, narrow windows, screened with cloth against the frigid night air. In the huge central fireplace, the great yule log was already lit, its fire warming the room.

Above the main floor, Sir Wilfrid had a minstrels' gallery, and Myles could see the musicians moving about, instruments in their hands. One had a harp, another a small drum for beating out time. A third man held a stringed fithele and bow, and his companion had a reed pipe.

Myles was not the first to arrive, for other guests milled

about, speaking in hushed voices as they awaited their host. At the far end, Myles could see other young noblemen in conversation, their manly laughter filling him with good cheer, and nearer to him, Lady Alice Derosier and Lady Elizabeth Cowton smiled invitingly.

Where was Lady Giselle? It might do her good to see that other young noblewomen thought him quite worthy of interest and attention. It would do his father and his brothers good, too. Then they might appreciate him.

No matter. Once he was married to Sir Wilfrid Wutherton's niece, they would have to admit he was a worthy member of their family.

He thought of the twelve gifts he had brought for his intended bride, one for each day beginning with Christmas and ending with Epiphany. Surely she would be pleased to receive them, and surely she would appreciate that he was a man of breeding and property who should be respected, given the costly nature of his gifts. That should curb whatever tendency to sarcasm might be lurking in the young lady's tongue.

More contented, he sauntered down the hall, growing increasingly aware of delightful aromas wafting in from the corridor that led to the kitchen. Sir Wilfrid must be happy in his seneschal, for the fellow seemed to have arranged everything with care and an eye to detail. Or perhaps there was a lady in Sir Wilfrid's life, someone to provide a woman's insight—and other things—since Sir Wilfrid had no wife.

He could not fault the man, for life was lonely without a woman....

Now what had brought that thought to his mind? He had no trouble finding a willing woman when he wanted one, and he had no need to tie himself to any woman, unless it be for power and gain, two things an alliance with Sir Wilfrid would provide.

Then he thought of Giselle's lissome figure and smiled,

for there would be other benefits to this proposed alliance that he could anticipate with pleasure.

Meanwhile, upstairs in the small tower room that was Giselle's own during her time with her uncle, Giselle was entertaining no such contented, happy thoughts. She was wondering if the beef would be roasted, not burnt, the fish tender enough and if Iestyn was going to be able to prepare all the sauces so that they weren't spoiled when it was time to be served, if they would have sufficient bread and salt and what she could do if she realized they were running low, and then finally, she was wondering if she looked as pretty as she possibly could.

Although her appearance was of far less concern than the feast. After all, the preparations and serving of the many courses could have a very real effect on her future. Her appearance need only be adequate.

Or so she tried to tell herself. After all, Sir Myles's approving looks and flattering remarks were probably completely insincere.

"Mary, what do you think of this headdress?" she demanded critically of her maidservant.

"Why, I think it's very fetching, my lady," replied her maid, somewhat stunned. In all the time since Giselle's arrival in the early autumn, she had never once asked Mary for her opinion, about clothing, millinery or anything.

Giselle pursed her lips thoughtfully as she regarded the cap made of velvet in a deep, rich red, like holly berries and trimmed with dark green and gold embroidery. "But do you think it suits me?" she persisted, putting it on her head and regarding her reflection in the burnished glass she used for a mirror. Beneath the cap she wore her hair in long braids and tied with a matching red ribbon.

"I think that cap's very fine, my lady, and it looks very nice with your gown," Mary replied.

That was true, for the gown was also red velvet, with a

gold silk shift underneath, visible above the ornately embroidered bodice.

"The cap is not too extravagant? Or distracting? I don't
want people staring at me."

"Oh, no, my lady," Mary said. "I don't think they'll
notice you much."

That response was not quite what Giselle cared to hear.

"I will wear it with this scarf," she said decisively. She
put on a thin gold silk scarf, then the cap, so that her braids
hung below the headdress. "Yes, I think this will do
nicely."

"It doesn't matter what you wear, my lady. You'll be
the prettiest one at the feast," Mary said. Then the older
woman grinned mischievously. "I'm sure Sir Myles won't
take his eyes off you."

"I had better see that matters are well in hand for the
feast. Iestyn was worried about the salt," Giselle said pertly
as she hurried to the door, trying not to think about who
might be watching her tonight. "If we run out, I might have
to marry him!"

Mary's expression grew puzzled as her mistress rushed
out of the room. "She might have to marry the salter?"
she muttered as she picked up the rejected scarves and caps
and bands Giselle had scattered about the room as she had
tried to decide what to wear to the feast. "I thought she
was betrothed to Sir Myles."

Mary envisioned the wizened little man who sold the
Wuthertons salt, then laughed, shook her head at her own
foolish conclusion and went back to work, reflecting that
all in all, she was glad she was not a noble lady with so
much to occupy her mind, especially at Christmas.

Giselle was vaguely aware that Sir Myles, seated immediately to her left, was saying something that was supposed to be amusing, for she could hear his bantering tone
and her uncle's responding chuckle. However, her attention
was trained on the minstrels in the gallery. She was rather

unfortunately sure that the fithele player had enjoyed far too much wine, for his bow kept slipping from his fingers; indeed, the fellow himself looked in danger of slipping over the railing onto the floor below.

Perhaps she could signal the seneschal to have the fithele player removed, Giselle thought anxiously, if it could be done without a lot of unnecessary commotion.

She should have noticed the problem sooner, and she would have, if she hadn't been so busy looking at Lady Alice making a fool of herself trying to catch Sir Myles's eye. Lady Elizabeth also glanced at the high table with suspicious frequency.

Not that she cared if women were looking at Sir Myles, any more than she cared if several of the unmarried noblemen were also casting a fair number of curious glances her way. She had far too much to concern herself with than playing coy games.

She was also aware, with increasing annoyance, that her uncle, seated on the other side of Sir Myles, was constantly giving them both speculative glances.

Suddenly a warm, lean male hand clapped itself over hers. "Yes, Sir Myles?" she inquired, turning to him with a forced smile.

"You weren't listening," he remarked coolly.

She pulled her hand away and laid it in her lap. "No, I wasn't."

A brief flash of annoyance appeared in his dark eyes and for a triumphant moment, she thought she saw his true and arrogant self. "You must forgive me. My excuse must be the duties of the chatelaine and—"

"You are the chatelaine here?" he asked, raising one dark eyebrow. "I am most impressed, my lady."

She blushed at his compliment, and realized she had never noticed how compelling his voice was, deep and rich and intriguing. She couldn't help wondering how it would sound whispering endearments.

Not that she wanted to ever hear such things. Not for some time yet, at any rate.

She wished he wasn't so handsome, either, and that her hand would stop tingling as she inadvertently recalled the sensation of his touch.

With something akin to desperation, she glanced at her uncle. Unfortunately, he was now engaged in animated conversation with the nobleman on the other side of him, the elegant Sir George de Gramercie.

Obviously she was going to have to fend for herself.

"I trust you will do so well as my chatelaine," Sir Myles commented placidly. "Of course, my hall is quite a bit larger, and there will be many more guests at our Christmas festivities. I fear your duties will not allow you much time for sport."

Or visiting her uncle, or Lady Katherine, or any of her friends, she finished for him inwardly, anger and dismay rising in her breast.

The damp must have seeped into her brain and frozen there, for her to even temporarily contemplate matrimony as a desireable state.

Suddenly, she no longer cared how handsome he was, or how wonderful his voice. He was a braggart. A smug, arrogant braggart.

"You will forgive me for saying so, my lady," he continued, obviously oblivious to the turn of her thoughts, "but I fear one of your musicians will not be able to play for us tonight."

"Yes, I noticed," Giselle said with no attempt to be polite. "I will—"

"Allow me," Sir Myles declared, rising before she could protest. He sauntered down the hall, greeting several of the knights and ladies, and pausing to speak with Lady Elizabeth and Lady Alice, as if this was his hall, not her uncle's.

The minstrel will be asleep on the floor before he gets there, Giselle thought peevishly, and she seriously considered going to the gallery herself. Before she could do so, however, her uncle leaned toward her and said, in a slurred drawl that had much to do with the fine wine he had provided, "Well, what do you think of him, eh, my dear? Is he not a handsome fellow?"

"And doesn't he know it," Giselle muttered, certain that she had Sir Myles's measure.

"I didn't have the heart to tell him of our bargain," her uncle continued, leaning even closer so that Giselle began to fear that he would fall out of his chair. "He's very set on this marriage, more so since he met you in the courtyard."

"Oh?" Giselle said, thinking Sir Myles's ardor had more likely grown when he saw her uncle's fine castle. "What did he say?"

Sir Wilfrid smiled and slowly waggled a thick finger at her. "No fishing for praise, my girl!" he admonished. "All I'll say is that he seems very keen. *Very* keen."

Giselle blushed, wanting to tell her uncle exactly what she thought of the young nobleman, yet knowing caution was the wiser course. Then she caught sight of a slight commotion in the minstrels' gallery and looked up to see Sir Myles gently but firmly escorting the lurching fithele player away with a minimum of fuss. She had to admit that she couldn't have handled the situation better herself.

More than that, once the two men were gone, the other musicians applied themselves to their task with a will. She had never heard them play better.

As servants hurried to take down the tables to clear the floor for dancing, Giselle thought she could make a slight effort to be a little kinder to Sir Myles.

Therefore, when he returned to his chair, she gave him a grateful smile and said, "Thank you, Sir Myles, for your assistance. I must ask what you said to them to make them play so conscientiously."

Sir Myles smiled at her, the effect spoiled by his conspicuous condescension. "I told them if they ever hoped to entertain at our wedding, they had best play well."

He was so completely sure of himself! She opened her mouth to make some kind of response when she caught sight of Sir George de Gramercie. He was a knight of good family, well-to-do, and while his fair looks were not a match for Sir Myles's darker handsomeness, he certainly wasn't ugly, either. She smiled a greeting and inclined her head as he bowed his.

"You seem to regard Sir George with great favor," Sir Myles noted.

"He is an old friend of the family," Giselle replied.

"An *old* friend of the family?"

"Yes, a friend of the family, but as you can see, Sir Myles, he is certainly not so very old. At one time I had hoped—"

"What?" The demand was made quietly, but a demand it was.

Giselle faced him, a scornful expression on her face that she took no pain to hide as she rose abruptly. "Excuse me, Sir Myles. I have duties to attend to."

He got up just as quickly. "I had hoped to dance with you, my lady."

"Some other time, perhaps," she replied. Then she ignored him and addressed her uncle. "I have to see to the alms, Uncle. Please excuse me."

"Of course, my dear," Sir Wilfrid said gruffly, nodding his head in approval.

Myles sat down and took a large gulp of wine. It didn't take a great deal of perception to see that something was amiss here, and not just with Lady Giselle. The marriage contract should have been signed that afternoon. Instead, when he had met with Sir Wilfrid in the solar, the man had talked on and on about matters of no significance until it was time to dress for the feast.

In fact, this visit wasn't going at all how Myles had planned. Or rather, not planned, exactly. He had assumed he would arrive, sign the contract, be his usual charming self and captivate Sir Wilfrid's niece with very little effort.

Instead, Lady Giselle was being positively hostile and Sir Wilfrid evasive.

Perhaps he had been a little arrogant and had bragged a bit, he admitted to himself. Why not, when he was clearly the best man in the hall and what he said was nothing less than the truth? Certainly Sir George de Gramercie was no match for him, in anything.

Myles regarded the red berries nestled against the dark green, thorny holly leaves laid on the cloth before him. The red reminded him of Giselle, both her gown and her lips, which he could easily imagine kissing. But like the holly leaves, she seemed to have some very sharp edges.

Then he considered his sudden, improbable resort to announcing his own worth to Giselle, all because she made him feel less sure of himself than he had in years. When she had looked at him with such stern disapproval, he had felt as he had when he was a child and his father had told him he would never be the equal of his brothers. And that he would never amount to anything much at all.

But Sir Wilfrid didn't think that. Indeed, Myles had thought Sir Wilfrid's agreement to the marriage had meant that he had finally gained all the approval he would ever need.

Unfortunately, that had changed once he had met Giselle. She was an intelligent woman, capable and clever—and apparently she didn't like him. Yet he would be an excellent choice for her as husband; anyone of any sense should recognize that. Why wouldn't *she?* Was there some lack in him that she could see?

Myles frowned darkly. No, surely not. Perhaps there was another man in her life. Not Sir George—somebody else. Somebody she might have met at the castle where she was fostered, perhaps.

Myles immediately turned to Sir Wilfrid. "Your niece has done an admirable job preparing for the feast, and the accommodations for myself and my knights are most excellent. You must be very proud of her."

"Yes, Sir Myles, yes, I am. She's a lovely girl and as smart as they come," her uncle replied, his words ever so slightly slurred.

"She must have had very good teachers."

"She's been fostered with Lady Katherine DuMonde these past ten years. A most exceptional widow!" Sir Wilfrid raised his goblet in salute, spilling only a little wine. "Strict, of course, Lady Katherine, very strict, but you can see it hasn't harmed Giselle. Girls can never have too much discipline, you know. Spare the rod and spoil the child, eh, Sir Myles?"

"I believe my father would concur with you on that point," Myles agreed, the chill of his reply quite lost on Sir Wilfrid. "Does Lady Katherine have any children of her own?"

"Not a one, poor thing."

"No sons?"

"More's the pity!" Sir Wilfrid answered with a chuckle. "They would have been fine soldiers. Disciplined from the cradle!" he said, flourishing his goblet like a flag of battle. "In the womb!"

Sir Myles smiled and joined companionably in his host's laughter, putting away all thoughts of his father's harsh punishments and wondering where else Lady Giselle might have met a young man.

Then he caught sight of Giselle making her way out of the hall toward the kitchen, and decided it really didn't matter. He wanted a woman with a considerable dowry, he wanted an alliance with Sir Wilfrid, and he wanted an intelligent woman to share his bed and bear his children. Lady Giselle was *exactly* what he required in a wife.

If there was someone else in her heart, Myles would simply have to see to it that the fellow was soon forgotten.

Chapter Three

Sir Myles was standing right behind her, just slightly to her left. Worse, Giselle could feel his gaze on her throughout the long Christmas mass, making it very difficult to concentrate on Father Paul's Latin or appreciate the beauty of the novices' chants as they filled the chapel.

She would have had difficulty anyway, for her mind was more than half-occupied with the business of the holy day. Already today there had been a crisis: an unforeseen shortage of hay. The head groom had appeared at her door at first light, anxious and apologetic. She had ordered him to dispatch three carts to outlying farms to make up the shortfall before telling him such a thing mustn't happen again. She wasn't as harsh as she might have been, given the situation and the early hour, for it was obvious he had not told her uncle. For that, she could be a little magnanimous.

On the other hand, she had no similar feeling to spare for Sir Myles. Why did he hover about her like a bee after honey? What did he hope to accomplish? Couldn't he see she had enough to do without his bothersome presence?

Why hadn't he spoken to her? What would she say to him if he did?

When at last the mass ended, she turned, ready to be barely polite to Sir Myles, and saw that he was already halfway to the door of the chapel. Then he stopped to speak with Lady Alice, who visibly preened under his gaze.

Perhaps he should ask to marry *her,* Giselle thought as she hurried past them. After all, Alice had nothing better to do with her time than find men amusing and interesting and attractive, much good may it do her.

Giselle just hoped Sir Myles stayed away from her the rest of the day, for tonight was the great feast of Christmas Day, and all her efforts today *must* go to making that a success.

He did not stay away. Nor did he speak to her. Instead, he had the most disconcerting way of appearing when she least expected him, and then going away without one word to her, as if he was some sort of spy, or guard.

He came to the kitchen when she was finalizing the order of dishes for the feast, ostensibly for a bit of bread because Lady Alice wanted to feed the ducks on the moat.

He entered the stables to see his stallion when she was determining that the appropriate amount of hay had arrived.

He was playing quoits in the courtyard when she was scurrying from storehouse to storehouse making sure they had plenty of wine and fruit.

He sauntered through the hall as she was supervising the arrangement of the trestle tables.

He was laughing with Sir Wilfrid when she hurried past the solar on her way to her room to dress for the feast.

In short, he was everywhere, and never once said so much as "Happy Christmas."

Which she knew shouldn't trouble her. It wouldn't have, except that she was chatelaine here, and his silence made her fear she had been too obviously rude last night. Perhaps he had told Sir Wilfrid of her discourtesy, but then her uncle would have summoned her to his solar immediately.

That did not happen, and the important feast passed so uneventfully, Giselle felt something akin to disappointment, which naturally had nothing to do with the fact that she

had seated Sir Myles to her uncle's right, while she was t
Sir Wilfrid's left. After all, she had no wish to be chastise
for not listening again, and if Sir Myles made no effort t
communicate with her, that was surely a relief.

Just as she was relieved to leave the high table as soo
as the final course of fruit was served, for she had to atten
to the wassail. It was her duty to make sure that the steam
ing bowls containing the hot, spiced brews were delivere
to the appropriate tables. For the nobles, the beverage wa
made of wine, with the costliest spices and best apples. Fo
those below the salt, the baked apples floated in ale. Th
servants' wassail was made of cider.

There followed the necessary and appropriate rounds o
toasts, and then the tables were removed to make way fo
the jugglers and acrobats Giselle had hired for this even
ing's entertainment. They were very diverting, especiall
since she didn't have to worry about Sir Myles. He wa
ensconced on the far side of the hall with several othe
young noblemen.

Over all, Giselle was pleased by the success of th
Christmas feast, and if she was at all piqued by Sir Myles'
behavior, she could take comfort in his apparent disintere:
in Lady Elizabeth and Lady Alice.

Although why his neglect of other ladies should comfor
her, she didn't care to consider.

The next day, Giselle feared that there would be a rep
etition of Sir Myles's odd behavior, and she spent the whol
morning in tense anticipation only to learn that he, alon
with several knights, had decided to ride out that day.

This was good news, she told herself, for that meant n
troublesome interference in her duties and, indeed, the re:
of the day passed quickly enough.

Just before going to her bedchamber to dress for thi
evening's feast, however, Giselle did make one change i
her plans. Since she had seen nothing of the irritating S
Myles all day, she supposed she would be able to tolera:

is presence beside her at the high table tonight, and informed the servants accordingly.

Quite pleased with her ability to rise above the petty annoyance occasioned by Sir Myles's conduct, Giselle entered her bedchamber and saw that Mary had laid out her favorite gown. It was made of deep blue wool, an indigo like the sky at sunset, and trimmed with bands of silver embroidery. She was to wear a scarf in matching blue with a silver circlet over her unbound hair.

She noticed, beside the gown, a painted wooden box the width and length of her hand. Curious, she picked it up and opened it.

Inside was the most hideous scarf Giselle had ever seen, in a shade of green that was akin to squashed peas. With an expression of distaste, Giselle gingerly removed it. The pity was, it was very fine silk, yet she could think of no color that would look more horrible on her.

She drew the scarf over her head and went to the looking glass, to see that she was absolutely right.

From whom had this gift come? Her uncle? He would never think of finery such as this, thank the Lord! Sir Myles? It had to be Sir Myles.

Naturally a suitor would give the object of his affection a gift for each of the twelve days of Christmas. This would be the first.

She sighed heavily at the realization that she would undoubtedly receive eleven more such gifts, and she had thought Sir Myles a man of some taste! His own clothes were well chosen to accentuate his looks and his build.

Of course, he had not seen her when he had selected this gift.

But he had seen her before he gave it. Surely he would have realized...

What did it matter what he realized? The scarf did not suit. Nor did she appreciate his recent possessive behavior. He had no right to watch over her every move, as if they were already married. Therefore, she would thank him as etiquette demanded, but only so far as etiquette demanded.

With that decision in mind, she put the scarf back into its box and secreted it away in her clothes chest. She had no wish to make explanations to Mary, who arrived moments later to help her mistress dress.

As she entered the hall and checked to make certain everything had been properly prepared, Giselle couldn't help noticing Sir Myles, standing near the hearth, his broad shouldered back to her. Indeed, he would have been hard to miss, for with his thick, wavy hair brushing his shoulders, well-fitting black tunic that reached to the top of his soft black leather boots, his narrow waist encircled with a belt of golden rings and his stance of easy, almost feline grace, there was not his equal in the hall.

No doubt he was quite aware of his personal attributes and thought those alone sufficient to make her feel flattered by his presence, or upset when he had chosen to go riding. He had probably been spoiled and complimented all his life.

Perhaps he could not be expected to comprehend her reluctance to marry.

Once he noticed Giselle, he immediately excused himself and strolled toward her. Then she saw a slight frown crease his brow and his full lips register what could have been disappointment.

Regardless of its ugliness, she might have worn the scarf, she thought with genuine remorse.

Before he reached her, her uncle and Father Paul bustled into the hall. Sir Myles hurried to stand at the table beside her, directed there by one of the servants. He said not one word of greeting to her.

Trying not to feel ashamed of her ungrateful thoughts, Giselle told herself she should be more concerned that everything be served at the proper time in the proper order.

and that all be cooked to perfection than giving and receiving greetings.

They ate in grim silence, until Giselle decided she had better say her thanks and be done with it. "Sir Myles," she said quietly when the second course of fish arrived, "I found a gift in my bedchamber today. Was it from you?" He gave her a wry smile and she was forced to admit to his handsome charm.

"Yes, it was from me. I trust you are not in the habit of receiving gifts from unknown men?"

"No, I'm not. Thank you." There. That duty was finished.

Myles turned his attention back to the perfectly cooked fish before him.

I suppose I should be glad she deigned to acknowledge my gift, he thought discontentedly, more aware than ever of her beauty. She looked like a goddess in that blue gown, and whatever dismay he had felt upon first noticing she wasn't wearing his gift had quickly disappeared upon realizing that the dark blue suited her to perfection.

Just as yesterday he had realized that he had never known a more competent woman. Giselle seemed to be everywhere, personally making sure that all was well in hand.

As his gaze roved over the assembled guests in the hall, he knew there was not another candidate for his wife who was so fitting as Lady Giselle, quite apart from the matter of her sizeable dowry and her uncle's influence at court.

He commanded himself not to make too much of Giselle's current behavior toward him. Of course she would be unused to gifts from men who were not her relatives. That would explain her blunt thanks.

He slid her a sidelong glance. How pretty she was, with that thin, transparent scarf hiding, yet not hiding, the curve of her soft cheek and the luscious redness of her lips.

The green of the scarf he had given her would surely make her pale skin look sallow.

Oh well. No matter. His other gifts were not scarves, and surely they would meet with a better reply.

Therefore, he would cease to concern himself with her previous response.

Besides, despite her manner when they were seated beside each other, Giselle had not been able to ignore him yesterday, try as she might.

Oh, no, my fine lady, he thought with more equanimity, the battle is just begun. And tonight, when I take your hand in a round dance, I will ever so gently caress it, giving you a promise of other delights to come.

If Giselle was disappointed that Sir Myles didn't seem to be paying much attention to her at all throughout the meal, it wasn't obvious. Instead, she watched the occupants of the hall carefully, noting what dishes seemed to be the most appealing, and if there was any strain among the different guests. Fortunately, it seemed that the Christmas season mellowed everyone.

Giselle wished she could leave the high table, where her uncle and Sir Myles seemed intent upon discussing the state of game in the country to the exclusion of all other topics, and join the other guests.

Soon enough, however, the musicians once again took their places, and at a nod from Giselle, the servants began removing the tables. Giselle rose, intending to see to the distribution of the remains of the feast to the poor of the village, when Sir Myles laid a detaining hand on her arm.

She looked at him with some surprise and could not resist saying, "I thought you had forgotten my existence, sir."

His slow, seductive smile made her warm in spite of her best efforts to remain unmoved. "Oh, I most certainly have not, my lady. May I have the honor of leading you in the first carole of the evening?"

Giselle wanted to refuse. She had things to do. She didn't want to dance. Not with him. Not in a circle holding on to the hand that was touching hers so lightly, and that was so hard to ignore.

However, she didn't have time to answer, because he immediately clasped her hand tighter and led her to the now empty space in the middle of the hall.

Giselle told herself there was nothing she could do now, not without making a spectacle of herself, especially as others hurried to join the dance.

"Your gown is very becoming," Sir Myles remarked, in a whisper only she could hear, as the musicians tuned their instruments and the dancers formed a circle. "And I quite like your hair that way. I can hardly wait to see it loose about your body. In our bed."

Giselle flushed hotly and opened her mouth to admonish him for his bold, impertinent remark when the dance began.

The carole was a complicated one, with steps from side to side, and forward and back, ending with all the dancers going around the circle at a breathtaking rush. Because Giselle had not danced very often, she was forced to concentrate on the steps so that she wouldn't falter. This was, of course, far better than looking at Sir Myles's fine profile, or enjoying the sensation of his admiring smile.

Sir Myles wasn't even winded as they came to a halt, while she was panting as if she had run from the hall to the chapel and back again. He bowed politely. "I thank you, my lady."

"I...I have to go," Giselle said, trying desperately to control her breathing, as well as the rest of her traitorous body, which felt so warm under his approving regard.

"Yes, I know," he said understandingly. "You have many duties to attend to."

That said, he bowed once more and sauntered away, toward Elizabeth Cowton.

Giselle sucked in her breath, told herself she didn't care who else he danced with, and hurried off to the kitchen, where Mary and several kitchen boys were awaiting her.

She took her cloak from Mary's arms and put it on, then

ordered the boys to bring the baskets of foodstuffs not consumed that night and follow her. She led them out into the cold, silent night. The stones in the courtyard were white with frost and slippery, and she reminded the boys to take heed. Icicles hung from the roofs of the buildings like long, white fingers. Overhead, the sky was clear, and the millions of stars shone brilliantly. The moon was nearly full, lending plenty of light to this pleasant, if chilly, task.

At the gate, waiting patiently despite the cold, were several of her uncle's poorer tenants. Each one held something with which to carry their gifts, either an old basket or shawl or piece of rag. Some held out the bottom of their tunic or skirt, if that was all they had.

At the front of the small crowd were the children.

With a congenial smile, Giselle beckoned them forward, calling most of them by name and giving into their eager hands a small loaf of brown bread and such meat and other food as they could carry. A few loaves fell to the ground, to be quickly snatched up again with a rueful smile, and more than one small voice lisped a fervent thanks that went straight to Giselle's heart.

Then she distributed the rest of the remaining food to the youths and adults. Each one bowed or curtsied, smiling and murmuring their thanks, as well.

Of all her duties during the Christmastime, this was the one Giselle enjoyed best. Unlike many of the nobles, these people were truly grateful for the food her uncle provided.

When she had given the last, she dismissed the kitchen boys and turned to go back to the hall.

She nearly collided with Sir Myles Buxton, who was leaning against the inner gate, a strange, intriguing expression on his handsome face—of approval, and something else.

Respect. Genuine, sincere respect.

Drawn by that look, she went toward him. "What are you doing here, Sir Myles?" she asked quietly. "I thought you would be dancing."

"I found myself curious to know what other pressing duty tore you from my side," he answered softly.

"I...I have to get back," she stammered.

He nodded and fell into step beside her as she turned toward the kitchen. His face was all angles and planes in the moonlight, and she couldn't read his expression.

"You do that very well," he observed.

"It is not difficult to give away food for which we have no further use."

"It is a rare person who can make it seem as if the giver of gifts is the one receiving the charity."

"Perhaps that is because I enjoy it. It makes me happy to see the children smile and to think that tonight, they will be well fed."

"You like children?"

"Very much. Don't you?"

"I've never given them much thought. I suppose so." He put his hand on her shoulder, so that she stopped walking. She faced him, alone in the winter-quiet courtyard. "Sir?"

Something was different. He was different, or she was. Whatever the cause, Giselle felt that something had altered between them, here in the intimacy of this moment.

Where was her previous dislike for an arrogant nobleman? More to the point, when had the arrogant nobleman been replaced by this respectful, soft-spoken stranger?

"I would like my own children," he said, and with more true sincerity than she had ever heard in his voice before. "I would like them to be *our* children."

Now, here, such a thing not only seemed possible but even desirable.

As marriage to him was desirable. As *he* was desirable.

Stunned by the force of this realization, so opposite to her resolve to save herself from the shackles of marriage for at least a little while, Giselle pulled away and hurried into the hall as quickly as a dignified lady could.

Chapter Four

He was doing it-again, Giselle realized as she stood in the chapel the next morning. Sir Myles stood silently behind her, saying nothing yet managing to disrupt her thoughts and prayers as effectively as if he were muttering in her ear.

Not that it required his physical presence for him to dominate her thoughts, as last night had demonstrated. She had been unable to sleep for what seemed half the night. Instead, she had spent the time pacing and thinking, thinking and pacing, trying to rekindle her determination not to marry *anyone* soon.

If only Sir Myles had proved to be what she had first taken him for, another hypocritical young nobleman. Then, it would be easy to maintain her resolve not to like him. With this new Sir Myles, she was finding that increasingly difficult.

She had finally concluded that the best thing to do would be to inform him of her wishes regarding marriage in general, and the bargain she had made with her uncle. If he was truly what he seemed last night, he would understand, or at least make an effort to.

With that in mind, she wanted to speak with him very much this morning, as soon as she could.

Unfortunately, when Father Paul finished the mass and

the people began to file out into the wintry air surrounded
by the haunting sounds of Latin chanting, she discovered
that Sir Myles had already left the chapel. Disappointed,
she continued toward the hall, intending to change before
getting down to the business of the day.

Then she spotted Sir Myles, suddenly and unexpectedly,
near the entrance to her uncle's solar, perhaps waiting for
Sir Wilfrid. She glanced about and was relieved to see that
the hall was relatively empty. "Sir Myles!" she called out
softly as she hurried toward him.

He smiled when he saw her and she tried not to feel the
warmth of it, although her whole being seemed to respond
to the affection it promised.

"I would speak with you, sir, if you can spare a moment," she said when she reached him. A quick look told
her no one was in the solar and she gestured toward the
empty room.

"Anything to oblige, my lady," Sir Myles replied. He
stepped aside to allow her to enter first. "Indeed, I am
delighted to have another private moment with you."

He followed her into the small room, which contained a
large, somewhat scarred oak table, with a heavy chair behind it that her uncle usually occupied, and another before
it, for visitors. A brazier was already lit in the corner, as
Giselle had instructed, for her uncle might want to play a
game of chess here with one of his many guests.

The room was illuminated by three small, very narrow
windows—little more than slits—that kept out most of the
wind, even today. Rushes sprinkled with fleabane covered
the floor, except in the places where her uncle's hounds
usually lay. There the bare stone floor showed through. Because the sky was cloudy, two flambeaux were also lit and
burning in sconces in the thick stone walls that were bare
of tapestries, in accordance with her uncle's preference.

Sir Myles closed the door. Giselle wanted to protest but
thought better of it. Her arrangement with her uncle was
unusual, and perhaps required secrecy if it was to continue.

Then Sir Myles reached into the pouch at his waist and handed her a large, ornate and singularly ugly brooch made of pale green, blue and yellow gemstones. "For the second day of Christmas," he announced grandly.

Full of her own concerns and caught off guard by his gift, she glanced down at his offering, heavy in her hand. She preferred small, delicate pieces of lesser value but more beauty. "Thank you," she mumbled, wondering how much it had cost and regretting the waste of money.

Then she looked at his face, and in his eyes, she saw very real anxiety. About a brooch?

"Thank you," she repeated, shocked that her acceptance of it seemed to mean so much to him and trying to sound more sincere. "It's...it's..."

"Must you be so ungracious, my lady?" he demanded, the apprehension in his expression suddenly replaced by fierce anger. "Is this how you have been taught to accept a gift?"

Confused, ashamed and upset, Giselle did not take refuge in tears. Instead, she lifted her chin and said, "I think it was most improper of you to shut the door. Is this how you have been taught a gentleman behaves?"

His dark brows lowered ominously as he glared at her, as if marshalling all the force of his masculinity against her. "I think I need hardly point out that coming in here was your suggestion, my lady. It was a most wise and prophetic notion, however, for I don't think you would like any stray servant or guest to overhear what I am about to say."

"I don't have to listen—" she began. Then she heard the sound of footsteps nearby and the noise of servants making idle chatter. She had absolutely no wish to be seen in such circumstances with Sir Myles, lest they be misconstrued. "Please say what you will and let me be about my business!"

Instead of answering right away, he slowly surveyed her from head to foot in a most impertinent manner. She flushed hotly as he abruptly turned on his heel and went behind the table, where he sat in her uncle's chair.

"Have you nothing to say to me, after all?" she charged when he still did not speak. "If not—"

"Sit down, Giselle," he ordered brusquely.

She gasped. "Who do you think you are to—"

"Sit down!"

Giselle marched to the other chair and was about to throw herself into it when she recalled Lady Katherine's constant admonition that a lady always acted like a lady if she wanted to command respect. She halted and slowly, demurely, in her most graceful, ladylike manner, slid into the chair. "I thanked you, which is all that is required when a gift is given, or so I thought."

He didn't appear to be moved by her dignified response. "Who do you think *you* are to accept my gifts with so little grace?" he said, glaring at her with a condemning expression on his handsome face.

She crossed her arms and did not reply. She must have been mad to feel for him as she had last night, or influenced by the moonlight.

"Are you trying to annoy me, the man you are going to marry? Where is the sense in that? I took you for an intelligent woman when I first met you, but I am beginning to think I was mistaken." He continued to stare at her, tapping his booted foot impatiently.

He was as upset as any little boy who doesn't get his own way, Giselle suddenly realized. She recalled how Lady Katherine treated the spoiled girls who arrived to be fostered with her.

"Oh," she wailed dramatically and put her hand to her forehead, "forgive me!" Her apology oozed insincerity. "I did not abase myself! I did not imply that never in the history of the entire world has such a gift been given! I didn't kneel at your feet and kiss the hem of your robe! Oh, how terrible I am!" Her voice grew colder. "Of course, you did not select these gifts to be demonstrations of your wealth. Certainly they were not intended to be manifestations of your taste! Alas, that I could have been so blind.''

His mouth twisted into a sardonic smile. ''I do not find this little display amusing, my lady.''

''Nor did I find your gifts pleasing, my lord.''

''Obviously.''

''I will gladly return them.''

His eyes narrowed. ''They are betrothal gifts. You cannot give them back.''

''I can if I decide I will not marry you.''

His gaze searched her face. ''What are you talking about? The agreement has been made.''

''But not signed.''

''What of that? It is going to be signed soon enough, of that I am certain.''

She felt a moment's doubt. Sir Myles had spoken to her uncle in the solar for some time on the day he had arrived, or so Mary had said. Could it be that her uncle had decided he need not abide by his bargain with her?

No, that she could not believe. Her uncle would have told her if he had changed his mind, and the reason why.

''But you have not signed the contract,'' she affirmed warily.

''A small detail that will be corrected soon enough.''

Giselle kept her face impassive. ''I would not be so sure of that, Sir Myles.''

He rose from the chair and adopted the stance she remembered from that first day when he had climbed onto the yule log. ''What nonsense is this?'' he asked angrily. ''Your uncle has said nothing to me of a change in our agreement.''

''Nevertheless, there has been a change.'' She regarded him as steadily as she could, despite his powerful and somewhat threatening presence. ''He has given me the right to refuse.''

''*What?*''

"My uncle is going to allow me to refuse you, if I don't find you agreeable."

"That is the most ridiculous thing I have ever heard in my life!" Sir Myles declared.

"Be that as it may," she said firmly, "it is true."

Then something completely unexpected happened. Sir Myles's gaze faltered and he looked at the floor. "And you do not find me agreeable?" he asked softly. "Any more than my gifts?"

She was quite prepared to say that she did not, except this change in his behavior confused her yet again.

What kind of man was this? Proud and insolent one moment, respectful and even anxious as any woman could wish the next.

"It's not that you're not agreeable, exactly," she said slowly. "You're certainly very handsome and manly. It's just that I don't wish to marry soon. I hoped my bargain with my uncle would give me a little time for liberty."

He sighed, and then he came around behind her and began to brush his long, lean fingers over the back of her chair. "And this aversion to matrimony has nothing to do with me in particular?"

She rose and placed her slender hand lightly on his arm. "No, and I'm sorry," she said softly. "I've been rude and unmannerly. I...I wanted to explain myself to you this morning.

"You see, Sir Myles," she began slowly and with unexpected shyness, "I was a long time under the fosterage of a very strict lady. That wasn't so very bad, because I had friends there. But one by one, they married, and it was as if they had died. We never heard from them again. I can only think that was because their husbands frowned upon such visits, although I don't see why. So you see, I was in no hurry to be similarly imprisoned. Then I learned that my uncle had betrothed me even before I came here."

"I suppose I would be disappointed if someone had

made such an arrangement for me under similar circumstances,'' Myles said with an understanding smile.

"I was more than disappointed, Sir Myles," she admitted. "I was angry. And I knew that I could not, by law, be forced to marry against my will. So I made a bargain with my uncle. If I do a fine job as chatelaine during the twelve days of Christmas, then I can refuse his choice."

"Do you still wish to refuse me?" Myles asked softly. He looked at her—and in his eyes, she thought she saw a calculating expression that chilled her to the bone.

While Myles held his breath as he waited for her response, afraid to break the mood he had established, and telling himself, as he had been since she began her explanation, that his anxiety was unfounded and that with care, he could overcome her foolish whim not to be wed.

She looked up at him doubtfully, and before she could speak, he pulled her into his arms and kissed her, certain that after that, she would forget all thoughts of refusing to agree to marry him.

Indeed, he forgot all thoughts of anything but how wonderful it was to hold her in his arms and taste her lips with his own.

It took all his self-control to break the kiss at what he judged the proper moment, so that they had kissed long enough to excite her and yet not so long as to be overwhelming, for either of them. "Forgive me, my lady," he whispered. "I was swept away by your—"

"Stupidity?" she declared, stepping abruptly away from him with a disgusted expression. "Do you think I don't know a clever show of playacting when I see it? Do you think those eyes of yours do not give away everything? I wouldn't marry you now if you were the last man in England!"

For an instant, he was completely dumbfounded.

"Do you think I am some silly girl to lose the measure of freedom I have won because of your charm or your

looks? That because of a moment's intimacy in the courtyard and one kiss, I will resign myself to your will?''

Who do you think you are, boy? His father's harsh words
seemed to ring out in the air between them, so much so
that Myles almost covered his ears with his hands.

Instead, and with surprising speed, he grabbed her and
pulled her back into his embrace, staring into her suddenly
frightened eyes. "It really doesn't matter what you want,
my lady," he said. "The marriage agreement has been
made, and I intend to see that it is kept! No one spurns
Myles Buxton! No one!"

He let go of her just as quickly. "Lady Giselle," he said,
fighting to make his tone more reasonable, to hide his anger
and his anguish, as she rubbed her arms where he had
grabbed her. "You had best understand this. Your uncle
and I both know that this is a most advantageous match,
and neither one of us would care to see it broken."

"What of love, Sir Myles?" Giselle charged. "Does it
mean nothing to you? For I assure you, I could never love
a hypocrite like you!"

His lips curled into a grin that was more like a scowl.
"I would never have guessed that from your kiss," he
noted haughtily. Suddenly he pulled her into his arms again
and, as she struggled to get free of him, his voice dropped
to a husky whisper. "You will not marry without love, is
that it? Then I promise you, my *arrogant* young lady, that
before the twelfth day of Christmas has passed, you will
be passionately in love with me. *Passionately.*"

He pushed her away and she stared at him in astonishment. Then her eyes narrowed like an opponent on the field
of battle. "Is that a challenge, sir knight?"

"If you choose to think so."

"I do—and I accept. But what if I am *not* passionately
in love with you by then?" she demanded scornfully.

"Then you do not have to marry me."

She smiled slowly and with such a look in her eyes that
Myles feared he had made a grievous error making such a

concession. Nevertheless, he would not back down, just as he would never admit that his father was right about him.

"I trust you realize you begin with a serious disadvantage," she said. "I do not like you."

"A little adversity makes the challenge that much more interesting, and the triumph all the greater," he replied.

"If it pleases you to think so," she said as she sidled toward the door, "although I would not be too swift to celebrate your triumph. Now if you will excuse me, I have many things to do."

She hurried away as if she half feared he would ravish her on the floor, nearly slamming the door behind her.

Myles slumped onto Sir Wilfrid's chair with a weary sigh.

Myles was still sitting there several minutes later when Sir Wilfrid opened the door and halted on the threshold.

"Sir Myles, what brings you here?" Sir Wilfrid began pleasantly as he entered, trailed by his two favorite hounds.

Myles got to his feet. "I want to know what the devil you're playing at," he demanded, coming around the table. "What is this nonsense about letting your niece refuse my hand? Does your word count for so little that it can be disregarded on the whim of a woman?"

Sir Wilfrid frowned and he loudly cleared his throat as he crossed the room and sat in the chair Myles had vacated. "Sit, please, my young hotspur," he said, gesturing at the other chair. "And listen before you say more you may come to regret."

Myles had a good mind to walk out of the solar. He had been insulted by this alleged bargain between Sir Wilfrid and his niece and, worse, made to feel a fool. The only thing that prevented him from doing so was the certain knowledge that if he did, he would not stop until he had left Wutherton Castle far behind, which would mean acknowledging defeat, and that he would not do.

"Was it Giselle who told you of our agreement?" Sir Wilfrid asked in a reasonable tone.

"Yes."

"What exactly did she say?"

"She said that if she did well as chatelaine over the twelve days of Christmas, she would be allowed to refuse your choice of husband for her, if she wished."

To his very great surprise, Sir Wilfrid's initial answer was a nod and broad grin.

Myles leaned forward and splayed his hands on the top of the table. "And you intend to abide by this ludicrous arrangement?"

"Now, now, Sir Myles, calm yourself," Sir Wilfrid said placatingly in his gruff voice. "You have not listened carefully enough, a fault not uncommon among the young, in my experience. She may refuse *if* she does a fine job, and *if* she wishes. Consider how easy it is for things to go wrong during twelve days of feasting and celebration. Consider, too—although I'm sure your modesty forbids—the groom in question. Now then, how much risk is there in letting Giselle think she has some choice?"

Mindful of her current opinion of the groom, it struck Myles that the risk was great, indeed. Nevertheless, Sir Wilfrid clearly favored the match, and the hint that he would be able to find some fault in Giselle's efforts should have been comforting.

Myles told himself that he was also attaching too much importance to Giselle's acceptance. Surely it was Sir Wilfrid's opinion that mattered most.

Sir Wilfrid sighed. "I dote on her, I must confess, and think of her as my own daughter. When she asked this of me, I couldn't find the will to refuse."

Myles recalled Giselle's eyes when she had talked of her time with Lady Katherine and her hopes for freedom, and realized it would take a very strong man to resist that particular young lady's pleading eyes and soft voice.

"I should also tell you Giselle's life has not been easy,

despite her wealth. She came to me after her parents died, when she was very young. If my dear wife had been living, I would have kept her here, but I knew nothing about raising a girl. That's why I sent her to be fostered with Lady Katherine, who, while the most admirable of women, is very...rigorous. Giselle's sojourn there was certainly not filled with idleness and gossip.

"I'm sure this agreement we have comes as something of a shock to you, but I'm equally certain it's all just a ding in the armor, eh? What's the harm in giving way a little, when it pleases her and costs us nothing—and there's not much else of which that could be said when it comes to women, is there, Sir Myles?"

Myles forced a smile onto his face.

"Come now," Sir Wilfrid said, heaving himself out of his chair, "what do you say to some hunting? It'll do us all good to ride out, I think."

Myles did not disagree.

"You go on ahead. I have a few small matters of business to deal with, and I'll join you later in the far meadow."

The younger man nodded, bowed and left the solar.

Sir Wilfrid went to the window and watched the group of noblemen gathering outside the stable. Then he realized Giselle was standing near the kitchen talking to a rather motley group of strangers. Entertainers, by the look of their wagon and the bundles tied upon it.

Suddenly Sir Myles burst out of the hall and marched toward the noblemen.

To Sir Wilfrid's dismay, a quick glance at Giselle showed she was paying him no attention, although the woman seated on the cart nearest her was staring at Sir Myles as if she'd never seen a man before.

What was wrong with his niece? Was she determined to be pigheaded about this notion of freedom? Didn't every young woman want to be married, and wasn't Sir Myles the answer to every maiden's dream?

Finally Giselle deigned to cast the briefest of looks over

her shoulder as the noblemen mounted their horses and rode out of the gate.

With a disgruntled frown, Sir Wilfrid marched to the door, threw it open and grabbed the shoulder of a shocked Mary as she passed by with a load of coal for the brazier in Lady Giselle's bedchamber. "Put that in here and fetch my niece at once!" he ordered.

Chapter Five

After her disturbing exchange with Sir Myles in the solar, Giselle had been delighted to be distracted by the news that the mummers had arrived and were waiting in the courtyard.

Nevertheless, as she hurried to greet the traveling band of players who would entertain the company in the hall that night, she couldn't rid her mind of Sir Myles.

Why was he so persistent, if her bargain with her uncle angered him so? Why did he issue his challenge, especially when he would surely realize, now more than ever, that his chances of winning were slim, indeed?

Perhaps the apparent disappointment on his face and abrupt change of manner from angry arrogance to apologetic self-doubt had not been feigned. Maybe she had been mistaken and that had not been calculation in his eyes.

Oh, she was imagining excuses that he did not deserve! He had been acting a part, as if he were one of the players.

She spotted the band of players gathered near the kitchen, their breath white puffs in the cold air as they stamped their feet to stay warm. Two small wagons bearing assorted baggage, a woman nursing an infant, and a girl were also part of the group.

Lady Katherine had considered mummers suitable entertainment, provided their selections were based on the Bible and Giselle knew these particular actors well, from their leader, Matthew Appleton, to the youngest performer of them, Matthew's son, Peter, a lad of fourteen who played the women's parts, for of course no woman could playact.

The only females in the company were Matthew's wife and daughter, and they did the things wives and daughters usually did in a household, plus looked after the costumes and the necessary properties, all while traveling about the countryside.

"Good day, my lady, and happy Christmas!" Matthew called out when he noticed her. He made a sweeping bow, still graceful and lithe for a man of nearly forty. The others followed suit. "You are looking very well, my lady. Isn't she, Martha?" Matthew said to his wife as Giselle drew near.

Martha, a pleasant-faced woman a few years younger than her husband, smiled.

"We thought you'd be a married lady now, though, didn't we?" Matthew noted, his brow furrowed. "And to a most fine nobleman, for so we were given to understand."

Martha nodded and looked concerned.

"Who gave you to understand this?" Giselle inquired, attempting to adopt a bantering tone.

"Well, my lady, it was Sir Myles Buxton."

At the mention of that gentleman's name, Martha and her daughter smiled approvingly.

"Is he not here, my lady?" Matthew asked.

"Yes, he is," Giselle answered lightly. "You know him well?"

"We've performed for him many times, my lady," Matthew said enthusiastically. "A most kind, charitable fellow, and with a right wonderful sense of humor—for a nobleman."

Kind? Charitable? A wonderful sense of humor? These were qualities Giselle had not noticed, or had not an opportunity to, perhaps.

"Yes, indeed, my lady," Martha seconded, apparently

sensing Giselle's doubt. "Why, no matter how much Matthew acted up, pretending to be Sir Myles when we performed at Buxton Hall, Sir Myles took it all with very good grace. And paid very well, too, I must say."

Giselle could not imagine anyone doing justice to Sir Myles's natural grace or self-assured manner. However, she had no wish to discuss Sir Myles anymore. "Sir Wilfrid will pay well, too, never fear. You may join us in the hall for the feast before the performance."

Matthew and Martha and the rest of their company were all smiles. "We had no doubt of being well treated, did we, Martha?" Matthew said with a glance at his wife. "Being in the hall tonight is most welcome, too. Apart from the food, which I'm sure will be excellent, we can study your guests, the better to entertain them."

Giselle slowly became aware that no one else was listening to Matthew. They were looking at something over her shoulder, and Martha in particular had an approving expression on her face. Giselle followed their gaze, to behold Sir Myles striding toward the stables attired as if for hunting, with his cloak thrown carelessly back over one broad shoulder.

Well, she never thought he wasn't a good-looking man. It was his manner that left much to be desired.

They all watched as he easily mounted one of the finest stallions she had ever seen, a large black beast that he apparently controlled solely with his knees. Several other male guests were likewise mounted or preparing to, obviously intending to ride out hunting.

That was good, because it would replenish the larder, already depleted to some extent. It would also take the annoyingly distracting Sir Myles out of her way for the rest of the day.

Then Giselle felt a spark of devilment. "I would dearly love to see you play Sir Myles," she said impulsively to Matthew, smiling sweetly.

Matthew directed a knowing look at his wife, which Gi-

elle ignored. They could think what they liked, as long
s Sir Myles was mocked. Despite the man's apparent
equanimity when he had witnessed Matthew's past perfor-
nances, he might not be so easy when *she* saw the imita-
ion.

"Delighted, my lady!" Matthew cried. "Shall he be Sir
George slaying the dragon?"

"Whatever you consider appropriate," Giselle said.
'You are all to sleep above the maid's quarters. If you wait
ere, I shall send someone to show you the way."

"Thank you, my lady. We shall not disappoint you."

"I'm sure you won't."

"My lady!" a very flustered Mary cried. The maidser-
ant's skirts swirled around her thick ankles as she rushed
oward them. "My lady! Your uncle wants you. In his so-
ar. Without delay!"

Giselle quickly bid adieu to the startled mummers and
ollowed Mary, the servant's panic infectious. "What did
e say? Why does he wish to see me?"

"He didn't tell *me*," Mary said anxiously. "But he's
ight angry! Growled like a bear! Told me to fetch you at
nce!"

Giselle cast a wary eye at the gate. Perhaps Sir Myles
ad voiced his displeasure at her agreement with her uncle
o Sir Wilfrid before he had departed. If so, she thought
with more anger than dismay, he no doubt had kept his
mpertinent challenge to himself.

Insolent, selfish man!

"Oh, I wonder what can be the matter!" Mary cried
new. "You've done everything wonderful well, my lady.
Surely he can't have found fault with you!"

Giselle hoped that was not the cause of this sudden summons. There had been a few mishaps, like the yule log
getting wedged in the entrance and the lack of hay, but
othing more serious than that.

Once inside the hall, she gave her cloak to Mary with
rembling hands and proceeded to the solar, pausing to

catch her breath outside the open door. When she felt a little calmer, she entered.

Her uncle was seated behind the table, his huge hunting hounds slumbering at his feet, a goblet of mead at his elbow, and a fierce expression on his face. "Shut the door," he ordered.

She hastened to obey.

"Why don't you like Sir Myles?" he demanded the moment she had closed the door.

She turned to face him, and Sir Wilfrid saw the defiance that was her inheritance from her mother, his sister. God's holy heaven, why did she have to have that portion of Livia's character?

"He is the finest knight in the land, and the best-looking, too," he said. "Every maiden within a thousand miles would beg to be his wife."

"Then they may have him."

"Giselle!" Sir Wilfrid rumbled, his frustration winning over his desire for diplomacy. "It took a great deal of effort to arrange this marriage and I am not about to let it be destroyed by anyone's whim, not even that of my beloved niece!"

She took heart at his last words. "I'm sorry to upset you, Uncle," she said placatingly, "but please try to understand. He acts as if...as if he can just come here and crook his finger and I will be his."

The foolish young whelp! Sir Wilfrid thought with some disgust. Perhaps the coolness between these two youngsters was not totally Giselle's fault, after all. Anyone could see that Giselle was the type of woman who would want gentle wooing, and perhaps Sir Myles had been too overbearing.

Convinced he saw part of the trouble, Sir Wilfrid's voice softened. "Considering that the marriage contract is all but signed, perhaps that isn't so strange."

"But it *is* discourteous and most impertinent."

"Is that all he is guilty of, in your sight?"

"The gifts he bought for me—he only chose them to

how his wealth. There was no thought of me at all!'' Even as Giselle voiced her complaint, she was uncomfortably aware of how childish she sounded. She felt even worse listening to her uncle's next words.

"He didn't buy those presents for you. He won them."

"Won them?"

"In tournaments. Every time he defeated an opponent, he demanded a prize suitable for his bride."

"But he didn't get them for *me*," she protested feebly. 'He's never even seen me before.''

"God's teeth, girl!'' Sir Wilfrid all but shouted. "What do you want the man to do? Get down on his knees like a moonstruck calf and beg for your hand? I never should have made that bargain with you. You were anxious to hate him on sight. I must be in my dotage!''

Giselle truly did not enjoy upsetting her uncle, so she said with more hopefulness, "I don't *hate* him, Uncle. He's just so...so conceited and sure of himself and I want some measure of liberty before I marry.''

"I've a good mind to forgo our agreement, since you aren't playing fair.''

"Uncle! Of what are you accusing me?''

"You aren't giving the fellow a chance! You looked like a woman about to be executed when you danced with him, and he's the finest dancer I've ever seen. You've rebuffed his gifts—''

"Did he tell you that?''

Her uncle glared at her and she blushed, knowing she should not have interrupted him. "No, he didn't tell me that. He didn't have to. You haven't worn one new bit of finery, so either you gave them back or might just as well have. Well?''

What could she say? He was quite correct.

Her uncle took a deep breath. "Listen to me carefully, Giselle. If Myles Buxton acts like a conceited, arrogant nobleman, it's because that's how he was taught noblemen should behave if they desire attention. If you want him to

understand you, you should be willing to do as much fo
him."

Her uncle was right, and she knew it.

Nor was she so stubborn as to refuse to acknowledg
that. Instead, she sat opposite him and regarded him steadi
ly. "Who taught him to behave so?"

Sir Wilfrid smiled slightly. "Ah, now you begin to won
der about him. You should have asked me sooner.

"But since you finally have, I shall tell you. His fathe
and his older brothers, that's who. If you think Myles act
the selfish princeling, you should meet *them*."

"That's no excuse," Giselle said, her tone petulant de
spite the remorse she was beginning to feel.

"Perhaps not. But know you this—his life has not bee
as easy as he would have you believe. His father doted o
his brothers, never him. Myles was treated as second-best
always, no matter what he did or how well he did it."

"Why?" she wondered aloud, finding it hard to believe
that any nobleman would not be proud to have such a son

"I suspect it's because of all Charles Buxton's sons
Myles was the only one to take after Charles's wife—and
how that man loathed her."

"*Loathed* her?" Giselle shivered, imagining life as
woman chained in marriage to a man who hated her.

Before she could say that this was precisely the situatio
she wished to avoid, her uncle continued. "It was quite
mutual, I'm sorry to say, although neither one was force
into the marriage."

"They chose such a fate? Why?"

Sir Wilfrid sighed wearily. "The woman Charles wa
first betrothed to, and whom he loved dearly, or so the
say, died before the wedding. I suppose after that, he didn'
expect to be happy, so he took the first rich woman offere
to him. As for Edith...she was not young, and I daresay
she thought it was him, or the convent."

"I am not so desperate, Uncle," Giselle reminded him.

"No, nor is Myles."

Her uncle rose and came to her, pulling her into a fatherly embrace. "He's a good man, my dear. You deserve the best, Giselle, and whether you think so at the moment or not, Myles Buxton is the best."

"But I don't understand. If his parents were not happy together, why would he insist that we marry, if I do not want him?"

Sir Wilfrid shook his head. "I have no idea, but I would consider his persistence a great compliment." Then he chucked her lightly under the chin. "A girl could do a lot worse, Giselle. Give him a chance, eh?"

Sobered by her uncle's words, aware of how little she really knew about Myles Buxton, Giselle nodded. "I will try."

That evening, Giselle was in a fog of confusion. She had tried to think of some explanation for Sir Myles's persistent wish to marry her, given his past and their last confrontation. Still determined to avoid marriage for as long as she could, she had nevertheless decided to try to learn more about Myles, without actually encouraging him.

Unfortunately, tonight he had not come to take his place at the high table. He lingered below the salt with the mummers, talking to Matthew and the others in animated whispers and laughing amiably.

Then a servant came to tell her Sir Myles had decided to eat with the players, if she didn't mind.

Mind? Of course she minded! He was a noble guest, and people might think *she* was responsible for this slight. She couldn't help but feel insulted and upset by his actions, and she wondered how he ever expected to make her love him by doing such a thing. But he was her guest, so she simply smiled and acquiesced.

At least the feast was going well, the day had passed without further problems, and the musicians were playing excellently. The scent of roasting apples and cinnamon filled the air, as well as the pleasant aroma of mulled cider

and wine. The dogs, sated with scraps from the tables, ha
ceased roving about the hall and lay slumbering by th
hearth where the great yule log still burned, their state no
much different from that of Sir Wilfrid, whose eyes wer
more than half shut.

She forced her attention to the center of the hall, wher
several of the guests were dancing. Sir George de Gramer
cie was leaping about with great vigor, to the delight o
those dancing in the circle with him, especially Lady Eliz
abeth and Lady Alice.

Well, for once Sir Myles was not the center of attentior
She wondered how he felt about that, but when she looke
where he had been seated, Sir Myles and the mummer
were gone. Matthew and the others would have left to pre
pare for the night's entertainment; she had no idea wher
Sir Myles might have gone, and told herself she didn't care

She sighed wearily and contemplated asking to be ex
cused before the mummers appeared. She had already dis
tributed the remains of the feast to the poor, so she did no
even have that to look forward to. She might as well go t
bed.

Before she could make this request of her somnambulan
uncle, however, the musicians played a tremendous fanfar
and Matthew appeared, dressed in a long red cloak trimme
with ermine and sporting a waist-length and quite fraudu
lent white beard.

"Saint Nicholas!" the waiting crowd murmured with ap
proval.

Then Peter arrived, dressed as a young woman and ac
companied by another mummer who was obviously sup
posed to be the husband or lover. The lover departed and
with actions, the "young woman" indicated that she wa
miserable.

"It's Saint Nicholas and the three sisters," Sir Wilfri
said, awakening with a snort and sitting straighter.

Giselle smiled wanly. The story of the saint who ha
given three sisters dowries so that they wouldn't be force

to prostitute themselves was most appropriate for Christmas; still, she wished they had picked something that had nothing to do with dowries or weddings.

Another couple from Matthew's company appeared, playing another of the distraught sisters and her betrothed. Saint Nicholas watched with great concern as they acted out their troubles.

Then came the third sister, whose entrance was greeted with a flurry of laughter, giggles, guffaws and snide glances at Giselle. It took her only an instant to see why, for the third sister, the one bustling about like a busy chatelaine, was being portrayed by none other than Sir Myles Buxton.

He wore a gown and a long, brown wig and minced about in a way that would have been comical if he wasn't making fun of her. The fact that he was also a good head taller than the man who was obviously supposed to be his betrothed added to the humor. Giselle, however, was determined to find nothing amusing about this impudent mockery.

Then she had another realization, one that contrived to bring a smile to her lips. The man playing Sir Myles's betrothed was imitating Sir Myles, from the swagger of his walk to the arrogance of his mien. He seemed completely oblivious to the loving "woman" scurrying around him, instead marching about like some kind of wooden soldier.

Not a bad imitation, Giselle thought with a smirk.

At last Saint Nicholas provided the dowries, to the delight of all the sisters. Here Sir Myles did something she could not have foreseen. The third sister hesitated a moment, as if reconsidering marriage with the martinet. The "groom" attempted to carry off his bride, only to be smacked soundly on the head. The groom then made a very good show of apologizing and was apparently forgiven, for "she" at last embraced her future husband, actually picking him up off the ground, to hearty applause.

Then, to Giselle's very great surprise, Sir Myles looked

at her and grinned, as if seeking her approval or forgiveness or both.

This action was more flattering than anything he had ever said to her and suddenly Giselle was no longer offended by his performance. She would have been, of course, had the third sister thrown herself at her betrothed with wild enthusiasm. Instead, the supercilious groom had been properly humbled.

But give Sir Myles the satisfaction of seeing her approval? Not yet, she thought, lowering her head to hide her smile.

It seemed only just, given his confusing behavior, to let him be perplexed about her for a while.

The next morning, Myles stared sullenly out the window of the barracks being used to accommodate noblemen and their entourages.

Mercifully he was alone, the other knights having already dressed and gone to the chapel for mass, or those that were not so inclined were in the hall, awaiting the first meal of the day.

He welcomed the silence, tired of their jovial good humor and remarks about his performance last night.

His gaze roved over the hall and the stables and the busy comings and goings of the servants. Sir Wilfrid had every right to be proud of his castle, for it was more than a fortress. It was a home.

He had never really felt at home anywhere, and certainly not at his father's castle. How could he, when he was always being criticized and made to feel a burden? It had been his ambition, when he married, to create a home such as this, and to be a better parent than his father had been to him, with a wife he could cherish and respect.

He thought he had found such a wife.

With a disgruntled frown, Myles glanced over his shoulder at the gown he had worn last night and then hastily tossed on his chest when he retired. In truth, he had thrown it aside angrily, convinced he had made a serious error in judgment by appearing in the mummers' performance. Giselle had sat stone-faced throughout, then disappeared without a word.

He had been a self-indulgent fool whose only thought when he had arranged to perform with the mummers had been to enjoy himself and take his mind away from Giselle Wutherton. He had mentioned something to Matthew about appearing as busy as Giselle, but he had not consciously decided to imitate her, at least at first, and he hadn't known Peter was going to imitate *him*. Then, once the mummery was under way, he had simply gotten carried away.

It was no wonder Giselle had been angry.

Unfortunately, he couldn't deny that he wanted her more than ever. Now he knew, without doubt, that her acceptance of his hand in marriage would be the greatest prize he could ever win, and the only thing he would ever need to prove his worth, if only to himself. Indeed, if he were to marry anyone but Giselle now, he would always feel his bride was nothing but second-best, a realization that made him understand something of his father's constant anger with the son who was so like the wife he had taken reluctantly and only out of a sense of duty to produce heirs. His mother, who had died when Myles was but five years old, had apparently married Charles Buxton as a last resort, fearing a life shut up in a convent.

He did not want a fate similar to his parents' to befall him. Or Giselle, either.

They could be happy together, if she would look beyond her own presumptions. And he could keep a tight rein on his temper.

She had appeared to be very lonely at the high table last night, as lonely as he had ever been. How much he had wanted to speak with her, but he didn't dare, and not just because of his performance. Surely now she would consider every overture he made as nothing more than an attempt to win his impulsive challenge. She was as proud as he was, so he knew very well the obstacle he had placed between them.

If only there was some way to repair the breach. Perhaps the gift he had sent her this morning at first light would help. Or perhaps it would offend her, as his others had.

He sighed and looked at the sky, as gray and forbidding as his mood.

Perhaps his father had been right, after all. Perhaps he was nothing but a worthless fool. Obviously Giselle believed that, too.

He had to show her that was not true. He would find a way to her heart and prove his merit, to her and everyone else. Her love would be the best gift he could ever hope to receive.

Was Christmas not the time for gifts and miracles?

Suddenly the door to the hall opened. Giselle paused on the threshold and threw the hood of her cloak over her head before she hurried toward the chapel, but there had been time for Myles to see something that brought a relieved smile to his face and made him dash from the barracks without even stopping to grab his cloak.

Chapter Six

Giselle tried not to feel disappointed, but it wasn't much use. Sir Myles wasn't in the chapel, and she had worn the scarf just to show him that she forgave his outrageous behavior last night.

She had immediately recognized the present Mary had brought at dawn, and had thought his offer of it touching, as she had his decision not to bring it himself. That showed a certain amount of humility, as well as a recognition that she might have found his performance last night less than delightful.

She would have, had it not been for the searching, diffident look he had given her. Enough time had passed, she thought, to let him see that she had been amused by his acting and that he was forgiven for mocking her.

She listened to Father Paul say mass, his words ringing in the incense-laden air as he prayed, and despite her resolve to pay attention, she couldn't help glancing over her shoulder to see if there were any latecomers.

There was, and he was standing near the door and smiling at her—only at her, of that she was sure, and with genuine approval and pleasure.

She was very glad, then, that she had worn the scarf.

Her heart began to beat rapidly and erratically, all hope of concentrating on Father Paul disappearing like snow in spring. She could hardly wait for the mass to be over, and when it was, she went to Sir Myles at once, in spite of the curious scrutiny of Elizabeth Cowton and Alice Derosier. She also knew she had the most idiotic grin on her face, but she couldn't help it.

Sir Myles took her arm and led her outside, slightly to the side of the chapel and out of the crowd.

"I have to thank you for your present," Giselle began the moment they were alone. "No, forgive me," she stammered as he continued to regard her with an intensely interested expression in his dark brown eyes. She touched the blue silk. "I *want* to thank you for the present," she finished breathlessly, quite unable to speak in more measured, unemotional tones.

"It is a better color, I grant you," he replied softly. "It does suit you admirably, even if it is presumptuous of me to say so."

She flushed, warm despite the cold December air. "Yes, it certainly is. It suited you last night as well, my lord, although it may be presumptuous of me to say so," she added mischievously.

His smile widened, and there was pleasure in his eyes. "Then I take it I am forgiven for any offense I may have given?"

"You looked so silly, how could I be angry?"

"You might have smiled once or twice, instead of making me fear I had offended you beyond forgiveness."

"I didn't think you were paying any attention to me at all, or cared very much *what* I thought."

"I was, my lady," he said softly. "And I most certainly care."

Giselle swallowed hard, suddenly remembering more vividly than any demure young lady should the sensation of his lips upon hers.

"I confess I was being completely selfish," he said. "I sought solely to amuse myself. It was only as the performance progressed that I realized I was being...rude."

"I am not totally lacking in a sense of humor, Sir Myles," Giselle replied. "Especially since I was not the exclusive prey of the mummers."

"I had no idea Peter was going to do that."

"Otherwise you would have prevented him from mimicking you?" she asked archly. "That hardly seems fair."

"If I had known you would enjoy it, I would have asked that the whole performance be about the arrogant, pompous Sir Myles attempting to woo a reluctant maid," he answered.

Giselle stared at the frost-hardened ground, unsure how to respond. Unsure of many things, her feelings for Sir Myles most of all.

"I have another gift for you today, to make up for the others that met with less favor," he continued. "It is in the stable."

"The stab—?"

"I assumed you enjoy riding. You seem to dislike being confined, to promises or anything else."

He assumed—again. Suddenly she was aware of how very vulnerable she was to his charm and his looks and this deferential manner of addressing her.

Which would probably disappear the moment they were wed. He would become an authoritative, repressive and confining husband. Despite her misgivings, she curtsied and said, "I thank you for your gift, Sir Myles."

"I was going to ask you to go riding with me this afternoon, since the day is a fine one, if a little cold."

"I could not, even if I wanted to. I have much to do," she replied, her tone as chilly as the air, for she could not rid herself of the dread that his current behavior was intended only to woo her into marriage.

"Ah, yes, the duties of a chatelaine." He gave her a shrewd and questioning look. "But is it not also the duty of the chatelaine to make sure her guests enjoy themselves? A large party intend to ride out, and I believe your uncle will not take it amiss if you join us, to insure that we are all having a fine afternoon."

Giselle regarded him pensively. She wanted to go riding, to be out of doors and having a pleasant time instead of being concerned only with household matters.

He was right, too. A good hostess should make sure that her guests were happy, and perhaps she could best do that by joining them, although she would do her utmost to stay away from Sir Myles.

After all, she would be back in plenty of time to see to the evening meal. "Very well, Sir Myles," she said. "I will ask him."

"Good. Now you must allow me to escort you to the hall," he said, taking her hand and placing it on his arm.

His muscular arm.

He gave her a sidelong glance and smiled. "You know, you are absolutely right. That other scarf would have looked quite hideous."

Giselle wanted to feel offended. Instead, all she could do was nod and try not to think about his arms or lips or eyes, or anything else about his body.

Which proved to be quite impossible.

Safely in the midst of the boisterous, pleasant party, Giselle sighed with happiness as her new mare walked along the road. It was indeed pleasant to be absolved from any duties for a little while, even if she had to be discomfited by Sir Myles's presence. She was no closer to understanding him than before, and she was beginning to fear she was too weak where he was concerned.

Especially when it appeared that Sir Myles was ready and capable of amending his ways in an attempt to please her, and when he chose the perfect gift for her, with true consideration for what she would like.

In one way, she could even learn from him. He was far more able to laugh at himself than she was.

Her resolution regarding marriage might crumble like the

old byre they had passed some way back, if he continued in this fashion. Or had he not arrogantly told her he would make her love him. Whenever she felt her resolve weaken, she must remember that.

A lone bird wheeled above the bare branches of the trees lining the road, a speck of darkness in the clear sky, which had brightened from the dull gray of morning to the special bright blue of a cold winter's day. The snow gleamed whitely, and here and there were patches of the dark green of holly and pine, the scent of the evergreen as strong as that of the incense in the chapel.

Once or twice she caught sight of mistletoe attached to a tree, its pale berries like wax against the bark. Cecily had told her that the druids had used mistletoe to cure a woman of barrenness.

Which made Giselle think of babies and recall Sir Myles's face when he had spoken of children, *their* children, in the courtyard.

She swiveled a little in her saddle to see where he was and inadvertently caught his eye. To her chagrin, he nudged his horse forward to join her, as if her look had been the same as a summons to him.

"You seem very pensive, my lady," Sir Myles remarked when he was beside her.

"It is a lovely day. I was watching the bird."

"Envying it its freedom?"

She slid him a sidelong glance. "Not especially, but now that you say that, I suppose it is true."

"I envy it, too."

"Why? You are free."

"No one is truly free, my lady. I have to answer to my father, who is my overlord, as well as the king, and make certain that my people prosper."

"Oh, yes," she agreed, although in truth, she had never considered that his life was not one of unending pleasure and self-indulgence.

Myles turned to her with a rather inscrutable smile. "I like your uncle. He seems a good man."

"He is," she replied matter-of-factly.

"Then I envy you," he answered in a similar tone, free of any self-pity.

She remembered what her uncle had told her of Myles's family and a new idea presented itself to Giselle. Could it be that Myles wanted not just her dowry, but a family, too, one that would treat him better than his own? "He thinks highly of you," she remarked.

"Yet he is willing to cast me aside as a husband for you," Sir Myles noted.

"I think that you may blame on both his fondness for me and his desire to do right. But I'm sure he likes you."

"I would far rather hear you say that *you* like me."

"I thought you had already decided I must," she said with a hint of mockery.

He didn't reply and Giselle immediately regretted not being more circumspect. If her uncle had spoken truly about Sir Myles's family, and there was no reason to suppose he hadn't, Myles Buxton had not enjoyed a blissful childhood.

In truth, he might have suffered far more than she had. It could even be that while she saw marriage as causing her to lose something, he saw it as a way to gain what he lacked. And if he thought she alone could provide that, no doubt she should be truly flattered, as her uncle had said.

They rode awhile in silence, with Giselle occasionally watching him out of the corner of her eye while she mused upon this idea, which would explain why he continued to pursue her despite her rebuffs. "You seem thoughtful, too, Sir Myles," she said at last.

He looked at her with a surprised and wary smile. "Forgive my preoccupation, my lady. I assure you, I was not contemplating my own attributes, or planning ways to force you into marriage against your will."

"Oh, no. That is, I shouldn't have said that, my lord."

"Yes, you should, if you thought it the truth," he replied calmly. "I have had worse things said of me, my lady."

Again Giselle recalled her uncle's words, and decided to try to begin the conversation anew. "I am not used to seeing you look pensive."

He gave her a sardonic smile. "I was thinking about love."

"Oh?" She blushed and desperately wished she wasn't.

"Yes. Elizabeth Cowton is very much in love."

Giselle frowned and said nothing, trying not to feel disappointed. After all, she should be relieved there was another woman who wanted him, if she did not, and she should be glad he was being honest with her.

"Not with me," he added, after what seemed a very long moment.

"Elizabeth Cowton's feelings are none of my business," she said quickly.

Too quickly, to judge by the shrewd glance he directed at her. "Alas! I was hoping you might be jealous," he said wryly.

"Why would I be? I imagine many women find you attractive."

"But not you?"

Giselle flushed hotly and her grip tightened on the reins.

"Unfortunately, Elizabeth's dowry is very small, and her beloved's family is not in favor of the match."

Giselle frowned with dismay. "It is a pity that marriage should depend so much upon money."

"Life without wealth is not easy."

"No." She regarded him with some curiosity. "You sound as if you speak from experience, yet your family is very rich."

"My father is." He stared straight ahead. "My brothers lack for nothing. My circumstances are slightly different. My father has given me an estate, but as for money, that must come from other quarters."

Moved by the seriousness of his tone and impressed by his apparent lack of bitterness, her heart went out to him.

Even then, her mind cried a warning. She should feel nothing for Myles Buxton, *must* feel nothing for him, or her freedom would be forfeit. "Such as your wife's dowry?" she suggested.

He turned to regard her steadily. "Yes."

"So when you marry, you will gain wealth, while I will lose mine without ever really possessing it. My uncle controls all my money now, and when I marry, my husband will."

"You don't believe your husband will let you have some say in how your money is spent?"

"You are going to tell me that you would allow me that privilege, I suppose?"

"Yes, I would," he affirmed, and she heard his sincerity.

"Yet you think it ludicrous of my uncle to allow me some discretion in the choice of my husband."

"That's different."

"I do not see why," she retorted. "Besides, I know full well how it will be. You are acting all kindness and generosity before the marriage, and you will be quite different afterward.

"My friend Cecily's husband made no end of generous promises before they were married. She wrote me all about him, telling me how kind, how sweet, how wonderful he was. Oh, she was going to be so happy!"

"Am I to understand she is not?" Myles asked when she paused to draw breath.

"No, she can't be! I have not had one word from her since she's been married, nor has she ever come to visit, and I've invited her more than once. I'm sure her husband prevents her, for Cecily and I were like sisters. I know she would come if she could."

"Granted there are some men who say one thing before marriage and another after, but I am not of that ilk," Myles said. "I promise you that you will have as much freedom as any married woman may reasonably desire, when we are married.''

Giselle shot him a questioning look. ''You will decide what is reasonable, I suppose.''

''Who else?''

Her only answer was to press her lips together in anger. To be sure, he had been kind and generous, but undoubtedly that would only last until they were safely wed. Then she would lose even the small measure of freedom she had at present. And he was so handsome, he would probably have a lover in every town under his rule. Oh, she never wanted to marry, not Sir Myles or any man!

''Shall we see how this mare gallops?''

''No,'' Giselle replied peevishly. All she wanted to do now was get back to the castle.

Suddenly Sir Myles reached out and slapped the mare on the buttocks, which made the beast break into a startled gallop. Giselle cried out and held on for dear life as the mare ran off the road and into an opening in the trees.

''Something's spooked Lady Giselle's horse.'' Myles called out to the company who had all been too occupied with their own conversations to see what he had done, a fact he had ascertained before slapping the mare. ''I'll stop her!''

He kicked his horse into a canter and followed, determined to have it out with Giselle Wutherton once and for all, challenge or no challenge.

Giselle finally managed to slow the mare, and when the horse halted, she slipped from its back, breathing shakily but happy to be on firm, if snow-covered, ground. It was a miracle she had not struck a tree branch and been knocked off her horse.

Sir Myles appeared, pulling his stallion to a stop and dismounting with a flourish.

''Why did you do that?'' she demanded, her hands on her hips. ''I could have been killed!''

"I thought you were a good rider."

"My skill would have had nothing to do with it, if an oak tree had been in the way."

He tossed his horse's reins over the bare branches of a nearby bush and walked toward her. "Then I must beg your forgiveness, my lady. I can only plead a tremendous desire to be alone with you as my excuse."

Giselle swallowed hard, realizing for the first time that they *were* alone. In the woods. Just the two of them. "We should rejoin the others," she said, moving close to her mare.

"Not just yet," Myles said, coming toward her and putting a detaining hand on her arm. "I want to talk to you without interruption."

"You didn't have to risk my life," Giselle noted angrily as she faced him, uncomfortably aware of his proximity.

"I didn't think I was."

"Be that as it may, Sir Myles, what do you have to say that is so important that you must risk injury and scandal?"

"I want to tell you that I truly want to marry you."

"You made that plain enough before, the last time we were alone in my uncle's solar, when you seemed so certain I would love you."

His brow furrowed and she thought she saw genuine concern in his dark eyes. "I know I've blundered—"

"Yes, you have!" she said, triumphantly interrupting him, for once. "You interfere in my duties, follow me about like an annoying shadow, you *tell* me I will love you and then you wonder that I do not leap into your arms with gratitude!"

His frown deepened. "I am trying to apologize."

She opened her mouth to tell him she didn't want his apologies, but something in his eyes made her hesitate. What was it? Dismay? Disappointment? Fear?

"Sir Myles," she said in a somewhat calmer tone. "I don't want to be married to *anyone*. Can't you understand that? I want to be free, at least for a little while."

His frown became a scowl. "Because your friend married a less than accommodating husband?"

"Because...because I'm afraid."

He drew back with a look of genuine astonishment. "Not of me?"

"I'm afraid I'll find marriage a worse prison than Lady Katherine's."

His gaze searched her face. "Do you truly believe that I would treat any wife of mine with so little regard?"

At this moment, she doubted it. Yet, at one time she would have said that Cecily's husband would not have treated *her* badly, either.

"I want you to be my wife, Giselle," he said huskily, reaching out and tugging her into his warm and strong embrace. "You, Giselle, for yourself. For your intelligence and kindness, as much as your beauty. Because I can imagine our lives together, and know it will be wonderful. Because I want to have children with you."

Then he bent his head and kissed her. Not fiercely, like before, but tenderly. Lovingly. As if to promise that he meant everything he said. Tempted beyond her resolve by his gentleness, Giselle abandoned herself and her fears to savor his touch and his caress.

How easy it would be to give in to him! How simple to agree to be his wife.

Part of her wanted to do so very, very much, recognizing that she was more than half in love with him already.

But what of freedom? another part of her urged. You cannot be sure that he will not change toward you once you are wed! Delay! Delay!

She pulled back and tried to keep her regard steady as she looked at him. "Sir Myles, I—"

He stared at her suspiciously. "You still doubt my sincerity? Or do you think I am not worthy to be your husband?"

"Yes! No! I don't know!"

"Enough!" he declared, his voice as cold as the snow

beneath their feet as he moved away from her. "I hav
tried. I have been as patient as I know how to be, but
refuse to be subject to any woman's whims and indecisio
for days, especially when I had been assured the marriag
contract was as good as signed!"

"Sir Myles!" she cried as he marched to his horse.

"No! No more words. No more talk!" he growled as h
prepared to mount, glancing at her over his shoulder. "
am not some boy you can play like a fish on a line!" H
leapt upon his prancing stallion. "I am Sir Myles Buxtor
and if you do not think me worthy of your hand, there ar
plenty of other women who *will!* Now, my lady, mount.
will take you back to the others, but I will have no mor
speech from you."

For an instant, she was too astonished to move, and n
only because of his harsh tone and imperious manner. Wha
shocked her was the burning anguish in his eyes as h
gazed at her.

"Do not tempt me to leave you here," he warned, look
ing away.

Quite convinced that he might very well do so, Gisell
went to her mare. He made no move to get down and hel
her, so she hiked up her skirts as much as modesty per
mitted and climbed into the saddle. Once mounted, she di
not wait for any further commands from him, but turne
her horse back the way they had come and nudged her t
a walk.

Giselle said nothing as they returned to the road an
rejoined the party. She dared not, for she feared that if sh
spoke even one word, she would burst into tears.

Chapter Seven

On the morning of the eleventh day of Christmas, as Giselle lay sleepless shortly before dawn, she was eagerly, if morosely, anticipating the end of the celebrations. What had at first seemed an exciting test was now merely tedious and too much hard work.

During the past few days, she had had plenty of time to think about what had happened between Sir Myles and herself. Not during the day, when her duties kept her most thankfully occupied, but at night, when she couldn't sleep, or early in the morning.

She had tried to convince herself that her state of ennui had little to do with Sir Myles's absence after their foray into the woods, and that his abrupt departure was all for the best. Everything he had done had probably only been intended to guarantee that the marriage contract was signed, so that his pride did not suffer. He made no real effort to understand her concerns or her feelings...just as she had made no effort to understand him, either, at least at first.

Despite her efforts to deny that she was at all to blame, she was once again forced to come to this conclusion.

She knew now that she had blundered from the moment of their first meeting. She should have been more amiable and pliant, until he came to know her better. Then, when she had told him of her fears and concerns, perhaps he would have understood, or made more of an effort. Instead she had acted the shrew, with results that she should have foreseen.

She should have been more patient, too, until she had learned more of other men, as she was doing now. There were plenty of noblemen in attendance for Christmas and it seemed, unfortunately, that several of the unmarried ones were anxious to take Sir Myles's place, once it was clear he was gone away. They all seemed to assume they stood an excellent chance of marrying her, yet not a one of them excited her as much as Myles Buxton had, even when she had been doing all in her power to ignore him.

With a weary sigh, Giselle rose from her bed and went to the narrow window of her bedchamber. The first streaks of dawn colored the eastern sky, which was the gray of slate this morning. The day was going to be as gloomy as she felt, she suspected.

If she had any comfort in all of this marriage business, it was that her uncle didn't seem to hold her accountable. Indeed, he had been gentleness personified to her, with no word of reproach or curiosity, not even when Sir Myles failed to appear in the hall after their ride.

With another sigh, she began to brush her hair. Today, as always since Sir Myles had gone, she would put a smile on her face and busy herself with the needs of their guests and the preparations for another feast. She would try not to gasp with anticipation every time she heard a horse in the courtyard. She would attempt to ignore her sense of remorse and to persuade herself that she was glad that Sir Myles had apparently found it so easy to leave her and abandon their betrothal.

Why should he not, when he so obviously felt insulted by her reluctance, as he must have felt when he heard of her agreement with her uncle? How that must have shocked him. If she hadn't been so selfishly concerned with her own desires, she might have handled the situation with better grace, and considerably more delicacy.

Sir Myles Buxton must hate her now.

Mary arrived to help her dress, and soon enough mass was over and the fast broken. By then, a light snow was beginning to fall, and Giselle realized that all the guests would have to remain inside if the snow continued or grew worse. She quickly set about supervising the removal of the tables and ordering preparations for some simple games. She also thought it wise to tell Iestyn to have apples ready for roasting, and to heat some wine, in case a few of the hardier men decided to ride out, after all.

Once that was done, she was forced to think about what she would do for the rest of the morning.

She could sit in the hall with the other noblewomen, sewing and exchanging meaningless pleasantries. Unfortunately, that would mean enduring Elizabeth and Alice's pitying looks, and the constant sense that they were studiously avoiding any and all mention of Sir Myles, lest they wound her tender feelings.

Staying in the hall would also require her to meet the speculative gazes of the unmarried noblemen and to try to ignore their attempts to capture her attention.

Such a morning would surely tax her thinly worn patience past its limit. Therefore, she decided, she would get her cloak and go for a short walk, despite the snow.

The stones of the courtyard were already covered in a thick white carpet of snow when Giselle went out, and it was beginning to fall faster and thicker. Soon they would be in the midst of a blizzard, she realized, and so she dared not leave the castle, in case she got lost in a storm.

More disgruntled than ever, she began to turn back, pausing when she heard the portcullis rattling upward. Who could be coming at this time of day, and in such inclement weather?

The cloaked figure of a woman had no sooner appeared than the stranger rose from her saddle and emitted a squeal of recognition. "Giselle!"

Giselle gave a shocked gasp, then cried out, "Cecily!" and happily ran to meet her frantically waving friend.

Only to skitter to a stop when she saw who had ridde in behind Cecily. It was Sir Myles Buxton, who entere the courtyard as if he hadn't departed without a single wor of farewell to anyone and been gone these several days.

As a stable boy came running and took hold of the bridl of Cecily's horse, Giselle tried to decipher Sir Myles's in scrutable expression, to no avail. Behind him came mounted troop of ten soldiers wearing the colors of th Louvains, Cecily's husband's family, as well as anothe packhorse, loaded down with so much baggage Gisell wondered how long Cecily meant to stay.

Or perhaps some of it belonged to Sir Myles and h intended to remain some time past Christmas....

Her heart leapt to think so. Truly there was not his equa in her uncle's hall, and probably all England, for looks (presence or even manner. He was a proud man, to be sur but she knew now, not unjustifiably. Her uncle had spoke the truth when he had said she should be pleased by hi persistence. She smiled and held her breath for some mar of greeting on his part and hoped he had returned becaus he had reconsidered his hasty departure.

When he barely glanced at her, she regretted her previou behavior to him all the more.

By this time, a groom had appeared, who helped Cecil dismount. Then she called out Giselle's name, again claim ing Giselle's attention. "It has been so long!" Cecil squealed excitedly as Giselle approached her.

Giselle had forgotten how high-pitched Cecily's voic could be when she was excited. Nevertheless, Giselle wa truly happy to see her, and wondered what part Sir Myle had to play in this sudden and unexpected event.

Cecily embraced Giselle rapturously. "My dear, dea friend! How long it has been!" she cried as Giselle trie to draw breath, and not incidently see where Sir Myles ha gone. She really should welcome him. It was her duty, at the very least.

Then she noticed something about Cecily that made her pull back and regard her friend with both envy and delight. "You are with child!"

Cecily's smile was pleased and rather smug. "Indeed I am. Bernard is so thrilled! Of course, he takes all the credit, but I tell him, my dear, surely I have something to do with it! Isn't that like a husband?" Her face took on a condescending expression. "You'll find out eventually, I daresay," she finished.

Despite Giselle's annoyance, which she was sure was only temporary and occasioned by the fact that Sir Myles had not yet greeted her, she managed to smile and then glanced about once more, searching for him. He was dashing up the steps to the hall with his easy, athletic strides.

With a significant look at Sir Myles, Cecily took Giselle's arm and steered her toward the hall. "Now you simply *must* tell me all about Sir Myles. Such a handsome fellow, and so determined! He simply *insisted* that I come to spend some time with you before Epiphany. He would not *hear* of a refusal, and he's the kind of man you don't refuse, is he not?"

"He knew how much I longed to see you again."

"And I, you, my dear!" Cecily replied, squeezing Giselle's arm. "But there was never the time, really. I was so busy with my household duties and Bernard and meeting the tenants and then we journeyed to London where I met so many courtiers—I'll tell you all about it—well, I simply couldn't spare a moment," she finished with a beseeching smile that had something of smug self-satisfaction in it, too.

Giselle regarded Cecily with surprise. "I assumed Bernard would not *allow* you to come to see me."

Cecily giggled. "Oh, dear me! Bernard not allow me? I can see you don't understand the relationship between a husband and wife, my dearest friend. Naturally he was reluctant to let me visit. He cares for me so much, you see, he couldn't bear to be apart from me, and he *hates* to travel. Well, I didn't want him to be miserable on account of me, so I thought I had better stay home! I assure you, my dear, Bernard tends to my comfort as much as any woman could wish.''

Giselle suddenly felt as if she had been the victim of a monstrous fraud. She had been so sure that it had to be Bernard who kept Cecily from coming to her only to find that was not the case at all. Indeed, Giselle was beginning to understand how a newly married woman might find it easy to neglect her old friends for her new husband, especially if he was as desirable as Myles Buxton.

By now they had reached the hall, and once they had removed their cloaks, Giselle immediately spotted Myles. She wanted very much to go to him, if only to welcome him properly, but Cecily had a firm grip on her arm.

"Now you must tell me all your news," Cecily continued in her high-pitched and rushed tones, glancing at Myles. "I simply must know all about you and Sir Myles. Are you to be married? Has he made an offer? What does your uncle think? It will be a wonderful match for you if he has. Really, such a good-looking fellow, and so polite! A bit quiet, though. He scarce said two words to me the whole journey here!''

No doubt because you wouldn't let him, Giselle thought with growing frustration.

Cecily stopped talking and gave Giselle a brief hug. "It *is* good to see you again, Giselle. I really have missed you. Do you remember how we used to imagine sneaking out of our quarters and running away disguised as boys?''

Caught unaware by Cecily's affectionate gesture as well as the sincerity in her voice, Giselle felt a flush of guilt. She had missed her friend, and she was glad to have her here for the holiday.

"This is a delightful hall!" Cecily declared, looking about her. "So nicely decorated, too. All your doing, I'm sure. I long to meet your uncle and all the noble company.

Our life is so quiet, but then,'' she finished with a giggle, "we are such an old married couple! Do you know what Bernard said to me the other day? It was so sweet..."

Giselle listened as Cecily rambled on, all the while trying to catch Sir Myles's eye.

She didn't succeed, and by the time she had showed Cecily to the guest quarters, relived some of their pranks at Lady Katherine's and hurried back to the hall, he was nowhere to be found.

It was only by asking one of the servants who tended to the knights that she was able to discover that Sir Myles did not plan to leave the castle until the next day, because of the weather.

Giselle hoped it would snow for a fortnight. Then she hoped Sir Myles would join them at the high table.

Unfortunately, and after Giselle had spent longer on her toilette than she ever had in her life, Sir Myles did not come to the hall for the feasting or the dancing or the entertainment.

Did he want to leave without speaking to her? Did he hate her that much? But if so, why go to all the trouble to bring Cecily?

Also unfortunately, her uncle had obviously heard of his return, and was likewise disappointed by the nobleman's reluctance to partake of Sir Wilfrid's hospitality.

"If he's such a fool, who wants him allied to us in marriage?" he grumbled after the abundance of food had been cleared away. "What did he expect of a well-brought-up young woman? That you would disgrace yourself and your family by panting after him like a bitch in heat? I tell you, I'm glad he's not here, unmannerly lout! He's ruining my Christmas!"

By this time, Cecily had realized that whatever had happened between Myles and Giselle, it wasn't good. She seemed to feel the best thing to do was to talk loudly, over the muttering Sir Wilfrid, and to act as if rejecting Myles was now the wisest course of action possible.

"The servants tell me he's gone to take his meal at an inn in the village, my dear," Cecily reported, for once saying something Giselle wished to hear. "And he's to leave at first light. Really, such eccentric, uncouth behavior! I was quite wrong about him, Giselle, and I think you should say a prayer of thanks that you are not to be wed to him!"

At last the mummers finished their performance, Cecily declared it was time she retired, and Giselle was able to return to her bedchamber.

Wearily she allowed Mary to help her disrobe. Although it was nearly midnight, she dismissed her maid with a brief reminder to awaken her at dawn the next day, Epiphany, the twelfth day of Christmas. Giselle felt completely and utterly exhausted, but several of the guests—besides Sir Myles—would be leaving tomorrow since the snow had stopped, and she had to make sure their departure went smoothly.

Once Mary was gone, Giselle slowly went to the small table where her brushes and combs lay. On it was a covered box about a foot square, with a small piece of parchment attached.

The parchment bore an inscription: "A final gift. Set them free, as you are. Myles." Lifting the covering, Giselle found a cage containing a pair of turtledoves. They awakened at the influx of light and began to coo plaintively.

Giselle's attention returned to the message, for there could be no mistaking the meaning of Myles's words.

He was setting her free. He was confirming the end of their tentative betrothal, because he thought that was what she wanted.

Wasn't it?

She set the cage down and covered it again, silencing the doves, before walking to her window and gazing out at the snow-covered courtyard. She idly watched the few sentries on the battlements. They were not in any state of watchfulness, for no trouble was expected and certainly not at this time of year, or after such foul weather.

Didn't she want to be free of Sir Myles Buxton? Had she not often proclaimed her desire to have some liberty before she wed any man?

Then another figure caught her eye—a man coming through the gate and striding toward the stables.

She knew that stride. Without pausing a moment to think about what was proper or dignified or expected of a young noblewoman, Giselle grabbed a thick woolen cloak, snatched up the cage and ran from her bedchamber.

Myles entered the warmth of the stable and closed the door behind him. The familiar aroma of hay surrounded him, and his horse whinnied a greeting.

He noticed none of these things as he sighed heavily.

He never should have come back here. He never should have seen Giselle Wutherton again.

He loved her. He respected her. He wanted her. He needed her.

If he had required any confirmation of his feelings, his brief journey with Cecily Louvain would have provided it. Every moment in her presence provided incontrovertible evidence of the difference between Giselle and all the other simpering, helpless young ladies Myles had ever met.

If only he had not acted so arrogantly at the first! If only he had proceeded with patience and delicacy, gently wooing her. If only he had spent more time trying to understand her yearning for freedom!

What would it have cost him to wait a few months to announce their betrothal? Had she been asking so very much?

Instead, he had lost his chance, and he regretted it so much he could not endure being near her, knowing that she would never be his wife. Better by far to avoid her, and best of all to leave at first light. For that reason, he had elected to sleep in the stable, so that he could leave as soon as possible.

He hoped she appreciated his last present, and wondered if she had any idea of the cost to the giver.

With such thoughts for company, he saw that his stallion was properly bedded down, procured two blankets and proceeded to make his bed on a pile of straw. Then, as he unlaced his tunic, the stable door creaked open. A shaft of moonlight illuminated the figure who slipped inside and closed the door behind her, holding something in her hands.

"Giselle?" Myles whispered incredulously.

He was extremely aware that his heart was racing and that she had never looked more beautiful or more desirable. Her long, waving hair was loose about her, and her slender figure was wrapped in a cloak as if it were a royal robe. His brow furrowed as he tried to imagine what had brought her here, at this hour, and alone.

"I wanted to speak with you and you didn't come to the feast." As she came closer, he recognized the cloth-covered parcel in her slender hands.

She held her freedom. The one gift he could give her that she would not refuse.

"I wanted to thank you properly for bringing Cecily, and for the mare and all your other presents." She was near enough for him to see clearly. Near enough to touch. "Thank you."

"I wanted to make you happy," he replied softly.

"You have."

He swallowed hard. He had thought he was already suffering, but at her words, which seemed to him to be the confirmation that she was pleased to be released from their betrothal, he began to understand what true suffering was. He turned away so that he didn't have to look at her.

And then she reached out and touched him. Gently. On his arm.

Unwillingly, yet powerless to resist, he faced her. Her

gaze was puzzled, and he wondered that she couldn't see his anguish, so very real to him.

"Sir Myles," she whispered, holding out the cage, "I do not want this last gift."

He stared at her as he struggled to comprehend her meaning. "You don't want the birds? Then let them go."

She nodded wordlessly and went to the door, where she released them into the dark night and then watched them fly away. As she did so, he realized that beneath her cloak she wore only her shift and thin slippers.

"You had better fly, too, my lady, before you are discovered here," he said brusquely.

She slowly turned to face him once more. She closed the door and walked toward him with a determined expression he knew very well by now.

"I have released you from our betrothal," he whispered. "Now you had better leave before you are discovered here, alone with me and in such attire, or your uncle may try to force a marriage between us."

"Were you planning to depart tomorrow without speaking to me?" she asked, ignoring his warning.

"Yes. What is there to say?"

"I did not think you were a dishonorable man, Sir Myles."

"I did not ask you to come here in your shift," he said hoarsely.

"That is not what I meant. I was speaking of your challenge."

Giselle held her breath while she waited to see if he would understand her meaning, or if she had done another foolish thing by coming here.

"What about the challenge? It is over, finished, done. I have lost, and so you are free."

"I agree I am free in one way, Sir Myles," she concurred softly, "but I must tell you that in another, I am not. I see I shall have to tell you plainly, sir, that you have triumphed. I am passionately in love with you."

For a moment, she feared he was going to say he didn't care. But only for a moment, for in the next, he pulled her into his embrace and kissed her, the heat of his passion reaching out and enfolding her, until she burned with equal fire. "Giselle, Giselle!" he murmured as his lips trailed across her cheek, only to return to capture her mouth again.

She held him tightly and felt his heart beating as rapidly as her own, his arms holding her as if he never wanted to let her go. But he did, drawing back slightly. "Are you sure? You were so determined—"

"Can you doubt it?" she demanded with a smile. "I am as determined in this, Sir Myles, I assure you, unless you do not want me anymore?"

"Don't be ridiculous," he said, returning her smile, his eyes full of happiness. "I've never wanted anything so much in my life as to have you for my wife."

"Then I think I am not the only one passionately in love," she observed with a low chuckle as she sighed and leaned against his broad chest.

"I acted like a conceited fool, Giselle. Can you ever forgive me?"

"I have, if you've forgiven me for trying to find fault with you from the moment I met you." Her hands traveled up his back, feeling his muscles beneath his tunic. His body felt so perfect against hers, hard and strong and desirable. With tender yet powerful yearnings building within her, she lifted her face for his kiss.

Their lips joined, their breath mingling, and she felt his hands caressing her. Cajoling her. Asking her...

As her own hands began to respond in kind, he moaned softly, then reached around to lift her hands away. He stepped back, a warning look in his dark eyes. "Giselle, unless you wish to consummate our relationship right here and now, I am going to have to beg you to leave."

She moved away from him, regarding him steadily. He was right, and she knew it. Just as she knew that he truly loved her, and that they could be wed as soon as they wished. Her uncle would certainly not stand in their way.

Myles stared in awe as Giselle reached up and undid the ties of her cloak so that it fell to the ground. "I have a gift for you, my love," she whispered.

"What—?"

"Take it. Take *me.*"

After that, there was no more resistance, and certainly no remorse, as he lowered her to his bed in the straw.

Sir Wilfrid frowned at the couple standing before him. "But, my dear," he said, feigning a dismay he certainly didn't feel, "I thought you wanted the right to refuse."

"I have changed my mind," his niece announced.

"A woman's prerogative, Sir Wilfrid," Myles observed.

"Yes, Uncle. A woman's prerogative," Giselle confirmed.

Sir Wilfrid could guess how she hated to fall back on that excuse, but it told him more about Giselle's feelings for Sir Myles than a thousand words could have. "You wish me to sign the marriage contract, then?"

"Yes, Uncle."

"And are you still willing to be wed to my niece, Sir Myles?"

"I am, sir."

"Very well," the older man replied. Then he smiled. "I am very pleased for you both," he said, an unmistakably gleeful tone creeping into his words.

"Uncle?"

"Yes, my dear?"

"I...that is, we...we would like to be married as quickly as possible. Perhaps even today."

"What?" This request was beyond Sir Wilfrid's most imaginative expectation.

"I see no reason for delay, Uncle," Giselle said firmly, all the while keeping hold of Myles's arm. "We were going to have the feast of Epiphany anyway and we can just as soon make it a wedding feast. I'm sure Father Paul will be agreeable to a marriage blessing at the mass. It is not so difficult a thing for him to do. And so many of our friends are here anyway, it will save them all an additional journey."

Sir Wilfrid leaned back in his chair and regarded the couple before him. So young and so eager. So happy and so desirous. So full of joy and love. So disheveled, and was that straw in Giselle's hair?

Suddenly an idea came to Sir Wilfrid, based in no small part upon a very memorable incident in the courting of his own beloved wife.

That Myles Buxton would have no scruples about waiting for the wedding night was not at all surprising. But that Giselle would ever consider—

Sir Wilfrid felt the most outrageous, undignified urge to laugh. She *must* love the fellow, and things couldn't have turned out better if Saint Nicholas himself had lent a hand.

Sir Wilfrid coughed and struggled to maintain a dignified demeanor. "If Father Paul has no objections, I see no reason for refusing to allow you to wed today."

"Thank you, Uncle!"

Sir Myles's smile was a little more shrewd than Giselle's. "Thank you, sir, for agreeing to a speedy marriage," he said with a touch of his old arrogance, but only a touch. "I care for her very much, and I believe your niece will make a most exceptional wife."

Sir Wilfrid rose and scratched his beard as he strolled toward the window. "I think you were both hasty in another matter." He glanced back at them, noticing that they were now fidgeting like naughty children, and again he had to strive to keep a smile from his face.

Then he chuckled companionably. "Well, far be it from me to condemn you, for I'm sure it was all your doing, Giselle."

She opened her mouth to protest, but he held up his hand for silence. "Quite frankly, I think being in love has addled your wits. If I didn't suspect something, why else would I agree to such a swift marriage—unless I could also see that you two are truly in love with each other?''

"Sir, we—" Myles began.

"You owe me no explanation beyond what I have already surmised, Myles." His expression grew grave, but there was a twinkle in his eyes. "Giselle is a very determined young lady with very determined ideas, as I have plenty of cause to know. I only hope you appreciate that, Sir Myles."

"Sir Wilfrid, I have no doubt that she will be the perfect wife for me."

"Just as I know Sir Myles will be the perfect husband for me," Giselle said staunchly.

"I don't think you quite follow me," the older man said as he winked roguishly at Sir Myles. "I hope you know what you are letting yourself in for. I believe I shall have a grandniece or nephew before next Christmas, and another on the way."

"Uncle!" Giselle gasped, blushing as red as the holly berries decorating the hall.

"And a good thing, too, since it will keep you both out of mischief. Now away with you. All this celebration is very tiring to a man of my years."

Smiling happily, the young couple made their obeisance and went to the door. They paused on the threshold and turned back.

"This has been the happiest Christmas of my life," Giselle said softly, her voice catching as she smiled tremulously at her uncle.

"And mine," Myles echoed.

Sir Wilfrid's eyes were suspiciously moist as he cleared his throat gruffly. "And I daresay we'll all have a very happy New Year."

*   *   *   *   *

The Twelfth Day of Christmas

Author Note

It isn't surprising that the thought of Christmas brings mind my two favorite historical time periods for setting Medieval and Victorian England.

There is something so medieval about Christmas. Pe haps it's the candles and the familiar rituals of the Chris mas service, or the scent of the holly, mistletoe and pin Maybe it's the fire in the hearth and the sight of the we coming lights of home beaming across the snowy groun Or the gathering of family and friends, enjoying our ow modern version of wassail.

And is there anyone who doesn't recall the Victorian e of Charles Dickens's *A Christmas Carol* as December 2 draws near? What would our Christmases be without Eb nezer Scrooge and the Crachets, even overcommercializ as they are.

My first sale to Harlequin Historical was like receivin the best Christmas present ever. And I must confess I st feel as if I'm being given a wonderful gift every time have the opportunity to write a new book.

But Christmas is not only about receiving presents, an as Myles has learned in *The Twelfth Day of Christmas*, t best gifts come from the heart. Nothing would give m more joy than to think that you consider each of my stori as my gift to you, whatever the season.

Which brings me to Sir George de Gramercie, seen dancing so energetically at Sir Wilfrid's feast. Sir George is the hero in my next book, *A Warrior's Bride,* which will be available in December.

I've known the droll, elegant George for a long time. He's appeared in several other books I've written, most notably, *The Baron's Quest.* However, I thought it was about time he quit being a happy-go-lucky secondary character and settled down as the dutiful lord of a large estate. I also thought it would be fun to concoct a woman able to crack George's lighthearted, self-deprecating facade, and allow the hot-blooded, bold warrior inside to escape. I hope you enjoy reading George's story as much as I enjoyed writing it.

All my best for a Merry Christmas and a Happy New Year.

Whithpersea me of St George & Cæsar... ... dine

... Sir Smith... ... Sir George is to

have in any part home, & that one I think much will be

available in general.

... most ... work ... elegant forming for a long time

He'd offended or severed to be found. I've pronounced

... why. The forme's taken. However, I suppose I said

shall not laugh again a deeper up think you must...

sedet and sould do ... & the similitude of a large head

... and Dreadful I would fly his to oppose... I would all of

the crew ... highlighted, self-depreciating means...

show the Brethrend & folk warrior meant to oppose, I have

not stop reading George's ... ... meant and I enjoyed

reading it.

... ... best ... at Henry Christmas and a Happy New

Year.

A WISH FOR NOEL

Deborah Simmons

Chapter One

"Christmas! Twelve days of feasting and making merry! Tell me more of this keep of yours, Benedick. Mayhap I will find a pretty maid there to help me celebrate!"

Benedick Villiers eyed his squire askance. Alard had recently replaced the more circumspect Wystan, who had been killed in a skirmish, and he seemed much more a boy than his predecessor. They were all getting younger, Benedick thought grimly, while he felt old beyond his years.

Twenty-six now, he had been fighting for a full decade, hiring himself out as a knight to battle. This last had been little more than a border dispute, yet he had been captured and imprisoned for more than a month before he was ransomed. The dungeon had not been the worst Benedick had seen, but his stay there had sapped his energy. Glancing at his young squire, he longed for some of the boy's enthusiasm, even as he mocked it.

He had never been that cheerful.

"Do not get your hopes too high, pup," Benedick felt compelled to warn the grinning youth. "Longstone Keep is old, cold and damp, and no fount of revelry."

The boy laughed, not to be deterred. "You are modest, Benedick. Your fiefdom looks to be the finest in the land!" he proclaimed, waving an arm to encompass the gray outer walls as they approached.

Benedick grunted at the boy's ludicrous flattery and wished again for Wystan's more subdued temperament. Longstone was a small holding, nothing more, but he had fought long and hard to obtain it, bought with gold and bribery from one of the lesser barons in need of funds. It was his, the lifetime goal of a bastard born, and although he felt a grim vindication in its ownership, it had given him little joy.

"I have spent no time there, and have made no improvements," he told the boy. "Do not expect luxuries or the excesses of a court celebration." Benedick did not hold with frivolity, nor did he think much of holidays. A lot of pagan nonsense dressed up in Christian finery, he thought with disgust. The elaborate feasting and game playing he had witnessed on occasion made him uncomfortable.

He was more familiar with hardship and battle.

"Well, I for one, will look forward to some hot food and a warm hearth," the irrepressible youth replied.

"Aye," Benedick agreed as they rode through the gate. He did not seek gaiety or renewed energy or even peace at his keep, for he had too much blood on his hands, too many scars to ever feel truly at ease. Yet he had hopes for rest, at least, after all the years of fighting, and the comfort of a bed and a decent meal.

The bailey was busier than he remembered, and he took note of some recently thatched roofs and mended walls. His steward, Hardwin, had obviously done well, Benedick thought with approval, especially considering the limited funds he had been given. Perhaps it had been a good year, Benedick conjectured, hoping that a successful harvest would see them through the long winter ahead. Leaving his squire to tend the horses, Benedick ignored the curious stares of the peasants and strode to the square, stone keep he had not visited in five years. Stepping through the wide doors, he paused just inside.

And wondered if he was in the wrong place.

The hall he remembered as cavernous and dark was now clean and full of light and color. Fires burned brightly, and the late afternoon sun entered through the tall windows, sending shafts of warmth to highlight vivid hangings that covered much of the walls. The air he had once thought stale and foul was redolent with the scents of baking bread, spices and greenery.

It was everywhere.

Holly, ivy, bay and pine boughs hung from every wall and were scattered among the rushes on the tiles beneath his feet. A swath of scarlet cloth dangled like a banner from the beams above, and sprigs of mistletoe, twelve to a bunch, were placed over the archways. It looked like some kind of Christmas fantasy.

Benedick blinked at both the change in his surroundings and the decorations. Rarely had he seen such elaborate preparations for wintertide; never had he given leave for such in his own hall. But that was not all. Benedick gaped in astonishment as a woman hurried forward to greet him.

She was young and fair, with golden hair floating unbound down her back in great length of silken waves. She was pretty, lovely even, for her skin was unmarked, her small mouth daintily curved and her eyes were bluer than the skies.

She approached Benedick with a smile that revealed even, white teeth and spoke in a lilting voice that sounded both sweet and sensual to his ears. "Welcome home, sir knight," she said, gazing at him with a glow that he did not recognize.

That wasn't all he didn't recognize.

"Who the hell are you?" Benedick demanded.

Noel Amery tried to hide her shock at the sight of her guardian. Not only was his arrival unexpected, but he had changed drastically since she had seen him last. Admittedly it had been five years since she and her father visited their new neighbor, but those years wore harshly upon the man before her. Oh, he was still handsome, with his great knight's body and his chiseled features, but lines marred his face and he looked rough and unkempt, his dark hair ragged about his shoulders, his black eyes glittering with contempt.

Indeed, so fearsome was he that she nearly took a step back, but she held her ground and lifted her chin, for he had no call to be rude. "I am Noel Amery," she said clearly. "Your ward."

He stared at her disdainfully, and Noel felt her cheeks heat. His ignoble behavior was not that of her memory, nor even that of a knight, she thought angrily. Why, he studied her as if she were some camp follower, not his neighbor of long standing!

His black eyes assessed her, up and down, until Noel wondered if she had imagined their appeal. Was this the same man who had so infatuated her five years ago?

"I have no ward," he said coldly, and Noel nearly gasped aloud. Had he lost his wits, as well as his charm?

"Ahem, but you do, sir." Noel sent up silent thanks as the kindly steward, Hardwin, hurried into the breach. "'Twas more than a year back that I sent you the message that your good neighbor Master Amery died, naming you guardian of his daughter, Noel."

The knight's eyes narrowed, and Noel thought it best to explain further. "We have met before, Sir Villiers," she said, his surname sounding foreign to her ears when she had thought of him so often as Benedick. *Her* Benedick.

Obviously he was not.

Noel drew a deep, steadying breath, and continued. "My father and I came to welcome you when you took possession of Longstone. He was so impressed with you that he made arrangements for me to be put in your keeping in the event of his death." Although she tried to hide it, the accusation that Benedick had failed both her and her father was implicit. The big knight said nothing.

"You sent a message back for me to take care of the matter," Hardwin added a bit nervously.

Benedick's black gaze never left her, but he spoke to the steward in gruff tones. "And your idea of handling the matter was installing her in my home as chatelaine?"

Hardwin reddened, and Noel wanted to box Benedick's ears for his rudeness. "She, uh, had nowhere to go, sir, and we had room here, of course. There was none but a small staff at the manor, hardly fit to protect a young girl, especially an heiress of good family," he explained.

"I see," Benedick said, though he looked as if he did not. His attitude cut Noel to the quick, for she had worked hard to make his cold and uninviting keep into a nice home. Did he not see the improvements she had wrought, the ungrateful wretch?

"Surely you cannot claim that you liked your home better before I arrived," she said, unable to resist the barb.

He smiled, a barely discernible movement of firm lips that seemed to mock all that she had done. "I would not insult you so, mistress, but I am seeking a rest from my labors. I want not the responsibilities of entertaining a guest."

A *guest?* Noel's eyes widened in horror. During the past year, she had come to view Longstone as her home, not as some temporary abode, and herself as mistress, not a visiting interloper. All the while she had labored to make the keep a comfortable, fitting retreat, not just for Benedick, but for herself. After all, he was her guardian, if not more...

Although only twelve when her father had taken her to welcome their new neighbor, Noel had been entranced by the handsome, strapping knight. Yes, he had been rather distant and elusive, but her youthful mind had conjured deep mysteries lurking within his dark eyes. He had left not long afterward, off to make a name for himself, her father said, but the memory had stayed with Noel. And the few suitors her father suggested to her had never measured up to it.

Knowing of her infatuation and trusting the honorable man who fought so valiantly, her dear father had bequeathed her to him. And Noel had just assumed that when Benedick returned he would be glad of her father's bequest. She had assumed so very much, and so wrongly, that now she reeled from the force of her misjudgment.

"But I have made a home here, as you can well see!" Noel protested.

Benedick raised his black brows. "And you have another home, do you not?"

Flustered by his logic, Noel tugged on a long lock of hair. So often she had dreamed of his homecoming, but the reality was a nightmare. "No one resides there except a few servants," she said, thinking of the small, lonely manor, memories of her father lurking in every corner. Sad and empty. She swallowed hard.

Obviously unmoved, Benedick regarded her stonily, while Noel twisted a golden strand between her fingers. Slowly, inexorably, she began to realize that he meant to send her away, and she was horrified. Had she spent the past year nurturing a falsehood? In the long months since her father's death, she had clung to one thing, working toward the return of her knight, her Benedick, and now he would dash all her hopes and dreams in a single blow. She released the lock of hair and held out her hands in supplication.

"But the manor is unguarded. Surely you would not send me there to fend for myself?" she asked, frantically searching for an argument that would sway this hard stranger.

Again Noel felt the slow sweep of his scrutiny and flushed at his insolence. He was outrageous, and yet she could not summon the proper indignation. Instead, she felt the heady rush she had known when they first met, a strange flutter of excitement, as if he had reached out to touch her with his dark gaze.

"How old are you?"

Noel colored anew at his blunt tone. "Seventeen," she answered, her breath suddenly short.

"Very well, ward," he said, as if the word tasted bitter. "I will send some men along with you as protection...until I can find you a husband."

Noel choked back a cry of panic. He meant to be rid of her, not just for now, but for always! "You cannot mean it. Not after all I've done here to make a home for you, to ready the keep for the Christmas! Why, everyone's expecting me to oversee the celebrations. 'Tis tradition! I've got the Yule log all picked out and...'' Noel's voice cracked precariously, and she knew that any moment she would disgrace herself with tears.

Hardwin made a sound of protest, but he was quickly silenced by a glare from Benedick. Grimly the knight glanced around his hall, and Noel followed his gaze to where a phalanx of servants gathered, eyeing him warily. Angrily.

"All right," Benedick said, his jaw tight with obvious displeasure. "You can stay through Christmas, but after Epiphany, you must return to your home, for I will bide here alone."

Noel's heart leapt, but Benedick held up a hand as if to forestall her gratitude. "Meanwhile, I will see about finding you a husband," he added.

A husband! Noel's elation fled in the face of his smug smile. She did not understand any of this! Everything was going wrong. Why did he so want to be rid of her? Where was the knight she had known, solemn, but kind of heart? Darting a glance at his hard visage, Noel searched for the man she had first met. Although she could not see him, she sensed his presence, somewhere in there, behind those black eyes. What if he was trapped behind that rough exterior, unable to escape? But how was she to find him, if she was soon promised to another?

Undaunted, Noel smiled brightly up at her knight. "There is really no need for you to tax yourself with that effort, for there is a much simpler solution to all of our problems."

Benedick lifted both brows skeptically, but Noel persevered. "I don't want to leave Longstone, and you will need a chatelaine to take care of the keep and to insure that you receive the rest you desire. I would be most happy to remain here, as your ward, and provide these services to you without recompense, but if you wish me to wed..." Noel paused to give him an encouraging look. "I can simply marry you!"

He stared at her, as if stunned, and Noel's hopeful grin faltered in the face of his obvious astonishment. Could he not see the sense in her suggestion? It was a most reasonable proposal, she thought, but to her horror, instead of agreeing with her, Benedick threw back his dark head and burst into laughter. In fact, he laughed so long and so hard that tears came to his eyes, and Noel watched in disbelief as he wiped them away with the back of one long-fingered hand.

Crossing her arms over her chest, Noel tapped her foot in irritation as she waited for him to recover from his fit. She was trying not to view his outburst as an insult, but what else was she to think? Finally he sank into a nearby chair. The chair she had commissioned for him as part of a pair, so they could sit comfortably before the fire together when he returned. The chair she now wished would break into a thousand pieces, dumping his ill-mannered carcass onto the tiles.

"What is so funny?" she asked. "'Tis a good alliance. You increase your lands and gain a small manor house and a decent marriage portion. I have proved my skills in running a household." She hesitated, reluctant to boast but determined to sway him. "And I have been told that I am not too hideous to look upon."

His amusement disappearing abruptly, he eyed her with a surly expression. "I need not your father's holdings or your pitiful portion. I have a steward to run my keep and servants enough to see to my needs. And you, beautiful as you may be, are just a child and far too young for me."

"I am not!" Noel cried. She was a woman, full grown, and knew very well that other girls her age were already bearing children. Gathering herself together, she bit back her argument when Benedick held up a hand to stop her.

"Cease this foolishness at once," he said coldly. "I regret if your manor seems small in comparison to Longstone, but I'm sure that we can find some other landowner more than willing to give you the comforts you so desire."

Gasping, Noel glared at him in rigid outrage. "You think 'tis this old pile of stones that I covet?" she cried.

"Don't you?" he asked, his brows lifted in dark disdain.

"Bah! I have refused better offers!" she snapped, disgusted. Luckily Hardwin had long since moved out of range of their conversation, for Noel was oblivious to her surroundings. "Yes, I have made a home here, but for one reason only—because 'tis your home. Since the first time I saw you, I have wanted to marry only you. Obviously I was mistaken about the man I thought you were!"

Noel caught but a glimpse of Benedick's startled expression before turning on her heel to flee the hall. Hurrying, she made it to the spiral stair before losing her dignity entirely. Fumbling, she continued upward, out of sight, while she wept at the loss of her dreams.

When she reached her tiny chamber, Noel did not pause to admire her handiwork in making the spare room livable, but threw herself on the bed and cried as she never had before. Even after her father died, she had held in her grief as she held on to the image of her knight returning to claim her.

Now that idea seemed foolish, nothing more than the fancy of a child yearning after an illusion, for her handsome warrior had returned an embittered creature who would throw her, like a bone, to the first man who came sniffing around.

Noel wept until her tears were spent, then lay still, like a dead thing, feeling hollow inside. She might have lain there all night, wallowing in her misery, but for a loud bang that made her roll reluctantly onto her back. A shutter had come loose, letting a chill wind sweep into the room, and Noel shivered, too weary to rise and secure it. Staring idly, she saw the breeze stir a bough of holly that hung over her narrow door.

Christmas.

Swallowing hard, Noel was grateful that at least she

could stay on at Longstone until the holiday was over. Her eyes fixed on the bright greenery, she felt the magic of the season push aside her gloom. Gradually she came to view her tears as a silly indulgence. She was made of stronger stuff, she thought, as her usual optimism reasserted itself.

Make a wish, Noel.

She smiled slightly, for she could almost hear her mother's voice whispering the words. Ella Amery had made the fortnight a special time for everyone in the manor and doubly special for the daughter who had been born on Christmas Day. Although the air was cool, sweet memories warmed Noel. As she watched, the red berries bobbed as if touched by some unseen hand, and she heard the gentle command again, seemingly borne on the wind.

Make a wish, Noel.

Should she? Her mother had always said that Christmas wishes were bound to come true, especially for those few who shared that special birthday. Hope surged to life in her breast, and she sat up, wiping her tear-streaked face determinedly. After having waited five long years for Benedick, turning aside other offers in the interim, was she going to give up so easily?

But did she still want him? Noel frowned as she considered the question. Certainly he was more rough-hewn than she remembered, but he was still undeniably handsome, scars and all. And even though he seemed churlish and ill-mannered, he still made her heart pound as wildly as before. Perhaps she had imagined all those mysteries behind his dark eyes, but what if she had not? Noel shivered as she considered delving into them to find the man hidden away inside. He was there, she sensed it, and what if he wanted out?

It was a challenge, Noel thought with a grin, and she loved challenges. Hadn't she turned his dark keep into a home? Hadn't she taken over the running of the household, although little prepared for it? Her father had always said she could accomplish anything when she put her mind to it. He had never used the word *stubborn*, but had called her strong willed, as if that were a virtue. Smiling anew at the memory, Noel hugged her knees to her chest and contemplated her future.

It wasn't too late. She had until Epiphany to change Benedick's mind. Absently she twisted a long lock of hair as she wondered how to convince the hardened warrior to marry her. As he had so rudely pointed out, he didn't need her small portion or holdings. Like most men, he didn't put a high value on household skills, and from the looks of him, he had no need of a woman to satisfy him, either, she thought, blushing. A man like that would have ladies waiting in line for his favors.

If only she were more of a seductress and less of the young girl that he saw her as. Noel sighed. Wishing for the impossible brought her thoughts back to Christmas, and her eyes widened in surprise.

She could give him Christmas.

From his behavior, Noel suspected that he had never enjoyed the celebration before, never relaxed his stiff guard, never been touched by the magic of the season. She would give him twelve wonderful days, the best holiday ever, she decided with a grin.

And by the time she was done, she just might get her very own Christmas wish.

Chapter Two

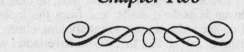

Benedick barely flicked a glance after the fleeing girl. She was a child and naught more than a nuisance. As for Hardwin... Benedick saw the steward's swift frown of disapproval and matched it with his own. The old man had taken much upon himself in his master's absence, and he would do better to worry about Benedick's wrath rather than the tears of a homeless wench.

A low grumbling made him turn, his warrior's instinct alert to the furtive exchanges and somber voices quickly silenced by his hard stare. Obviously the girl had many allies, and Benedick swore softly at the discovery. Had he left one battlefield only to find another? Would rest always be denied him?

"Saint Bernard's bones!" Alard's loud exclamation made Benedick decide to put off his reckoning with his steward until he was settled in at his keep. Still he gave the man a look that spoke of his displeasure, both with the matter of the girl and Hardwin's attitude toward her.

"'Tis a fitting home for a brave knight, Sir Villiers!" Alard said, turning around as if awestruck by the hall. Indeed, one would have thought the lad was viewing a king's castle. With a grunt of annoyance, Benedick shook his head.

"Put your eyes back in your head and attend me, lad!

he called, and with a nod of dismissal to Hardwin, he
headed for the dark, circular stair to the great chamber.
Even the dank passage of the steps seemed brighter, and
Benedick began to wonder if his memory served him well.
Or perhaps his recent lodging in a petty baron's dungeon
made all else seem an improvement.

Smiling tightly at the thought, Benedick swung open the
heavy door and eyed the interior warily, for even this room
was not as he recalled. The place had not only been
scrubbed clean, but the walls had been painted a pale yellow, new covers had been fashioned for the big bed and
the shutters mended. A welcome fire burned brightly in the
hearth and a length of carpet rested in front of it.

Benedick sucked in a breath. The effect was one of
warmth and welcome, of sunny greeting despite the low
light from the windows that signalled the fading day. Yet
Benedick took no delight in the changes. Instead, he felt a
surge of resentment that the girl had made her presence
known even here! What right had she to enter his most
private chamber? He would take Hardwin to task for the
matter, he thought, and woe betide any who would stand
in his way.

He remembered the condemning faces of the servants,
and he wondered if she had turned his entire household
against him. He was well used to enmity but had hoped for
more in his own keep. He ought to turn out the lot of them,
with her at the forefront.

Except he had promised.

"Saint Theodore's tooth!" Alard exclaimed from behind
him. "'Tis a bit better than our last encampment, eh?"

Benedick shrugged, his mind drifting back to the girl.
Noel Amery. He had given his word that she could remain
here until Epiphany, but if she wanted to leave earlier, he
would be more than happy to oblige her. His lips curved
into a tight smile. Once he stripped her of all authority, she
would probably run back to her own manor, her golden
hair flying behind her.

"Ah! 'Tis as soft as goose down!" Alard said, and Benedick started, alarmed that the squire's words so echoed his own thoughts. What did Alard know of the girl? But when Benedick swung around, he found the boy admiring, not Noel, but the great bed. In fact, he was lying upon it, grinning outrageously.

"Up, you!" Benedick said. "Your place is on a pallet before the door."

Alard grinned, unapologetic. "I can dream, can't I?"

Ignoring the youth, Benedick returned his attention to Noel. A few days in his cold company and she would soon abandon her silly plan to marry him. A wife! That was the last thing he needed. He was a warrior, not some courtier who sang love ballads over a lady's hand. He had worked hard for everything he had, disdaining those who would wed for financial gain.

And he was far too old to gently woo a maid.

By faith, he felt centuries older than the young innocent who claimed to be his ward, and he had the scars to prove it! If he decided to marry, he would choose someone more mature, more experienced, a woman who knew how to pleasure a man. Aye, a widow, even. A proven child-bearer to get him an heir, or perhaps someone already equipped with sons.

That was what he needed, yet even as Benedick tried to picture one of the jaded, hard-eyed court women in his bed, he saw the girl who had greeted him below, golden hair spread upon his pillow in silken waves. Fresh faced and smooth skinned, she had borne no children, nor had she known a man, from the looks of her. A virgin. The knowledge was oddly stirring, and Benedick swore softly at his own weakness.

"All right!" Alard said. Obviously the youth thought the oath was meant for him, and Benedick did not deny it. "I will take myself onto a hard mat at my master's feet," the squire grumbled.

Benedick grunted. "'Tis a berth I know well myself." He tried not to wonder where Noel was sleeping.

"But 'tis one you will not have tonight, so why do you

grumble so? You are home, at last, and 'tis a fine place, indeed. How could it not be to your liking?'' Alard asked. He paused meaningfully. ''Was not your lady wife eager to see you?''

Benedick's eyes narrowed dangerously. ''What?''

''The beauteous woman I glimpsed in the hall, slender and fair as an angel. Is she not your wife?''

''No! You know full well that I am not married.''

''Your leman, then?''

''No!'' Benedict snarled. ''She is my ward, and hardly a woman, but a child.'' Young, innocent and full of foolish dreams, Benedick thought as he tossed his pack upon the bed and pulled out the few possessions he carried with him.

''She looked a lady full grown to me,'' Alard said with a sigh. ''I saw the curves beneath her gown, the silky length of her hair, and the delightful sway of her—''

Benedick cut off his squire's words with a growl of warning. Although well used to Alard's randy talk, he would have none of it applied to his ward. The boy's lusty look made Benedick's normally cold blood boil, and he had to stop himself from grabbing the mouthy youth by the throat.

''Keep a civil tongue in your head,'' Benedick warned. ''And your hands to yourself. Aye, even your very thoughts away from her. She goes to a man of property, not a squire without a farthing to his name.''

Benedick's eyes narrowed. An heiress, Hardwin had called her. Her wealth meant little to him, but now he wondered just how much of a temptation she would present to penniless rogues like Alard.

''If I find you even looking at her too closely, I'll toss you out on your ear,'' Benedick warned. By faith, he had best marry off the wench soon, else he might find this task of guardian onerous indeed.

''''Tis certain to test me sorely, but I will obey you, of course,'' Alard said, with a bow of acknowledgment.

''Do not test me sorely,'' Benedick snapped, displeased with the youth's levity. But a few minutes home and al-

ready he was saddled with a meddlesome girl and disloyal
servants. And he must ever rein in his squire. So much for
his much-needed rest!

Benedick scowled. To his mind, it was all the fault of
one Noel Amery. And he had to put up with her until
Epiphany! Running a hand through his thick hair, Benedick
grunted in dismay.

Surely this was going to be the longest fortnight of his
life.

Benedick stirred, a cocoon of warmth and softness surrounding him as he turned. Hair like liquid gold ran through
his fingers, and the scent of greenery and spices filled his
head, blended with a more subtle, womanly fragrance.

Noel.

She smelled young and sweet and fresh, like nothing he
had ever known in his hard life. And she was in his bed.
His body was suffused with a gentle heat, a sensation of
completeness, of repletion, although he could not remember
having lain with her. Better to renew his memory, he
thought with a smile, and drew her close, her silken limbs
sliding along his own, her skin sleek and supple and…

When Benedick's hand closed around his blanket, he
blinked in surprise, his eyes narrowing at the unfamiliar
room and the walls that gleamed with the faint light of early
dawn. Swiftly recognition returned, but with it came the
tantalizing recollection of his thoughts before waking. Noel.
In his bed. It had all seemed so real that for a moment
Benedick thought the girl was well and truly beside him.
He jerked upright in horror, his breathing labored.

A quick assessment of the chamber assured him that the
only presence was that of Alard, sleeping peacefully on his
mat in front of the door. Disgusted, Benedick ran a hand
through his hair. Noel, the feelings…it had all been a
dream.

He never dreamed.

With a rough shake of his head, Benedick swung to his
feet, firmly dismissing the entire episode. He was unaccus-

tomed to a bed, to the sights and smells of his own keep, decked out like some kind of child's toy for the holiday. The problems of a landowner weighed down upon him, with the meddlesome wench an unexpected addition. It was only natural that his sleep be disturbed.

"Up, you!" he growled at Alard as he grabbed his clothes.

"What? What is it?" the squire mumbled, rubbing his head. Although Benedick suspected the youth had consumed one too many cups of ale and now felt the effects of indulgence, he spared his squire no sympathy.

"'Tis dawn, and time to rise, as you well know," he answered tightly.

Opening one eye, the youth looked at him and groaned. "But we are not on the battlefield!"

"Still, there is much to be done."

Alard fell back upon his pallet with a ragged sigh and swiped at his face. "Last night you had the pleasure of a bath, clean linens, and the softest bed in all Christendom. How is it that you are up and about this early, and ill-humored besides?"

"I slept poorly," Benedick snapped as he bent to tug on his boots. But it was not really true. His usual heavy slumber had been replaced by a sense of lightness, of peace and contentment and sweet dreams. He scowled, unwilling to admit to such, even to himself.

"You?" Alard scoffed. "You sleep like the dead! I've seen you make a nest of rocks and profess them to your liking!"

"Then perhaps my own foul nature 'tis the cause," Benedick answered. "And unless you would see more of it, I'd advise you to rouse yourself." Pointedly he stepped over the youth's body and pulled open the door.

Expecting another one of Alard's rejoinders, he paused on the threshold, but the boy only studied him with a curious intensity. Unaccountably irritated by his squire's scrutiny, Benedick slammed the door shut behind him.

His mood was not improved by the sight of his hall. The

servants were just rising, and he had to fetch his own ale and bread. Although he had spent his life doing for himself, he resented the small effort in his own household. Calling angrily for his steward, he was further displeased to discover that Hardwin was still abed.

Taking his seat at the high table, Benedick drank his ale and watched the room stir to life around him. He had to admit that the place smelled better than most, no doubt because of the branches dangling from every archway and opening. It was ridiculous, of course, but fragrant.

Leaning back, Benedick relaxed once more in the chair he had admired last night. It was a nice piece, heavy and so large he could rest his head against its high back. He did not remember it from his previous visit, but his time here had been all too brief. Flicking his gaze to the smaller one where Noel had taken the light supper served before nightfall, Benedick felt a resurgence of tension. The meddlesome wench had made herself at home far too well for his liking—and that was not even taking into account the dreams that he would rather forget.

"Sir Villiers?" Benedick swung his attention to his steward. The old man appeared sleepy eyed and a bit disheveled, as if he had dressed hurriedly, but Benedick gave him no sympathy.

"I would have the keys to the keep, and then I would like to go over the accounts," he said coolly.

"But 'tis Christmas Eve, sir," Hardwin protested.

Benedick gave him a hard look for his insolence. "'Tis also the first opportunity I've had in five long years. I would have the records, if you please."

"Yes, of course, sir." The steward answered promptly enough, but he reddened slightly. "I will send for them at once."

Benedick lifted his brows in bemusement. "Don't you have them in your possession?"

Hardwin cleared his throat. "Noel keeps the books now and the keys."

Noel.

Not "your ward." Not "Mistress Amery." Noel. Had that infernal female invaded every segment of his life? He frowned, for he knew well the answer to that question. "Then see that you fetch them, immediately," he said through gritted teeth.

"Yes, sir!" Hardwin bowed and backed away, and Benedick waited, his temper festering. If the accounts were not in perfect order, he would send the girl home, promise or no promise. And before he was done, he would have a good reason why she had taken on tasks that were not her own.

Hardwin returned with keys and books in hand, in good time, and presented the most recent volume to Benedick without demure. Scanning over the pages, Benedick could easily read the small, well-formed letters and amounts. The expenditures were carefully detailed as were any incoming fees, rents and produce. Despite himself, Benedick was impressed. The girl had done a fine job.

Leafing back through the volume, he noticed the purchase of two chairs, sturdily built, for the good knight and his ward. Obviously that is why he had not remembered his seat. Benedick's eyes narrowed as he noticed a small mark beside the exorbitant price paid for the furniture. He could not decide whether it was a small *n* or another notation. And what did it record, an overpayment or some extra amount due the purchaser?

"What is that?" he asked, pointing to the mark.

Hardwin, who had been hovering around nervously, stepped closer. Then he pulled the book in front of him, leaned over and squinted at the page for a long minute.

Watching him, Benedick felt the fool, for he suddenly realized that his steward was no longer a young man. He had kept on all of the servants when he took over the fiefdom, without a thought to their age or abilities. Now he noticed the white of Hardwin's hair and the slight tremble of his hands. His joints were swollen, and from the way he looked at the parchment before him, he might be half-blind, as well! No wonder he had given over some of his work.

Finally, the steward straightened. "'Tis Noel's mark," he said.

"And what does it do here?" Benedick asked, suspicious.

"It means that she used her own funds." The old man stepped back, as if in disapproval, and Benedick echoed the sentiment. By faith, there was something totally unsettling about the girl buying him a chair, especially when he had more use for it than for her.

"She has her own money, sir, to spend as she wills," Hardwin reminded him.

Benedick's eyes narrowed, for the steward did not help the girl's case with his hasty tongue. "On my keep," he said. "And without leave of her guardian."

Hardwin reddened, effectively silenced, as Benedick glanced through the remaining pages. He found Noel's mark in several places, usually in connection with some frivolous purchase. Obviously Hardwin had no control over the girl's buying habits.

At least she had the good sense not to try to make him pay for that expensive carpet on the floor of his chamber. She could take the thing with her when she left, for he had no use for it! Did she think she would soon be sleeping in the great room? Had she stayed there while he was gone? Benedick's indignation gave way to a deeper disturbance at the thought, and he shifted, suddenly uncomfortable in his seat.

"Is something troubling you, sir?" Hardwin asked.

Yes, and her name is Noel, Benedick thought, but he shook his head. He would take the girl to task rightly enough, for he wanted no claims on his household. He would repay her for his chair and send the other with her when she left. And, after she was gone, he would find an assistant for Hardwin, someone young and eager, like Alard, to help him with his duties without shaming him.

"I will speak with Noel about these expenses," Benedick said. "Meanwhile, I will study the books at my leisure." Nodding his dismissal, he let the steward go and turned his attention back to the pages.

Soon deep in study, Benedick began to feel a reluctant admiration for the skills of the person who had managed Longstone in his absence. It was hard to believe that such a young girl was responsible. As his opinion of her improved, Benedick reminded himself that Noel Amery was hardly more than a child. Forcibly he pushed aside the nagging memory of a dream in which she was very much a woman.

Benedick was not sure how long he sat there, but his concentration was finally disrupted by the tantalizing aromas of cooking food and something else—fresh, clean, inviting and vaguely familiar. He lifted his head.

Noel.

She was standing in front of him, looking more beautiful than he remembered in a scarlet silk kirtle that clung to the curves Alard had so enthusiastically pointed out. Annoyed to discover his squire had been more than correct in his assessments, Benedick jerked his gaze upward only to blink in surprise. Her lovely face was so somber, he bit back a groan. Surely she did not plan to resume their argument? How like a female to gain a concession and then ask for more. Unfortunately, this one was bound to be disappointed, for he had no intention of giving her even one more day past Epiphany!

"I have to know something," she said, with an uncommon directness.

Ah, here it comes, Benedick thought, but there was nothing calculating or accusing in her eyes. They were bluer than the clearest lake, Benedick decided. Bluer than anything he had ever seen. And surely that hair was a shade of gold that he had never viewed before, shimmering over her shoulder like a bright wave, long and thick. Hazy remnants of his dream returned, and his fingers itched to see if those locks were as soft as he remembered.

"Is there someone else?"

Benedick's head jerked up guiltily at her words. Someone else, who? His bewilderment must have shown on his face, for she glanced away and then began again, as if it cost her in effort.

"Have you a…another woman you wish to marry?"

Benedick blinked, nonplussed by her question until he recalled her suggestion of the night before. Obviously she was unwilling to let go his keep, or him, as she had claimed then. Her words, forgotten, now returned to make him uncomfortable. Had she said she wanted only him?

Annoyed, Benedick shifted in his seat and glared at her, intent upon snarling a reply, but the bleakness of her expression stopped him. Something about her openness, her innocence, made him feel guilty. Yet he had done nothing except dream about her, and he was hardly responsible for that!

"No. As I told you last night, I have no use for a wife," Benedick answered, firmly putting an end to the foolish discussion. Surely the girl was not going to press him again? Such boldness of speech astonished him. He had never known a female to talk so freely, and yet it was oddly refreshing. He grimaced at the thought and told himself she didn't know any better because she was too young and unworldly.

"Good," she said, her lips curving into a smile that seemed to light up the hall as it grew. Benedick found himself staring and determinedly looked away. "I would not like to use my Christmas wish to the detriment of someone else."

"Christmas wish?" Benedick asked, his attention swiveling back to her. What was she about now? Did the girl ever make sense?

"My mother always said that Christmas wishes are bound to come true, especially for me since Christmas Day is my birthday. That is how I got my name, you see."

Benedick could only gape at her, unable to refute that kind of twisted logic. Christmas, birthdays and wishes were all equally nonsensical to his mind.

"I just wanted to make sure that you had no one else in your heart before I wished for you."

"You are going to make a wish for...that I marry you?" Benedick asked, incredulous. She was a child, just as he suspected, despite her fine record keeping. He grunted in contempt. Nothing ever came from wanting, as he well knew. Hard work, struggle and pain were the only ways to get ahead, and even then, a man might never find peace.

"I am considering it," she said, giving him another brilliant smile.

Determinedly Benedick ignored it and the warmth it seemed to invoke deep inside him. "Enough foolishness!" he said. "I want to talk to you about these." His mouth tight, he thrust forward the account book.

"Not now," she said, waving a hand in airy dismissal. "'Tis time for dinner, and afterward, you have something much more important to do!"

With a glance, Benedick realized that the trestle tables were filling with people, and he wondered just what it was about this dainty female that kept him so captivated he lost all sense of his surroundings. Not captivated. Irritated, he told himself with a grimace.

The meal was much better than the small supper the night before, and well satisfying to a man used to dungeon fare. As Noel pointed out to him, there were twelve dishes in keeping with the holiday, but he cared not for the number, only that there was plenty of pike, beef, venison, hare, cabbage and leeks, and a plum pudding. Even the presence of Noel in her presumptuous position beside him failed to turn his appetite, and he ate his fill, pleased with the food and the running of the household.

Nodding at Hardwin, Benedick commended the man, who reddened and looked to Noel, as if she were once again responsible. Frowning, Benedick turned narrowed eyes toward the girl, but before he could question her she had risen from her seat.

To his astonishment, she stepped to his side and took his hand, as if to pull him from his chair. He blinked in astonishment, for rarely did anyone touch him except Alard, who tended his mail. Her small fingers curled around his, warm and soft as silk, her skin white and smooth and unsullied.

"I have already chosen the Yule log, but, as master of the household, you must get it into the hearth," she said.

"What?" Benedick stared at her dumbly, his attention still fixed on the feel of her.

"The Yule log. 'Tis tradition!" she said, flashing those white teeth at him.

The Yule log? Before Benedick could gather his wits, she was calling to the others and pulling him to his feet. He stood, yet still she held his hand in her own. It was dainty, like a child's, but with a woman's strength. Benedick felt heat travel up his arm and through his body to other, nether regions.

Swearing softly, he jerked away, ignoring her frown of dismay, but it was too late to escape his part in this absurd ritual. Already a surprising number of people were crowding around him, drawing on worn cloaks and chatting excitedly. Noel called them by name, and they answered her, faces wreathed in smiles, from small children to those wrinkled with age.

These were the residents of his keep, Benedick noted, and they all looked to him, waiting, expectant. Someone even tossed his heavy cloak over his shoulders, and Benedick grunted, resigning himself.

He would fetch the girl her stupid log, and then he would retire to his chamber in hopes of finding some peace in his own home—away from his ward and the flummery of Christmas.

Chapter Three

Noel's "log" turned out to be a downed tree, with a trunk wider than a man's chest. Benedick stared at it in astonishment, while the other onlookers gave approving nods and praised Noel for her choice. Were they jesting?

"It's a...a tree!" he protested.

"Of course," Noel replied. "It must be large enough to burn all through the twelve days of Christmas." Her cheeks were pink from the cold, her eyes sparkling as if she enjoyed his discomfiture. Annoying wench! He felt like telling her that the task of lugging this monstrosity back to the keep would hardly endear him to her, but he didn't want to encourage her misguided wish to marry him.

"Like as not, it could burn through Easter," he muttered.

"No, it shall do very well," Noel said, gazing at the enormous length of wood as if she derived some deep, mysterious satisfaction from it. Benedick's eyes narrowed. Perhaps she hoped he would kill himself getting it to the hearth. Then she would have his home and all else!

His ragtag group of followers, enlarged by the addition of several peasants, declared themselves ready and willing to assist him and were soon wielding their axes under Benedick's direction. His surprise at their eagerness was swiftly tempered by the discovery that they intended to keep whatever limbs they managed to hack from the bole for themselves. He sent Noel a hard, questioning glance, but she only flashed her white teeth.

"'Tis tradition," she informed him. Scowling at her, Benedick hefted his ax, determined that anything removed by the sweat of his own efforts was going back to the keep where it belonged. Tradition or not.

Even with his helpers, stripping the trunk of its limbs was an arduous and time-consuming chore that took most of the afternoon. The rest of it—on into early evening— was spent rigging up ropes enough to drag the trunk back to the keep. It was no little feat, and by the time they pulled it through the doors, Benedick was well and truly sick of Christmas and all of its attendant rituals.

Unfortunately, just depositing the fateful log in the hall was not enough. Now he must get it in place, and although the old-fashioned hearth took up a goodly portion of one wall, naturally, it was not big enough to hold Noel's log. Glaring at her, Benedick leaned pointedly on his ax and wondered if he should throttle her now or later.

The angelic smile she sent him did little to improve his mood, for he was beginning to think that his innocent ward was not quite as beatific as she looked. His opinion was heartily confirmed by her next words.

"Just chop a bit off the end there, and it will fit nicely," she said, as if serenely oblivious to his mood.

"Humph!" With a grunt, Benedick did her bidding while mentally tallying up the days left until Epiphany. He had never been so eager for the new year's arrival.

"Wait! We have to save it!" Noel cried, looking horrified when he tried to heave the chopped pieces toward the woodpile. "We might need it later, just in case the Yule log burns out before the Twelfth Night."

Benedick lifted his brows and looked askance at her. Was she serious? "That thing will burn until doomsday," he muttered.

"Nevertheless, one can never be too sure," Noel said, sending him a bright smile that annoyed him all the more.

Sure, she was grinning. She hadn't done any of the sawing or hauling.

"Besides, it's part of the magic!" she said, in a breathless whisper hinting that all things were possible.

"Magic!" Benedick grunted. The girl was a blessed lunatic! Christmas wishes. Special logs. What next? He ran a hand through his hair, wondering how could he could escape her presence for the next eleven days.

"Now! Everyone gather around," she called, clapping her hands in a delighted fashion, and Benedick was suddenly aware that their audience had swelled. So many faces that he did not know—servants, peasants and freemen—surrounded them, and Benedick's eyes narrowed as he spotted Alard, close beside Noel. Too close, he thought, as the squire was jostled within touching distance of his ward. Where had the youth been this afternoon when he had been toiling over the tree trunk, Benedick wondered, giving him a glare. Alard only grinned impudently.

"Hardwin! Fetch the remnant!" Noel cried happily, and everyone stepped back so that the old steward could make his way through the crowd with much ceremony. Slowly, reverently, he held up a piece of cloth, and a hush fell over the assemblage as he reverently unfolded it.

Did the steward have some sort of relic? A tooth from some long-dead saint or a sliver of the Cross? Benedick was even more contemptuous of such foolishness than he was of the pagan rituals for which they were often used. He had yet to see an object that possessed any special properties, for good or ill. Nor had he known any so-called magic in his life.

"Ahh." A collective sigh arose from the peasants as Hardwin lifted his hand to display...*a charred bit of wood?* Benedick choked back his astonishment.

"'Tis a piece of last year's Yule log," Noel explained. Somehow she was no longer a part of the milling group but stood at the head of it, at his own elbow. "And you must use it to light the new one." Hardwin held out the treasured chunk to him tenderly.

"Me?" Benedick grunted.

"Of course! You are master of the keep," Noel said, investing his ownership with a sort of nobility that had heretofore escaped him. He watched her through narrowed eyes, but she only leaned closer, placing a hand on his arm. He looked down at the pale, delicate fingers, shocked at the intimacy. Why was she always touching him? Did she not know better?

"Do it, now," she urged, and for a moment, Benedick was hard-pressed to recall exactly what she was talking about. "To a new Christmastide!" she said, stepping back. And Benedick had no choice but to light the proffered remnant and put it to the massive trunk that nestled tightly within the hearth.

As the new log caught fire, a shout rose up around him that surpassed any victory call he had ever heard, and Benedick jerked back in surprise. Although he had sometimes been feted for his bravery in battle, those instances had been rare and never so rousing as this one. Suddenly he was surrounded by smiling, cheering people, and it gave him a strange sensation, deep in his chest.

His roving gaze abruptly focused on Noel. She stood out among them all, more beautiful, more full of life. Their mistress. Scowling, Benedick pushed aside the notion and turned away, his shoulders protesting the day of wood chopping. Absently he swung his arm upward.

He was getting too old for this.

As if she glimpsed his weariness, Noel sent everyone over to the trestle tables, and servants hurried back to the kitchens to serve the evening's supper. "Come, sir knight," she said, taking his hand. "You have done well this day."

Benedick grunted. He cared not for her opinion! He turned to seek the relative peace of his own chamber, but she tugged him toward the high table. She was touching him again. He looked down to see their fingers entwined, pale and dark, and he felt oddly light-headed.

"Your people are well pleased," she said, in that breathless, admiring voice, as if he had actually done something important. *His people?* Startled, he blinked, and realized she was right. Although no baron, he was lord of these lands and those who resided on them.

"And the celebration is just beginning!" Noel promised. Her eyes sparkled, and he saw that twelve candelabras had been lighted. More nonsense, Benedick thought in disgust. He ought to forbid it, or, at the very least, retreat to the quiet of his own chamber. He glanced toward the dark stair to his room, but Noel pulled him, inexorably, toward the noise and the lights and his chair. And he let her. As master, he supposed he ought to preside over the meal. It was Christmas Eve, after all.

The repast was smaller than the massive dinner, but with bread and meat aplenty, and afterward, there was singing. Relaxing in his chair, listening to the fine voices entwined, Benedick forgot his plan to retire early. He had seen grander entertainments and more luxuriously appointed halls, but there was something soothing about his own well-run household. When he had thought of Longstone, as he had done often while away, he never pictured it so warm, so full of life.

Unwillingly Benedick glanced toward the woman who stepped forward to praise the revelers, for he knew now that she was responsible for the changes here and that he would reap the benefits long after she left. Frowning, he tried to ignore a twinge of guilt that came with the knowledge. After all, he had not invited her to Longstone, and all these festivities were not necessary. They would manage just as well without the Time of Twelves, he thought grimly.

But would she? Benedick let his gaze rest on her up-turned face, shining with happiness. Even at seventeen, she was such a mixture of child-woman, moving around the room with the grace and beauty to rival any queen's, but infused with the gaiety of youth, guileless and carefree.

Benedick scowled at the thought of quenching that fire, although he knew that she must marry and pursue a life of her own. He would have to take good measure of the man who would wed her, for all too soon, Noel would have more to concern her than Christmas gifts.

Christmas gifts? Only the knowledge that she had undoubtedly spent her own money kept Benedick from protesting the precious waste of coin. But as she stepped closer, he could see that her presents were handmade: a sweet-smelling bit of dried flowers for a female attendant, an unguent for Hardwin's joints. Benedick relaxed back into his chair, content that she had not spent too much, until she lifted her head and looked at him, a grin as mischievous as any child's lighting her features.

He felt as if she had reached out and touched him.

Ignoring the warmth that seemed to infuse him at her regard, Benedick straightened as she approached and bowed her head before him in a gesture of respect. He noticed how the candlelight made her hair shine as it had in his dream, a shimmering length of molten gold, and then grunted at his own folly. Since when had he started thinking like a whey-faced troubadour?

"And here is your present, sir knight," she said.

"No," Benedick said, for he had no wish to take something she had meant for another. Nor did he have anything to give in return. "I have no gifts."

Noel shook her head as if to deny his words. "But you must give and receive twelve gifts!"

Benedick frowned, having had his fill of the so-called traditions she held so dear. "No gifts," he said.

"Perhaps if you gave twelve of your servants each a coin," she suggested, her eyes twinkling.

"No gifts," Benedick repeated through gritted teeth.

She clucked her tongue, as if to scold him, and Benedick sucked in a breath at her audacity. He was a man, a knight three times her size, and her guardian besides! Had she no sense? He opened his mouth to take her to task, but then she smiled, just as if she weren't maddening him, and held out her hands to reveal a dark green pillow, flat and square.

"Get up," she said.

Benedick blinked at her in astonishment, unable to remember the last time a female dared give him an order.

"Up!" she said, laughing as she grabbed him by the hand. Caught off guard by the gentle warmth of her touch, Benedick responded to the small tug of her dainty fingers and rose to his feet.

"'Tis a cushion for your chair," she said. Grinning, she put the pillow where he had been sitting while Benedick stared, stunned. Slowly the realization came to him that this was not something intended for another, for it fit perfectly in its place.

Although she had not known he would be here, sometime during the past year, Noel had crafted the small luxury with her own hands—for him. The knowledge touched Benedick strangely, for no one had ever made him anything. Nothing had ever been given freely to him in his long years of struggle.

"I cannot accept it," he muttered.

"Oh, but you must," she said, pushing him back down. He sank down upon the cushion, and it felt...wonderful. "I must give twelve gifts and this is one of them, so you cannot return it. There! Comfortable?" she asked.

Benedick could only nod curtly as she leaned over him, golden hair falling over one shoulder to tickle his chest. Her eyes were bluer than a hillside stream, her smile brighter than the sun, and his body tightened, unnerved by her nearness as he had never been by any other female. Her scent enveloped him, heady and more vivid than his dream, and just when he thought he would gladly succumb to that memory, she straightened, moving away from him and on to the next prize she would award.

Benedick leaned back, shocked by his reactions to his child ward. His breath was too hurried, and he concentrated on slowing it deliberately, as he tried to absolve himself of any guilt. Naturally a pretty maid would have an effect on him. He was but a man, healthy despite his recent imprisonment and not yet in his grave, for all his weariness.

Did Noel not realize that, the little fool? Apparently not,

he noted with some disgruntlement. Any other female who
claimed to want marriage would be sidling up to him, ad-
vertising her charms as a means to get his agreement. But
instead of swinging her hips or batting her eyes, Noel took
him by the hand as if he were an elderly uncle and helped
him into his chair like some graybeard!

Faith, but he was not *that* old. Benedick frowned at the
thought. His mood was not improved when he saw Alard
present the girl with a circlet of greenery, which she
promptly set atop her hair. It made her look like some kind
of wood nymph or Christmas angel, and Benedick caught
his breath, enchanted by the sight of Noel turning slowly,
laughter curving her dainty mouth.

With a grunt, Benedick shook his head. Had the girl no
modesty that she displayed herself so shamelessly for
Alard? And hadn't he expressly forbidden his squire to
have dealings with her? Yet there they were, leaning close
and whispering together. Light haired, young and similar
in height, the two looked akin in more than rambunctious
spirit, and Benedick felt a strange sort of uneasiness deep
in his gut.

It did not escape his attention that Alard had already
dragged several maids beneath the mistletoe in his efforts
to gain the requisite twelve kisses. When it looked to Benedick as if Noel might be next, he half rose from his chair,
a growl rumbling in his chest.

Noel must have heard him for she lifted her head and
moved toward him. "You've already had kisses aplenty
this night, squire," she called over her shoulder. "But what
of your master?" she asked, a teasing glint in her eye.
Stepping nearer, she reached out and took Benedick's hand
once again, pulling him toward an archway where the mistletoe dangled.

Alard made some rowdy remark, and Benedick heard
other voices, raised in encouragement, but all he could
think of was the way she led him across the room. Who
else had she kissed this night? He had seen her with a

couple of the children, the cook and Hardwin. Did she think of her guardian as equally harmless?

Benedick grew more irritated with each step, a glance at Alard's grinning countenance doing nothing to improve his mood. He thought of the young, enthusiastic squire embracing her next, and his blood fairly boiled. No doubt Noel eagerly awaited a turn with the handsome youth—after doing her duty by his master.

Frowning, Benedick let her position him beneath the pagan greenery. Then she rose onto the tip of her toes and brushed her lips over his cheek in the most tepid of unions. Did the wench want a husband or a father? Benedick wondered angrily. Did she truly wish for a marriage or a sexless union in which she ran the household while he sat in his cushioned chair?

Outraged, Benedick put his hands on her shoulders and held her in place. Did she think to find more pleasure with a boy half his age? His mouth quirked in bitter humor. There were some things to be said of maturity and experience, and obviously, his young ward needed a lesson in the ways of men.

Those blue eyes looked up at him with curiosity, but Benedick refused to lose himself in them. This time, he swore it was little Noel who would be light-headed before he was through with her. Focusing instead upon her shoulders, Benedick rested his thumbs against the skin above her kirtle and stroked lightly. He felt her relax beneath his hands and smiled grimly.

"Be wary who you would tempt, child," Benedick warned as he lowered his head. Noel's lips parted in surprise, and he took his advantage. Opening his mouth over hers, he kissed her hard. One minute, he was putting her in her place, the next he was sinking into her sweetness. She smelled like holly and Noel and tasted of elderberry wine. Warm. Moist. Delicious.

And she answered him. As soon as his tongue gentled from its first punishing assault, Benedick felt her give way beneath him, her hands sliding up his chest to curl around

his neck. The soft touch of her fingers on the flesh beneath
his hair fired his blood, and he backed her against the stone
of the archway. Her firm breasts pushed into his chest, her
slender belly pressed against him, and lust, long dormant,
clamored to attention. But it was more than that. A sense
of rightness, of homecoming, that Benedick had felt only
in his night vision surrounded him, feeding his hunger for
her, swamping him with sensation until he felt as if he lived
the dream.

The fleeting thought was so startling that Benedick lifted
his head, easing away from her. Dazed in mind and body,
he glanced down at the woman in his arms. She sagged
back against the wall, staring up at him with those amazing
blue eyes, filled with an innocent desire that was nearly his
undoing. Indeed, he might have reached for her again had
he not gradually become aware of their surroundings, and
the stunned silence that had fallen over the hall.

Benedick might not be an expert on all of Noel's beloved
traditions, but he knew that kisses under the mistletoe were
supposed to be those of friendship, not pulse-pounding desire. He grimaced but refused to feel ashamed. Noel was
still leaning against the stones, her breasts rising and falling
rapidly, her garland of greenery hanging askew, her eyes
liquid and yearning. And from the looks of her, he should
be well satisfied, for she had obviously discovered that he
was no doddering ancient. Unfortunately, Benedick had
also learned something.

His ward was no child.

Noel stared after Benedick as he stalked off. She heard
his squire's whoop of enthusiasm and the delighted murmurs of those residents who still lingered in the hall at this
late hour, but she paid them no heed. Her eyes were fixed
firmly on her knight. Tall, lean and muscular, he strode
away with an easy grace, his long, hard thighs eating up
the distance to the stairs.

Flushing, Noel remembered the feel of that body against
hers, strong and hot and thrilling. She gulped a breath, clos-

ing her eyes to savor the taste of him on her lips. She had
been stealing kisses under the mistletoe for years, but never
had she felt anything like this bone-melting craving. His
mouth had been dark and delectable and full of mysteries.

Mysteries that only he could teach her.

And his touch! Noel shuddered as her shoulders begged
for more, her skin tingling from where he had stroked it.
Everything, from the moment he had put his hands on her,
had been a revelation that rocked her to the core.

"I think you just got your quota of kisses for the night."

Noel's eyes flew open at the sound of the squire's dry
comment. Glancing over to find him watching her with a
curious, assessing gaze, she blushed crimson.

The youth laughed. "Don't worry. I think Sir Villiers
was just as shaken as you were by that little tryst." He
turned to look after the disappearing figure and grinned.
"Perhaps the great knight has met his match, eh?"

Noel only shook her head. Benedick wanted no match
with her. He had made that abundantly clear this morning.
And yet...she needed to think.

"Excuse me, I believe I will retire now," she said, nodding toward Alard. The youth waved her off with a knowing smile that flustered her, but as she made her way to the
steps, her thoughts swiftly returned to Benedick.

The kiss changed everything.

Oh, she had been infatuated with the handsome knight
for years, but it had been the innocent infatuation of a child,
with little relation to the adult emotions that coursed
through her now.

To her young eyes, Benedick had been attractive and
alluring, a man who had earned her father's respect, yet
what had she really known about him or his life? She had
nursed that memory, along with the desire to make a home
with the only person she recalled fondly.

When Benedick returned, Noel still found him handsome
and appealing in a gruff sort of way. Anxious to keep the
life she had made for herself here, she had clung to her
hopes for an alliance. But, suddenly, Longstone took on a

lesser importance, as she realized that there was something else she wanted more.

Benedick.

Once closeted in her room, Noel fell upon the bed in a near swoon. Faith, her heart was still racing. Her body ached in places she had never been aware of before, and her mind was in a turmoil. Why had he kissed her so, when he professed not to want her? Was he even aware of his effect upon her?

Of course, Noel's feelings for her returning knight had been subtly changing all day. After his initial ill temper this morning, Benedick gradually had become more...approachable. Obviously he had never known a true Christmas celebration, and so he had to be prodded into taking part, but despite a few complaints, he seemed to enjoy himself.

Ignoring his grumbling, Noel had dragged him into the thick of things, and in doing so she discovered a few facets to Benedick Villiers. He might be demanding, but he gave others their due. He worked hard, doing more than his share, and he treated his people fairly. His surprise at their attention told Noel that he was unused to caring of any sort. Sadly she suspected that the man hidden inside was in desperate need of cheers and laughter and...love.

Every time she watched him, Noel's heart softened even more, and when their eyes met, she sensed again the kinship she had imagined at their first meeting. Their bitter exchange of yesterday was forgotten, and she began to feel that Benedick was an old friend.

Except that he didn't kiss like one.

Noel smiled dreamily. Marriage to Benedick took on a whole new appeal at the memory of his mouth on hers, his hard body, his hot hands, his low voice, deep and disturbing.... But a man like that might treat every maid to such pleasures! Noel shuddered at the thought. What if their embrace meant nothing to him? What if he held to his decree that she leave after Epiphany?

Noel sat up abruptly, filled with a new desperation. She

was certain now that Benedick was her destiny. She wanted to stay here forever, to make a home with him, to discover the secrets hidden behind his dark eyes and the mysteries that only he could teach her.

She wanted to spend the rest of her life loving him.

There was only one thing to do. Drawing a deep breath, Noel put her arms around her knees, hugging them to her, and closed her eyes tightly. With fierce concentration, she put all her hopes and dreams and yearning into one whispered plea.

"Let my Christmas wish be that Sir Benedick Villiers marry me before Twelfth Night is over."

Chapter Four

Benedick knew a peace he had never hoped to find. Home at last, he was surrounded by comfort and warmth—the comfort of Noel's gentle touch, the warmth of her heat. She was in his bed, and he reveled in the glide of her silken skin beneath his hands, the dreamy look in her liquid eyes. It was a look meant only for him, and Benedick gave her what she wanted. His mouth took hers in a kiss that tasted finer than wine and just as heady...

Abruptly coming awake, Benedick blinked up at the ceiling. He lay on his back in bed, alone, in the chill of morning. With a glance, he noted that the fire had burned down, and despite a blanket of thick fur, he shuddered. The heavy curtains he had pulled nearly closed the night before did little to keep out the drafts, for he felt cold to the bone.

Bereft.

Benedick frowned. He shouldn't have kissed her. Now he knew what delights awaited the husband he must choose for Noel, and he liked not the knowledge. But neither could he succumb to his own lustful urgings. Noel was too fresh and innocent to be burdened with his darkness. It was a bitter truth, but Benedick faced it as he had faced many such in his life.

He would find her a young man of property who had never fought a day in his life, someone as bright and sunny as herself to give her many children. And he would be rid of her and these plaguing dreams. In the meantime, he would do best to remember that Noel was his ward and behave accordingly. He ran a hand through his hair and counted.

Only ten more days.

When he went down to the hall, Alard trailing sleepily behind him, Benedick found it humming with activity. Servants were up early, rushing to and fro, and Noel was standing at the great doors, greeting a couple of peasants enthusiastically.

Benedick's eyes narrowed as he approached, for the men seemed overly friendly for his taste. He had always been well aware of the differences between a landless knight and a lady, and these two looked even poorer than he had once been—definitely too penurious to be standing so close and grinning so widely. He stepped to Noel's side, intent upon sending the beggars off, but the words died in his throat when she turned to him.

"Sir Villiers," she said in a breathless tone that reminded him all too well of their last meeting—under the mistletoe. Glowing, she gave him a smile that seemed to reach inside his chest and tug on his heart. Placing a hand over the offending organ, Benedick tried to ignore its jerky betrayal. Surely no woman had ever looked at him like that, as if he were the answer to her prayers.

But then, maybe he was, Benedick thought with a frown. Didn't she covet his keep as her own? Dropping his arm, he studied her more closely. Was she really so happy to see him?

Ignoring his sudden frown, Noel gestured to the two men Benedick had forgotten. "This is Drogo and Edgar, freemen who work their own plots, as well as yours," she said. And schooling his features to courtesy, Benedick nodded in greeting.

"We are glad to see you back, sir," Drogo said. "'Tis a good sign that you arrived for Christmas."

"Aye, and Noel gives us a celebration like no other," Edgar added with a sigh. "Surely it must rival the king's own!"

Let us hope not, Benedick thought, for he had heard of Edward's lavish holiday entertainments. As if sensing his disapproval, Noel herded the men past him, sending them on to where the trestle tables were already laid out.

"What do they here?" Benedick asked, inclining his head toward the departing twosome.

"'Tis Christmas," Noel replied "Your people are all invited to partake in the feast. They are each gifted with a loaf of bread and a candle, and may stay until our own burn low."

"'Tis an extravagance," Benedick muttered, for he saw no reason for such expense.

"But 'tis—"

"I know. I know. Tradition!" Benedick said, holding up a hand to halt her speech. As if untroubled by his scowl, Noel only laughed. Then another peasant arrived, and nothing would do but that she must introduce the fellow and his wife. The couple was followed by another and another until Benedick resigned himself to remaining by Noel's side, greeting the guests.

She knew them all by name, of course, and they treated her with a respect and affection that Benedick had never seen at any other castle. Noel had done her work well, it appeared, and not all of it involved the account books.

Benedick did not know whether to be pleased or dismayed. What would these people say when he sent their beloved mistress away? Had she turned not just the residents of the keep but of all his lands against him? The scent of battle filled his nostrils, and he wondered if he would ever find his rest.

After filling quickly, the hall was more crowded than Benedick had ever seen it when he and Noel took their seats at the high table. Glancing around, he saw poor men elbow to elbow with residents of the keep, and simple, worn clothing next to bright silks. The servants hurried to present the twelve courses, so that they might join in, and even Alard had been drafted to help. Benedick was glad to see it, for the youth seemed to have too much time for dallying and too little to keep him busy.

Although not prone to gluttony, Benedick found himself making up for the past month of poor fare. Pigeons, mustard, goose, nuts and frumenty were among those dishes that joined the requisite boar's head, and he sampled them more than once. The spiced wine with honey was delicious, and when he leaned back, relaxed and sated, Benedick wondered how it would taste on Noel's lips.

Alarmed by the thought, Benedick straightened and glanced at his ward. She was smiling happily as the wassailers wandered among the celebrants, singing their twelve wish songs for health and prosperity. Following her gaze, Benedick watched one of the women hold up a tree branch they then commanded to be fruitful.

Benedick grunted in disgust. What nonsense! Some orchards gave fruit while others withered, and some men thrived while others died, but their fates lay not upon the whim of a wassailer. His contempt turned to annoyance when the singers reached his chair.

"We wish a joyous Christmas to Sir Villiers, our returning knight!" they sang, much to the delight of the other listeners. Benedick frowned, disliking the attention.

"May he have money and wine aplenty throughout the new year, A sturdy keep, a fine table and lovely Noel to bring him cheer."

Benedick smiled grimly as shouts of approval erupted around him. When at last they died down and the singers moved on, he glared at his ward through narrowed eyes. Obviously she was not as embarrassed as he, for she was smiling happily at the tribute. No doubt, she had put them up to this, Benedick decided, ill pleased by the discovery. Did she think he would be swayed by the sentiments of others? All his life he had fought for his own on his own, without regard to anyone else's opinion.

"Although I must commend you on your rhyming skills, I care not for your sentiments," he said roughly.

Noel's eyes widened. "You think I am responsible for the wassail?" she asked.

"Aren't you?"

She laughed gaily. "Nay. My wishes are my own, sir knight."

Benedick lifted his brows at the reminder of her determination to marry him. Surely she did not mean to persist when he had refused her, as if he had no say in the matter? Slowly he set down his cup and regarded her. "And have you made your Christmas wish, Noel?" he asked, his voice rigid with contempt.

"As a matter of fact, I have," she said, slanting him a grin that on another woman would have seemed wicked. "Why? Are you nervous?"

Benedick's lips tightened at the taunt, but he leaned back in his chair. "Nay, for I hold not with wishing or wassailing," he replied, meeting her gaze directly. "They are naught but a lot of meaningless words without power or substance."

Her smile faltered for a moment before reforming into a gentler curve, and her gaze softened. "But the magic is all around you," she said, waving a hand to take in the hall, crowded to the very walls with people. "What other time of the year does the peasant sit down to a meal in the keep? When else are men more kindred? Brotherhood and love," she said breathlessly, "are everywhere."

Brotherhood! If there was such a thing, Benedick had never seen it. And love! Not only did his ward still think to wed him, but now she was prattling about that much-lauded but nonexistent emotion. If she thought he might swoon at her feet, she might as well beg for the moon.

"Tell me, Noel, just how many of these Christmas wishes of yours have come true?" he asked smugly.

"None."

"*None?*" Benedick blinked at her calm reply. He had expected her to hedge or to claim at least one victory he could argue as coincidental, but none? How could even this guileless innocent keep believing in the face of such failure? He shook his head. She was not just naive but hopelessly gullible. Had Benedick not seen the evidence of her cleverness in the account books, he would have thought her witless.

Watching her blithely nibbling on a piece of spiced apple, Benedick pondered her manner, for she seemed neither heartbroken nor discouraged by her past defeats. Abruptly he wondered what requests she had made that she should show no regret. Had she asked for frivolous trifles like golden slippers or impossible things, such as healing the sick? The thought sobered him, and for the first time, he questioned how her father had died.

"What is it you have wished for that has been denied you?" he asked gruffly.

Noel gave him a shocked look. "Why, nothing!" she exclaimed.

"Nothing?" Benedick felt more befuddled than ever, dizzy from her nearness and her nonsense. He shook his head again, this time to clear it, then fixed her with a hard, questioning gaze.

"Nothing," she repeated. "Although my mother spoke often of the magic of Christmas, she told me never to waste my wishes on silly things, like gifts or riches. After she died, I wanted to beg for her return, but Father said that would not be right," she added wistfully.

"And your father?" Benedick could not stop himself from asking, although he did not want to see her pain.

It was fleeting, flashing over her beautiful face and disappearing in an instant. "His death was swift, for he was thrown from his horse and crushed. And by then, I was old enough to know better than to think he could be revived." She smiled, with a somber expression that made her look wise beyond her years.

At least she had some sense, Benedick thought, while the silence lengthened between them. Just as he began to feel a twinge of guilt for taunting her about her fancies, she took a deep breath. "So I have never had occasion to make a wish. You see," she said, giving Benedick a brilliant smile, "I've been saving it up for something that really matters."

Benedict nearly flinched. Obviously the little idiot had invested all her childish hopes and dreams in a wedding that would never occur. Although he couldn't help but be flattered, he was more appalled than anything else. Not only would he be responsible for sending Noel from the home she enjoyed come Epiphany, but he would destroy her most precious illusion, as well.

Unable to face her bright smile, Benedick looked away. He told himself that sooner or later, Noel would have to accept the harsh realities of the world. Faith, but he had been only five when his father had put his mother aside for another, little older when he had left her to seek his fortune. He tensed even now at the memory of those bleak years, of finally coming home only to find his mother's grave, of nursing his hatred for a father who died before Benedick could challenge him. Long-buried feelings, old emotions he had thought tamed, washed over him, overshadowing the warmth and gaiety of the hall.

Swallowing a thickness in his throat, Benedick glanced at his ward, who was being dragged away by a group of youngsters tugging on her gown, all seeking her attention. He could hardly blame them, for Noel grinned and held out her hands as if she were one of them.

With a startling abruptness, Benedick realized that he wanted to protect this shining child-woman from all the grim truths of life. The discovery dismayed him, and he looked away, his eyes almost stinging from her brightness. Ignoring the tentative efforts at conversation of those around him, he sat in silence, alone among so many, glum and brooding. And yet, his gaze was irrevocably drawn back to Noel.

Lithe and graceful, she led the children in a game that involved plucking raisins from a flaming bowl. Obviously the older ones had played before, because they were quite adept at snatching the prize without burning themselves. The younger ones were not so lucky, so Noel often delved in for them. Despite his own weary cynicism, Benedick nearly flinched when he saw her jerk back her hand as if hurt.

Half out of his seat in an instant, he halted as she lifted one slender finger to her lips and drew it into her mouth. Between giggles and protests, she sucked on that digit until Benedick felt his body harden in response. Letting out a low shuddering breath, he imagined her tongue on his flesh just so, her moist warmth closing around him, milking his seed...

With a groan, Benedick shot to his feet and strode through the hall, past the revelers and out into the fresh air. Perhaps a turn around the keep's defenses would clear his head—and cool his blood. The wind caught at the heavy cloak he donned, chilling his hot urges swiftly, but walking along the wall and nodding to the occasional guard only made him aware of the stark loneliness of a soldier's life.

It reminded him of all those other Christmases when, isolated and cold, he had watched other men's borders and fought for other men's lands, taking shelter for the fortnight before going out to kill again. He blew out a breath, white in the afternoon air, and shuddered as he stared out into the distance. For a long time, he stood there, weighing his life and the choices he had made.

Finally, in an effort to shake off the strange mood, Benedick lifted a hand to touch the stones that belonged to him, reaching for the pride of ownership that had once meant so much. But now that he was here at last, he could no longer conjure the fierce proprietorship that had kept him going for the past few years. Restless, he moved on, as if searching for something he had lost without knowing it.

Although Benedick would be the first to deny it, he kept looking back toward the hall that burned brightly with lights and warmth and celebration. And Noel.

It was late when he returned, supper having come and gone, and the once-crowded room more thinly populated.

After all his uncommon study, Benedick felt oddly unsure as he stepped back into the hall that was his own, but had yet to feel like home. Without realizing it, he looked for Noel, and as if he had called aloud to her, she was beside him at once, her smile both welcoming and concerned.

"Where have you been? Your people have been asking for you, and I was worried," she said, his eyes guileless and clear as she searched his face. "Are you all right?"

Benedick opened his mouth, but nothing came out. In truth, he knew not how to answer her, for he was not certain himself. It seemed that no matter what course he took, she would be hurt by it. He stared down at her, trying to absorb her sweetness, her goodness, and for a moment their gazes locked, his anguished and hungry, hers gentle and knowing.

"Come," she said, putting a hand upon his arm. "You have had no supper and must keep your strength."

"Why? Are we in need of another Yule log?" Benedick asked in a caustic tone.

Noel only laughed. "You tease me, sir knight," she said. The comment gave him pause, and Benedick shook his head, for he had never bantered with a female. His life had been lived among the coarseness of soldiers, his business that of killing, relieved by brief forays into the halls of others. It bore no resemblance to the fine chivalry that Noel, no doubt, imagined.

"Now, take your seat," Noel said, and she joined him at the head of the table. Soon cheese and bread, pudding and wine had been placed before him, and Benedick leaned back in his chair. The warmth of the room seeped into his cold bones, and he relaxed, enjoying the festive air that surrounded him.

Although most of the peasants had left, some residents of the keep still celebrated, and their laughter was strangely cheering. The food was good, the company lively, and beside him, Noel sparkled. Gradually Benedick's strange mood lifted. A man might get used to such ease, he thought abruptly, before swiftly dismissing the notion.

He was too old to change.

Still he had a mind to enjoy the holiday while he could, and he smiled indulgently as some of the day's gifts and kisses were exchanged. Slanting a glance toward his ward, Benedick wondered how many Noel had received and from whom. He shifted uncomfortably as he considered watching her give twelve kisses to others each day until Epiphany.

Benedick's eyes narrowed as he saw his worthless squire pull a giggling maid beneath the mistletoe, and he fervently hoped that his ward limited her partners to the very young and the elderly. Something akin to jealousy stirred inside him and was promptly quelled. He refused to covet his ward. Nor would he teach her any more lessons.

"I have a gift for you," she said, rousing him from his increasingly morose thoughts.

"Nay," Benedick protested.

"Yea," she said, laughing. Her eyes glittered like the bluest of lakes, and Benedick was sorely tempted to dive in. Instead, he tore his gaze away, down to the object she placed before him on the table.

It was a book.

"Nay," he repeated, startled at the sight. "'Tis too expensive. As your guardian, I will not permit such lavish presents!" Benedick pushed it away.

Noel pushed it back. "'Twas my father's, and so, cost me nothing," she said, smiling gently. "And now you must accept it."

Despite his misgivings, Benedick reached out a hand to touch the small volume. He had never owned a book in his life, had struggled to learn to read when already a knight, desperate to improve his lot. His fingers stroked the dark binding and then closed around it, as warmth beyond that of the fire seeped deep down inside him. He, who had so few possessions beyond his own armor, now held both a keep and a book. For a moment, Benedick was not sure which was the most precious.

"Now come," Noel said, taking his other hand in her own.

"Cease your constant pulling on me!" Benedick grumbled, unwilling for her to see just how much her gift had touched him. "I am no toddler or graybeard to dance to your whims."

But Noel ignored his complaints as usual. Still gripping the book, Benedick let her drag him toward the archway, and then he stopped, warily eyeing her position beneath the mistletoe. Alarm surged through him as she tugged him closer until finally he stood only inches in front of her. He lifted the slender volume before him like a shield.

"I would have my kisses, sir knight," she said demurely, but Benedick was not fooled. Her bright eyes twinkled, and her luscious lips fairly twitched with mischief. What was she about? Had she not learned her lesson last night? And hadn't he learned not to touch her?

"You have already given me enough," Benedick said roughly. "Mayhap you should seek your kisses elsewhere." He turned to go, but her fingers still clung to his.

"I am afraid you have spoiled me," she said softly. The breathless words sparked through him, and Benedick swiveled slowly, thinking he had not heard her correctly.

She grinned, almost wickedly, and squeezed his hand. "I want all twelve from you," she said in the most provocative whisper he had ever heard.

Benedick stared at her in horror; yet, despite his dismay at her request, his gaze dropped to her lips...lips that tasted finer than wine...lips he had imagined stroking another part of him... Benedick blinked, disgusted with himself. He was a lecher. There was nothing more contemptuous than an older man preying on a young girl, as his own father had done. Had he become that cold-blooded?

Frowning, Benedick ignored the clamor of his body, and laying one hand on Noel's shoulder, he brushed his open mouth against her forehead in a kiss that, if not quite chaste, would not lead to anything more. He expected to feel nothing at that simple touch, but her scent enveloped him, and he drew in a deep, shuddering breath, closing his eyes as if to take her into himself.

"Noel! Do you have a kiss for me?" Benedick lifted his lids at the sound of Alard's voice. Although the functioning part of his brain told him that it would be wise to hand her over to his squire, his fingers on her shoulder tightened, preventing escape.

"Nay," Noel said, her gaze never leaving his. "I would have another from my knight."

There was something in the way she claimed him as her own that both touched and annoyed him. "I will not marry you," he said.

"But will you kiss me?" she asked, shamelessly entwining her arms around his neck. A wisp of her bright hair fell forward, and Benedick lifted a hand to brush it away from her cheek. Her skin was flawless and silken, but his attention was caught by the golden strand, and he rubbed it, shimmering and alive, between his fingers.

Time seemed to slow and stop, the hall around him quiet and still, as he looked down at her. In that moment, it seemed as if he had waited his entire life for this woman, for a salvation that existed just beyond his grasp. Tempted but wary, he refused to reach out for it, but in the end, he had no choice, for it was Noel who lifted herself on tiptoe and pressed her mouth to his.

The minute Benedick felt the touch of her lips, his blood surged, his thoughts swam and whatever had held him back was swept away in a flood of sensation. He knew only her sweetness, her softness, her light to his darkness. And he took it, stroking her tongue with his own, sucking her warmth into himself. His fist closed in her hair, and he groaned, seized with a pleasure so hot and deep that he could not deny it.

Only the book between them prevented him from fitting her curves to his hardness. Only a last vestige of rational thought prevented him from taking her on the floor of his keep, surging into her body and knowing, at last, the denouement of his dreams. And only the delighted shriek of a maid and Alard's brazen jostling for position beneath the mistletoe brought the madness to an end.

Breathing hard, Benedick rested his forehead against Noel's. His knuckles, still clutching the book, were pressed between her breasts, and he could feel the rapid pulsing of her heart. The discovery made him shudder, and Benedick knew he must release her before temptation again stole his wits. But even then, as the sights and sounds of his surroundings came rushing back with vivid clarity, Benedick did not want to let her go. He wanted to hold her, claiming her as his own, taking her into his bed—and his life—forever.

It was the discovery of that fierce and startling longing, wholly unexpected and totally unacceptable, that made Benedick finally push her away. Without looking back, he left her, seeking the haven of his chamber and a peace he knew he would never find.

Chapter Five

Benedick stood in front of the hearth, alternately craving and despising its heat. He needed to be cold. Cold and composed if he was to face the truth, and do so he must, no matter how much it disgusted him. Groaning, Benedick ran a hand through his hair and admitted the unthinkable to himself.

He lusted after his ward.

The dreams had come again last night, vague erotic visions of Noel beneath him, naked and sweet, filling him with warmth even as he filled her with his seed. Muttering a foul oath, Benedick slammed his fist against the stones. He had awakened this morning, bathed in his sweat, his body rigid and ready, only to grasp nothing but his blankets.

And, if the dreams weren't bad enough, he had only to recall the reality that had taken place under the mistletoe. Not once, but twice had he lost himself in the taste and feel of Noel, forgetting his position, his decisions and all else, like a randy fool.

Things were getting out of hand, of that he was certain. The lesson he had sought to teach her had gone awry. Instead of backing away from his embrace, Noel now pursued him with renewed fervor. Benedick flushed at the thought.

By faith, he was but a man, and flattered by her purpose, but he could not encourage her vain quest for marriage.

Although he wanted to protect her from the harsh truth, Benedick could only go so far without sacrificing them both to another, grimmer, reality. He knew it was better that she take the blow now than later, for each day she seemed to grow bolder and more determined.

The time had come to talk seriously with her. And Benedick could not do it in the hall, surrounded by the very essence of her, with the greenery, the mistletoe and the reminder of her Christmas wish everywhere. Nor did he care for the presence of others, especially Alard, with his perpetual smirk.

So he had ordered her to meet him here, in the great chamber. This morning, when the remnants of his dream drove him to urgency, it had seemed the only solution, for the old keep had no solar. But now, as Benedick glanced behind him, he noticed that the bed took up an inordinate amount of space, taunting him with the memories of his visions.

Swearing, he leaned his arm against the stones and laid his forehead against it. Rest and quiet. That is what he had sought here. Instead, he was plagued with a hall full of noisy celebrants during the day and sleepless nights fraught with phantoms. Perhaps he would never find surcease, Benedick thought sourly, because he so little deserved it.

"Benedick?"

Startled, Benedick raised his head to see his ward standing just inside the doorway. He had not heard her arrival, but that was not what struck him so forcefully. It was her use of his name, breathless and intimate upon her lips, that spread heat throughout his body. She had always called him "Sir Villiers" or "sir knight" before, and the gesture of familiarity echoed his dreams like a haunting refrain. He tensed, as if to battle, though he was not sure whether the war was against her or within himself.

As he watched, Noel began to shut the door, but he stopped her with a sharp grunt. Already he regretted his choice of location for their meeting; he did not want to be tempted further. "Leave it, for I would not cloister you here. I only wanted some privacy in which to talk."

Her eyes were so blue and so full that Benedick nearly flinched at the sight. In them shone curiosity and sweetness and a gentleness such as he had never seen directed at himself. Faith, she was young and innocent!

Swearing, Benedick pushed off the wall. "I called you here to warn you that I will have no more displays like those under the mistletoe." He turned away as the images of her softness and heat assailed him. Stepping toward the window, he leaned into the chill to cool his unwanted ardor.

"As your guardian, it is my responsibility to find you a husband, and I do not want you going soiled to him. If you must have twelve kisses because of some ridiculous tradition, then limit yourself to the children or Hardwin." *Anyone too young or old to respond*, Benedick added silently.

"But—"

Benedick held up a hand, halting her protest. "I take full responsibility for my part in…things," he said awkwardly. "However, these kisses are to be those of friendship, brief and chaste. Therefore, you will not seek them from me or any other man."

"But I want to kiss you," Noel replied in that breathless voice that tightened his body. "And it will not bother my husband, for it is you I will marry."

"No." It was a harsh exhalation, sharp and painful, as he turned on her. "This foolishness of Christmas wishes must cease," he warned through gritted teeth.

Far from being frightened, Noel did not even look perturbed by his decree. "'Tis my wish to do with as I will," she said with a smile. "You may be master of this keep, but you have no sway over the season's magic."

"Magic!" Benedick swore again and stepped toward the hearth. For a long moment, he stared into the fire, seeing ghosts in the wavering flames and blood in the red embers. "I am old and tired, Noel," he said finally, "and not a fit husband for you." Lost in thought, Benedick was not sure what he expected, but certainly not her light trill of laughter.

"I would hardly call six and twenty ready for the grave," she replied. "And you seemed lively enough last night."

Benedick shuddered as her words reached out and caressed him, her voice threaded with both shyness and seduction. He slanted her a hard, warning glance. "I am a man, as any other, so do not tempt me."

Her eyes widened in surprise, but it was not fear Benedick saw on her face, and he nearly groaned aloud at the desire, fresh and newly minted, that transformed her features. "Noel," he whispered roughly, turning back to the fire. "You are young, vibrant and good—and deserving of the same." Although Benedick had thought them often enough, the words stuck in his throat.

"Perhaps I could just share some of my own abundance," she replied softly. Seriously.

Benedick bit back an oath. "You little fool! You have no idea who I am or what I have done! I am a bastard born. I fought my way up from nothing, and once attached to a household, I got ahead by fighting harder, better, fiercer than those who trained with me. I have hired myself out to battle every since. Sometimes I can even remember their faces, these dead men. And for what were they murdered, an acre of dirt? A rich man's greed?" he muttered.

Without waiting for her reply, he continued on, forcing himself to speak plainly. "I don't know what you imagine a knight's world to be, but I have made my living…I earned this keep…by killing, Noel. That's what I do."

Finally, Benedick turned to face her, prepared for the retreat he expected, telling himself it was for the best. But Noel did not flinch. No horror or revulsion showed on her lovely features, just a somber aspect that he rarely saw, along with that confounded gentleness.

"Not anymore," she said softly.

Although the absolution she gave him threatened to undo him, Benedick schooled himself to reveal nothing. But when she stepped forward, he panicked. Somehow, he knew that if she touched him, he was lost and all his fine resolutions with him. Without looking at her, he moved past her to the door only to pause on the threshold.

"As your guardian, I am ordering you to obey me," he said, assuming the harsh tone he had often used with his men. Turning his head, he regarded her with a bleak coldness that no hearth could ease. "No more kisses, Noel. No more gifts," he said firmly.

"And no more wishes," he concluded.

Noel watched him go, hugging herself against the sudden chill. When she glanced around, searching for the source of the draft, she found none. And then she knew: it had emanated from her knight.

Benedick's prohibitions hung heavy in the air, air redolent with the smell of greenery, and Noel smiled shakily when she noticed that he had not torn down the branch she had placed over the door. Christmas magic. It seemed to flicker before her eyes, struggling to life, and Noel sighed wistfully. It had better be powerful this year to combat Benedick's stubborn refusals.

It could be worse, Noel told herself with her usual optimism. At least he had not found fault with her. He had not claimed that she was ugly or ill-mannered or repulsive, and she would not have believed him, if he had. Benedick might have contempt for her youth, but Noel was old enough to sense that he was attracted to her. His kisses had proved it.

Noel shivered, suddenly warm again, as she remembered the feel of his hard body pressed close, the gentle touch of his callused hand against her cheek, the fantastic pleasure of his mouth upon hers. And Benedick had been just as moved as she, for she had heard his rapid breathing and a stark groan that had made her shudder with delight.

The first kiss was so startling in its revelations that Noel had not been sure of his attachment, but she had come away more certain the second time. Smiling at her first, heady surge of feminine power, Noel brightened. Oh, she had been daring last night all right, but obviously she had pressed Benedick too far, too fast.

Now what?

Noel's smile faded when she realized that she could more easily change his opinion about her than about himself. For it was himself Benedick had maligned. Unfairly, Noel knew. No wonder this man seemed so different from the young warrior she had met. Benedick was tired, not in body but in spirit, and Noel knew that such wounds were less easily cured.

Yet she had no doubt that she could do it, if he let her. Even now, she ached to go after him, to put her arms around him and give him the comfort he so desperately needed. But not yet. He looked to be a man already pushed to his limits. She would have to give him some time, but that was something of which she possessed very little.

There were only eight days until Epiphany, and then both her time and her wish would run out.

Benedick tried to concentrate on the accounts in front of him, but he kept wondering where Noel was and what she was doing. Since she given him neither kisses nor gifts for the past few days, he should have been well pleased that she was finally obeying his dicta.

Only he wasn't.

In fact, he was like a man bedeviled. Befuddled by lack of sleep, he increasingly felt as if he were no longer in control of himself. Even as he counted the days until he would be free of her, Benedick sought her out, drinking in her presence like a thirsty peasant. She alternately enthralled and dismayed him until he knew not what to think—or to feel.

Now, poised over his books, he thought he could smell her perfume, the fresh, clean scent of her, and he drew in a deep, unsteady breath. Perhaps his mind, unused to such things as leisure time and plaguing dreams, had begun playing tricks on him.

"Benedick?"

At the sound of her voice calling his name, Benedick looked up, both relieved that she was not a figment of his imagination and dismayed by his body's swift reaction to the sight of her. His gaze rode up her gown, searching the opening of her fur cloak for the lemon silk below, then traveled up her slender throat to her lovely face. She was smiling, and a familiar warmth gathered in his chest and traveled outward as if Noel herself had gathered him close.

"Come now, put away those dry books, for 'tis a holiday. It snowed during the night, and now we are off to gambol and skate upon the pond," she said.

"What?" Blinking to clear his thoughts, Benedick could not believe he had heard her correctly, but then very little of what Noel said seemed to make sense to him.

"Come skating with us," she said, holding up a set of animal bones that had been fashioned into slender points. "The water is frozen over, the sky has cleared, and it is fine weather to be out and about. 'Tis tradition," she said. Her innocent eyes were wide and sparkling, as if she thoroughly enjoyed teasing him, and Benedick scowled, prepared to deny her when Alard appeared. Dressed for the cold weather and moving entirely too close to Noel, he obviously intended to go with her. Benedick realized he would have to assign the errant youth more duties, at least until Epiphany.

"Saint Norbert's knee! You'll never get Benedick to come with us," his squire said. "He doesn't know how to have any fun!"

Fun. Benedick snorted in contempt. His life had ever been one of struggle and battle, not holidays and their requisite foolishness. He had no time for such nonsense, and he opened his mouth to tell Alard so, but the sight of the two of them together stopped his pithy retort. He liked not the cozy friendship between them, especially after he had warned his squire away from his ward. Perhaps he would join them, if only to keep an eye on the insolent Alard.

"He knows how to play," Noel replied in a breathy tone that made Benedick glance at her sharply. Coming around the table, she took his hand, tugging on him, as usual. "He has been too busy being brave and valorous, but now that he is home to stay, he can enjoy himself."

Benedick refrained from pointing out that his idea of enjoyment was rest and warmth and quiet, not a deliberate trek into the cold. He let her pull him to his feet, his hand unaccountably loath to slip from hers, and lead him across the hall, but he drew the line at sliding around some pond like an unruly child.

"I will not skate," he said.

"Oh, very well, just come along then. It's too stuffy to remain inside on such a beautiful day!" Noel replied. Before he knew it, Alard had tossed him his cloak and disappeared out the doors, along with another youth.

Noel led him a different direction, into the garden, where the herbs Hardwin claimed she had planted lay covered with snow. A tall ash lifted its black branches into the sky, and bushes and benches were softened by their white covering.

"If you will not skate, then you must take the consequences," Benedick heard Noel say from behind him. Then suddenly he felt a smack upon his shoulder. He turned his head to see flakes of white falling from his cloak. Had she struck him?

"Come now, surely you know how to make snowballs?" she said. She had pulled on her gloves and was patting something between her hands. "Now, watch carefully," she instructed. When the lump was small and hard, she tossed it at the low stone wall.

She missed, her attempt landing in a clump of dry stalks of vegetation before the stones. Despite himself, Benedick laughed at her efforts. She turned to him, arms crossed in front of her, her toe tapping into the white around their feet. "I suppose you can do better?"

With a snort, Benedick reached down, palmed the snow and struck the center of the wall in one swift movement.

"Humph. Not bad for a beginner," she said. With a flash of even teeth, she smiled up at him, then reached down for another attempt. Benedick tried not to notice the way strands of gold escaped the hood of her cloak or the unconscious grace of her movements. Or the sweet curve of her behind when she bent.

Her second ball landed short of the first, and Benedick found himself wondering what the devil he was doing. He had come along ostensibly to watch Alard, who was nowhere in sight. "This is a pointless exercise," he said gruffly, jerking his attention away from the sway of her hips.

"It is not," she argued. "Can't it qualify as some sort of knightly practice?"

Benedick thought of his kind of practice—killing—and grimaced. "Yes, ofttimes in the thick of battle did we pelt the enemy with balls of snow," he muttered.

Noel's trilling laughter told him she was not offended by his sarcasm. "We'll need a big target," she said, looking about the small garden. "Turn around."

Automatically Benedick let her hands guide him, so that she stood behind him, then he jerked in surprise when he felt a hard whack on his back. Obviously she planned to use him as the "big target."

Slowly turning, he prepared to berate her for such childish nonsense, but she was giggling with delight, her blue eyes sparkling, her grin so bright that he was struck dumb. Enchanted, more likely. He scowled.

"Come now, sir knight! Can you do as well?" For a moment, all Benedick could do was survey the tempting sight she presented, all pink-cheeked and fresh, lifting her skirt to expose one slender, curved ankle before disappearing behind the large ash.

Annoyed at himself for gawking like a dim-witted lad at her antics, Benedick skimmed some snow off a bush and packed it tightly. The minute she stuck her head from behind the tree, he tossed it. Unfortunately, she, too, was armed, and he got it right in the chest.

Her aim was improving.

As Benedick stood there listening to the sound of her

laughter, he knew just how ridiculous it was to participate in her follies. He ought to quit now, regain his dwindling dignity as head of the household and return to his account books. His body was well past the age for games and his soul had never embraced frivolity, yet a flash of her blue eyes, daring him to play with her, made him linger.

She peeked out again, volleying another ball in his direction and Benedick took off after her, catching the edge of her cloak. She escaped with a whirl and a giggle and tossed snow into his hair. It felt good, cold and invigorating, and he lunged after her.

Grabbing only at air, Benedick heard himself laugh, and the discovery made him light-headed. And lighthearted. As he put up an arm to shield his face from a flying ball, he felt young again, as if she had infused him with an energy that gave him a different past and a new future. For once, Benedick forgot all else. He just wanted to reach out and seize the moment. Seize her...

Another miss, and he had her, his fingers closing around the soft fur of her cloak and reeling her in like a fish on a line. Grinning, he hefted a fistful of the chilly flakes in one hand, and watched her laughing protests as she tried to escape. Then, suddenly, she surprised him by falling backward as if in a swoon.

Leaning, Benedick caught her with one arm and stared into her delicate face, concerned. Then her lashes fluttered open. "I surrender," she teased with a smile. Disgusted, he dropped her, squealing, onto the soft snow, but she grabbed his cloak and pulled him down on top of her. Automatically Benedick put down his hands to take some of his weight as she chuckled beneath him. He was a heavy man and would not hurt her, even in jest.

Noel apparently had no such qualms, for she managed to tug strands of his long hair to drag his face closer. "Got you!" she cried delightedly. Although it pained him not that slight jerk went deeper than his scalp. Benedick felt as if something shifted deep inside him as he looked down at her. Her lashes glistened wetly, her eyes glittered with mis chief and her pink lips were parted in a soft smile. Flexing his elbows, he let his chest come to rest against hers, reveling in the gentle give of her breasts.

She did not look alarmed. Nor did she eye him with lascivious intent. Her clear gaze met his with a sweetness that made his throat ache, and somehow one of her gloved palms came to rest against his cheek. "Benedick," she whispered.

He wanted her. Not just her body, but Noel, every bit of her, until he possessed her light, her joy, her very soul. Pressing his sudden hardness into the juncture of her thighs, Benedick took her mouth with his own, and the ensuing heat threatened to melt the snow that surrounded them. It went deeper than the kiss and the alignment of their bodies to his very heart, as if it, too, had been covered in ice.

And Noel was skating on it.

Benedick felt her fingers curl into his hair, heard the tiny sound she made, and knew the heady wonder of pleasing her. He brushed his lips against her cheek and her moist lashes and licked away a snowflake that had settled on her brow. She shuddered beneath him.

"Benedick," she murmured, and he pressed his face against her white throat, seized with desire so strong that it made him weak, a need that surpassed the physical. Here, at last, was the haven he had so long been searching for, and he knew that if he would let her, Noel would welcome him home at last.

But he could not let her.

He was too old to change, too grim to romp in the snow, too coarse to give her what she deserved. The knowledge made Benedick lift his head and, with great force of will, he eased away from his ward. Below him, Noel blinked dreamily, her eyes drowsy with longing and gentleness and something else that he had never seen.

Benedick stared, and for one brief moment, he was tempted to believe in all of it: Christmas magic and wishes and even love, that most elusive of prizes. But he knew better. Rising to his feet, he pulled Noel with him and dusted off her cloak. Despite her protests, he sent her inside to dry, while he walked away, drinking in the fresh air in an effort to clear his mind.

He called for his mount to be readied and charged off across the white ground as if fleeing his own keep. And maybe he was. When he finally reined in the massive destrier, Benedick began to feel more in control of himself. This was a world he knew, of horses and hard riding, not tenderness.

Scowling, he paused to examine his behavior toward his ward, and found himself wanting. He ought to be discouraging her youthful fancies, not giving in to them and his own lecherous leanings. He was no better than his father!

Except it hadn't felt like that at all.

Benedick shook his head. Lust was a part of it, to be sure, but there was so much else that he did not even begin to understand. All his fine intentions and logical arguments faded away when he saw Noel, when he held her, and then...she became the beacon for a new world, shining and bright and beckoning.

Chapter Six

Benedick stood at the window, relishing the chill wind. The snow had melted, leaving sodden fields and patches of ice, and the white world in which he had frolicked with Noel, snatching a kiss in its pillowy softness, seemed as much of a dream as all the others.

And just as insubstantial.

Drawing in a deep breath, Benedick watched a lone soldier high on the wall. Not so long ago, that had been him, a young lad striving to be stronger, swifter, fiercer and more clever than all the others. And he had succeeded, all too well, growing impervious to cold, to weather, to feelings of any kind. He had killed not only others, but parts of himself. And now it was too late to call back those pieces that were missing.

"Reminiscing?"

Benedick started at the sound of Noel's voice, so close and oddly baiting. He turned his head toward her in question, but she looked the same as always, guileless and beautiful, if more somber than was her wont.

"Reminiscing?" he asked, lifting his brows.

"Yes," she said, with a nod toward the soldier. "You claim you want rest and ease, and yet you fight me every time I try to tempt you to it. You wrap your past around you like a cloak, clinging to it as if for protection."

"'Tis all I know," he said gruffly, swiveling his attention to the outside once more. The last thing he wanted now was another lesson in Noel's philosophy. Play and wishes were fine for her, with her angelic appearance and fairy ways, but he was more fit for grim reality.

"Nonsense. You can read and write and balance accounts. You can mete out justice fairly, and you are a leader of men. This is your keep, and you can see that its people thrive in the years to come. Look to the future, Benedick."

Her soft admonition irritated him. What did she know of anything, a pampered girl of seventeen summers? He had seen things, done things, that would make her quail. Aye, that would make a grown man weep!

"Go away," he said curtly. "Your prattle becomes tiresome." He stared stonily out into the bailey and wished her lilting voice and merry habits gone.

But Noel was never tractable. "I see," she said sharply as she stepped in front of him, blocking his view. Crossing her arms over her chest, she glared up at him, with a boldness that astonished him.

"Now let me make sure I understand. You spent half your life working to improve your lot in the only way possible, through the noble knighthood, and now you would spend the rest of your life atoning for it."

Benedick flushed with rage. Did the wench dare to mock him?

"Do you know what?" she demanded, tapping her slipper against the tiles as if she were the one rightfully indignant. "I think you want to suffer, as some kind of penance! But those men whose deaths are on your hands would not respect it. Only an honorable life, well lived, will serve their memories."

Benedick gaped at her, too outraged to speak.

"Embrace life, Benedick!" she said with gentle urgency, and she laid her slender fingers upon his arm as if to coax him. "If not with me then with another woman, but marry and fill the hall with your heirs and pass on to them all that you have struggled to gain—and all that you have learned.

as well. Give to your family and your people and yourself. You are a good man, Benedick—''

She paused suddenly, to study him intently, and he felt the light pressure of her fingers as they tightened upon him. "Why do you not know that?" she whispered. "Is it because of your father? Do you think that a bastard born cannot deserve what you have fought so hard to win?"

Benedick trembled in furious denial, his heart pounding and his breath catching at this small woman who dared speak to him as no one ever had before. The gentle understanding he glimpsed in her eyes only mortified him, and he grappled for words strong enough to extinguish it, to turn her and her worthless wishes away once and for all.

"You are a good man," she repeated softly. "And you have earned your rewards. Seize them with both hands before they are gone to dust."

She whirled away then, her pale fingers slipping from him, her hair flashing brightly behind her as she hurried from his side. Staring after her, speechless, Benedick was just as enraged by her sudden departure as by all the accusations she had thrown at him.

She was wrong! He was no monkish man to lock himself away, wasting his time in flagellation. She knew nothing of his torment; how could she judge him? His fingers closed into a fist, and he struck at the stones that lined the window.

He had come here seeking rest, and he would have found it, if not for her infernal interference. He could have no ease because of her and her ceaseless revelry, her countless traditions, her continual presence, teasing and tempting him. Lifting his arm to the stones that lined the window, Benedick rested his forehead against it and released a ragged breath. She was wrong, and he knew it.

But what if she wasn't?

Another day gone.

Benedick laid his head against the pillow, expecting a sense of relief, but it did not come. Lately he was not so eager to see the arrival of Epiphany, only two days hence, as he once had been.

Ever since Noel's outburst, Benedick had tried to ignore the questions she raised, but some of her accusations struck too close to the truth to be dismissed. He was forced to admit that the shame of his birth had long hung over him. He had worked and fought and struggled to prove himself, but to whom? His parents were dead. Perhaps it was time he took a long, hard look at his life.

Unfortunately, every time he did, he saw Noel.

No doubt, that was because she made such a nuisance of herself. Each time Benedick turned around, she was there, tugging on his hand, trying to get him to join in a child's game of Bee in the Middle or dragging him out to gift the birds with a wheat sheaf—another one of her Christmas traditions.

She had many of them, and as master of the keep, he was expected to participate in all of them. After a while, Benedick stopped arguing with her about it and suffered his "fun." Perhaps she was right, and he had denied himself for too long. It was a startling concept, for he had never known anyone who was truly content, but the more time he spent around Noel, the more he wondered if he was embracing grim reality a bit too fiercely.

Slowly he began to realize that a little celebration and revelry was not amiss, but wrapped up in his acceptance of Noel's philosophy was acceptance of Noel, for how could he find happiness on his own, without her direction?

And there was the rub.

For Noel was not his to hold, and in a few short days, she would be gone. In the meantime, Benedick had formed a rather uneasy truce with his ward. He was willing to participate in her ridiculous traditions, play assorted silly games and converse at length with sundry villeins. Indeed, he allowed Noel full reign over his household, just as long as he was not alone with her.

Although not the kind to admit to his own limitations, Benedick did not trust himself where his ward was con-

:erned. He could no longer deny his attraction to her, for
t went beyond physical desire to a deeper yearning to
which he refused to succumb.

Yet, as long as Benedick kept his distance, he could
avoid temptation and preserve his ward's honor. He could
maintain control of his body and his mind, he told himself
firmly, even in sleep. And so, resolutely he willed away
dreams of Noel even as he drifted into uneasy slumber.

All too soon, the visions came, and this time they were
different. Instead of lying abed with Noel, he was astride
his great destrier returning home from a long, enforced absence. Around him, the world was dark and vague, and he
was alone.

Eager to reach his keep, Benedick sent the horse to the
top of the rise that led to Longstone, only to find some
other castle, crumbling and cold in its stead. Confused, he
traveled onward to familiar hills and a castle that looked to
be his own, but when he entered, it was nothing but a
timbered shell. Swearing wildly, he spurred his mount,
thinking to escape this maze, if not the dream itself, but
soon he faced the same lands. Another keep loomed ahead,
shrouded in fog, yet Benedick kept his distance, wary, until
a woman rose out of the mist.

Noel.

Cloaked in blue as clear as her eyes, she was so beautiful
that Benedick's breath caught and held. Then she ran toward him, golden hair flowing behind her, and her smile
of welcome made his heart pound with joy. Sunlight suddenly streamed around them, and he dismounted. Hurrying
to greet her, he reached out to catch her up in his
arms...only to awaken with his hands full of blankets.

Tossing them aside with an oath, Benedick sat up and
rubbed his eyes as if to remove the last vestiges of his
dream. Of course, the meaning of this little nighttime drama
was painfully clear. In fact, if Noel had been a different
sort of female, Benedick might have suspected her of taint-
ng his food with some kind of potion. But Noel was far
too sweet to do evil. As well, he had been eating and drink-

ing the same as the other residents, yet he seemed to be the only one beset by these visions.

Alard, worthless cur that he was, snored loudly from his position before the door, as if to confirm Benedick's opinion. Leaning back against the pillows, Benedick frowned at the irony. After years of uncertain berths, he was now cradled in a soft bed in a spacious chamber with a bright hearth, but he was unable to enjoy it.

Because of the dreams.

They plagued him nightly. And whether of peace and comfort or lusty pleasures, they always centered around a phantom Noel and lingered during the day, bringing his thoughts ever back to her. If he didn't know better, Benedick would have wondered if something outside himself was affecting his mind.

A sudden draft rattled the shutters and swayed the curtains around him, making Benedick chill. Indeed, it was lucky he did not believe in such things, for, if so, he might even have blamed his increasing sleeplessness on Noel— and her Christmas wish.

In a narrow bed in her much smaller chamber, Noel also was awake. Undaunted by dreams, she nevertheless lay with her eyes wide-open, her thoughts too frantic for slumber. Finally she abandoned her efforts, sat up and drew her knees to her chest. Hugging them tightly, she turned her attention to Benedick. Wonderful, impossible Benedick.

Ever since she had confronted him about his past, she had sensed the turmoil in him. It seemed as if he wanted to let go and enjoy the fruits of his labors, but something was holding him back. Although there were fewer scowls and grumbles and more of those reluctant smiles of his, he still kept his distance.

Noel sighed. She sensed that she was on the right track, that eventually Benedick would come to appreciate her, if not care for her. She had caught him watching her, sometimes with a fierce look that implied possession, more often with a wistful longing that broke her heart. He wanted her and needed her, if only he would reach out and take her!

She was impatient, even as she knew that the liberation of her knight would be a gradual process. Under normal circumstances, she would bide her time, hoping to sway him with gentle persistence. Unfortunately, she could not afford the luxury of waiting, for time was running out. There were only two days left until Epiphany.

Desperate measures obviously were needed.

She had tried reasoning with him, tried to pamper him, tried to get him to enjoy life, and she had succeeded to some degree, but her only real achievements were underneath the mistletoe and out in the snow. Despite whatever misgivings he harbored, Benedick desired her, yet he had forbidden her to kiss him and cleverly avoided being alone with her. Indeed, the hall was usually so crowded with holiday revelers from both the castle and without that the only real privacy to be found was in the few bed chambers.

Noel went very still at the thought. From what she had seen, Benedick was an early riser, eager to get on with his day, so the only time she could be assured of finding him in his den was late at night. When he was sleeping. In bed. Naked.

Noel swallowed hard. She was not so naive as to compare an embrace beneath the mistletoe to a visit to the great chamber. She knew very well that she had better be prepared to indulge in more than just kisses when she sought out Benedick's bed. If he didn't throw her out on her ear immediately, he would make love to her, and there would be no turning back.

Noel shivered. She ought to be shocked by the train of her own thoughts, but instead she felt a flood of tingly warmth. Pleasure, anticipation. A wealth of emotions begging to be set free by his touch. Benedick seemed so often to deride her innocence that perhaps seduction would prove she was not too young, too inexperienced to please him.

Noel caught her breath as she let herself consider such a course: Benedick's initial resistance, followed by his rough, demanding passion. Noel imagined touching his body, melting into the hard, hot heat of him, and her decision was made as swiftly as the images that flashed before her.

Dizzy with desire, she forced herself to plan carefully. She would have to divert Alard, who lay in front of his master's door. No elaborate plot was necessary, for she need only ply him with too much wine and he would sleep like a rock. Noel smiled slowly. Some wine might be in order for Benedick, too, to ease her way past his formidable defenses.

But once there, she had no doubt that her knight would welcome her into his bed. And his arms.

Benedick scowled as he watched Noel call for more of the strong wine. There seemed to be a lot of it flowing during the small supper and afterward. Alard was already laughing too loudly from his seat on the bench against the wall, where he was trying to entice a village maiden onto his lap.

Benedick groaned. What was his ward up to? Although her time here had nearly run out, she continued to hold herself with grace and beauty and an abundance of good spirits. Until today.

Although taut as a bowstring himself, Benedick had begun to notice a tenseness about her this afternoon that seemed to grow as the evening wore on. She kept darting quick, wide-eyed glances in his direction as if agitated by the very look of him. He frowned when her gaze slid away and color stole up her cheeks.

What was she up to? He was accustomed to her ploys. Sometimes, despite his warning, she tried to tease him under the mistletoe or drag him on a private stroll, but he would have none of it. Try as he might to ignore it, he felt a twinge of guilt about her banishment that made him all too happy to accede to her wishes for now. Yet the niggling doubt about his decision did not extend to pleasing her in private.

Leaning back in his chair, Benedick closed his eyes against the sweet, tempting sight of her, and acknowledged his own weariness. He was tired of fighting this attraction, tired of clinging to a life that had never given him satisfaction, and just plain tired. Last night, after the strange dream, he had stayed awake till nearly dawn. And now Noel was plying him with drink that was making him even more drowsy.

"More wine?"

The sound of her voice echoing his thoughts made Benedick blink. His lashes fluttered open to see her pushing another cup toward him while nervously tugging on a lock of her hair. She avoided his gaze in a way that was wholly unlike her, and his eyes narrowed. Was she trying to get him drunk?

Benedick straightened as the suspicion shot through him. The whole situation reeked of one of Noel's schemes, but why? Did she think to drag him insensate before the priest? The old man knew better than to marry them when Benedick was in his cups. What, then? Benedick watched her dart a swift glance at him and studied her. Her blue eyes glittered too brightly and her face was flushed as if she, too, had consumed too much, but he knew that she had not. When she passed him the wine with fingers that trembled almost imperceptibly, suddenly he knew.

She was going to try to seduce him.

Benedick's body rose enthusiastically to the idea, and he shifted in his seat, tugging at his braies beneath the table. He promptly quelled the niggling voice that told him to go along, wholeheartedly, with her scheme. For, if he did, he would surely end up married to her. And he didn't want that, did he? The answers didn't seem too clear anymore, and he ran a hand through his hair.

No matter, he told himself, for little Noel wouldn't have much success if she kept forcing wine upon him. He was not your typical drunk. He did not lose his inhibitions and dance upon the tables. Nor did he bark and growl and beg for a fight. He simply fell asleep, which ought to wreak havoc with dear Noel's plans.

As if suddenly noticing his rather vacant expression, she appeared at his shoulder. "You look tired. Let me help you up to your chamber."

Benedick wasn't tired enough to ignore the tension in her voice, and so he shook his head. "I'm going to sit by the fire," he muttered. Suddenly he didn't like the idea of sleeping through her seduction, especially when she might demand marriage in the morning anyway. Dragging his chair to the hearth, Benedick sat back and looked into the flames.

His will was weakening, he admitted with a disgruntled sigh. Just the thought of Noel coming to his room made him hard and hot. Lying with her in that great, soft bed would be more potent than any dream. Drowsy with drink, Benedick let the scene play out in his head. What would she wear? How would she act? Right now she looked as eager as a lamb to slaughter, and Benedick frowned. That's not what he wanted from her. What did he want? He wanted her gone, he told himself, but his resolve was fading. He wanted her...

Closing his eyes against the slow seep of desire, Benedick let himself drift upon a waking dream that dissolved into slumber. And soon, the visions he had tried so hard to escape claimed him at last.

This one was different, Benedick sensed that immediately. Instead of the usual warmth that permeated his being, he felt cold and distanced, an outsider, as he had been so much of his life. Blinking against the dimness of the world around him, he saw a hall that was strangely similar though different.

Greenery was everywhere, along with brightly colored swatches of cloth and glowing candelabras denoting the season, yet something was subtly altered. Around the high table gathered a group of people, and Benedick wanted to protest the crowding but could not find his voice. Moving closer, he saw that they were children of various ages, but why did they surround his seat? And why could he not see it?

In front of the table, a tall dark youth stood by a pretty girl with golden hair that seemed familiar, while two smaller children had their backs to him. Benedick saw another boy holding a baby, but the other side lay in shadow.

"Happy birthday, Mama!" they all shouted, and a woman rose from behind them. With a start, Benedick recognized her at once. It was Noel, only older. Still beautiful and graceful, but mature and womanly wise, she smiled and laughed so gaily that he wanted to go to her.

Instead, he remained silently rooted to his spot, while she moved among the children, drawing them to her with a loving gentleness that startled him until he realized they must be her own offspring. But how? And then she turned, a special smile reserved for someone seated in the shadows...in his chair!

Her husband.

Rage swept through Benedick as he tried to see man hidden there. *Come out of the darkness, you coward, for I would know you!* he shouted, though no one heeded him. His hand went to the hilt of his sword even as he knew that he could not kill the father of Noel's children. Their children. Beautiful and laughing, they filled the hall with life.

Jealousy consumed him, sharp and stinging, and he shouted for an answer. *Identify yourself!* When none replied, he turned to Noel. Her eyes sparkled with happiness, yet she seemed to know him not. *Who is he?* Benedick demanded, reaching out to force her response.

"Wake up," she said.

Benedick blinked. "Who is he?" he demanded as she knelt before him. Grabbing her shoulders in a savage grip, he leaned close, frantic to learn the truth. "Who is your husband?"

She looked startled. "Why, you are, of course." For a long moment, Benedick wasn't sure if he was still dreaming or if the dream had become reality. Then she smiled, her lips curving so near to his own that he nearly claimed them and her, too. Dazed by the powerful vision, he felt like weeping for the want of her, for the want of...everything.

"If I can convince you, that is," Noel said. "Now, come up to your chamber. You were asleep in the chair."

Shaken more than he cared to admit, Benedick focused on her voice, her face, until instead of the woman of his dream, he saw Noel, her eyes bright with intent.

His chamber.

"No," Benedick said unsteadily, as the present came flooding back, and with it, Noel's heady plan to seduce him. "I think I'll sit up here tonight."

"Here! Why?" she asked, obviously flustered. But her dismay only made Benedick more determined. She was young, beautiful, a virgin, and he knew that his drowsiness would disappear if he found her in his bed.

"'Tis tradition," he muttered through gritted teeth. She was positioned between his spread legs and the thought of her bending her head forward and that golden hair flowing over him like silk made him painfully hard. Along with the knowledge that she wanted him.

Obviously she wanted something—either him, the keep or marriage—enough to offer herself up for it. But hers was a gift he could not accept. Although his body throbbed with frustration, Benedick was not so base as to take a young girl of good birth he had no intention of wedding.

Unlike his father.

The thought brought Benedick to his feet, and he drew her up with him. "Go on, Noel. 'Tis late, and you must seek your rest."

Her eyes were as wide and blue as the ends of the earth must be and better than any dream. "But I—"

Benedick shook his head, even though his blood thundered and heated. "Catherine," he called over his shoulder to one of her attendants. "See Noel to her chamber and make sure that none disturb her sleep."

When the handmaiden drew her away, Benedick sank back into his chair and stared into the flames. Gradually the hall quieted down, the servants made their beds in the corners and he heard the soft sounds of their retirement. At his nod, Alard extinguished the last of the candelabras and lay down on a bench nearby. For once, the youth did not pester him with annoying queries or comments, and Benedick was grateful for it.

Even in the dim light of the hearth, where the Yule log still burned, Benedick could see the greenery everywhere, and he could smell the pungent odors of spices and boughs and berries, but without Noel's presence the place lost its festive air. It became only a room, dark and bleak and full of nothing.

Benedick sucked in a ragged breath as the memory of his vision returned. He felt a sudden tightening in his chest when he considered the choices it had offered him. Long into the night, well past the time when all around him slept, did he sit there, contemplating his past, his present and his future.

And he realized that he could lock himself away at Longstone with his scars and his memories, or he could become the man in the dream. He could be Noel's husband and the father of those children and embrace life with all the vigor he had once thought lost in battle.

And for one long moment, still in the darkness, he nearly wished for it to be so.

Chapter Seven

Noel stumbled to her chamber, bewildered and off balance. All day she had summoned her courage, expecting to be bedded this night. Instead, it seemed she had been oddly rebuked by the man she had intended to seduce. Had she gotten Benedick *too* drunk? Noel knew little of wine's effects, for her father had been a temperate man. And what was all that shouting about her husband?

"Are you all right, Mistress Noel?" Catherine asked. "You look pale. Here, sit down."

"I'm fine," Noel answered. Sinking onto the edge of her narrow bed, she was vividly reminded that this was not where she had expected to sleep. The knowledge made her breath catch on a sob, and she cleared her throat, pushing aside her tumultuous emotions, at least until Catherine was gone.

"Let me help you undress," the girl said, and Noel nodded. The daughter of her father's old steward, Catherine had been brought up in Noel's household after the man died. She was barely fifteen, but responsible beyond her years, and Noel had gladly brought her along to Longstone. Lately she had noticed the maid's eyes lingering on Benedick's playful squire, and she hoped that Alard did not break Catherine's young heart.

The thought swiftly brought her back to her own prob

lems, and Noel shuddered as Catherine tucked her into her own bed. Alone. "I will bring a pallet in here beside you," the girl said, studying her anxiously.

"No! You go on to sleep. I will be fine."

"But Sir Villiers told me to make sure none disturbed you," Catherine said, obviously torn between her duties. "Perhaps I will put a stool outside your door and sit for a while."

"Very well, but I would have you get a good night's rest, for tomorrow is…another day of celebration," Noel said, her voice breaking.

"Are you sure you are well?" Catherine asked.

"Yes. Go on now," Noel urged. Closing her eyes, she waited until she heard the door shut, and then she turned her face into the pillow, but she did not weep, for fear Catherine would hear.

Finally Noel sat up, hugging her knees in the darkness and fighting back tears of frustration and bewilderment. Her scheme to seduce Benedick had gone strangely awry, and now she had but one day remaining before Epiphany. One day in which to work some sort of miracle, or else…

Her wish was not going to come true.

Stifling a sob, Noel told herself that it was time to face the truth. She had gambled her future and lost. Maybe Benedick was right, and she was a fool for believing in wishes. Maybe her mother was wrong, and there was no such thing as Christmas magic. The whole season might well be a sham, a jape in which people played at kindness in order to revel and feast.

Immediately Noel was seized by guilt for such thoughts. They rang of disrespect for her mother, if not blasphemy. And her entire being rebelled against such a calloused view of the world. Determinedly she clung to her vision of a holiday filled with goodwill toward men and miracles beyond the ken of mere mortals, for if she couldn't believe in Christmas, then, surely, there was nothing to believe in. But if wishes were real, then why had hers gone so terribly amiss?

Perhaps she had only herself to blame, Noel mused. Instead of asking for something like health or contentment, she had been selfish—and she had involved someone else. Had she really the right to decide Benedick's fate for the benefit of her own?

Wiping away a tear, Noel realized that she had no business taking over Benedick's life. It was one thing to wish her own happiness, another to foist her hopes upon him. In her own defense, she thought that he needed her, but she could not be sure. She knew only that he wanted her.

Noel's lips curved into a shaky smile as she recalled that even tonight when he sent her away she had felt the pull between them and seen the fierce longing in his eyes before he shuttered them. His behavior had been so odd that she wondered if he knew somehow what she was planning and refused her, not because of a lack of desire, but because he guessed her game. And did not want to marry her.

Ashamed of her scheming, Noel flushed. Perhaps Christmas wishes only went so far and hers had butted up against Benedick's implacable will. If so, who was she to try to overcome it? The question made her pause and reconsider her objectives.

Finally Noel drew in a deep breath and made the most difficult decision of her life. Sitting there in the dark silence of the night, she resolved to take back her wish. She would enjoy what little time she had left but look for no miracle to extend her stay. And then, she would leave on Epiphany and not look back.

And she would do so, knowing that her heart would remain here at Longstone forever with the knight she loved.

The holiday celebrations were slowly coming to end, and although Benedick knew he ought to be grateful, he felt a stinging, wistful regret. Despite his initial misgivings, he had come to enjoy the so-called traditions of the season. He relished the twelve dishes at supper, even though they were becoming less elaborate, for he knew that all too soon the winter stores would dwindle in the long wait for spring.

And afterward he waited along with the rest of the keep residents to see what new revelry Noel had planned for the evening. As he looked around the benches that lined the walls, Benedick realized that sometime since his return, he had begun to think of these men and women as his people, to take a certain pleasure in their smiles and their happiness. Having known no ties, except perhaps to his former squire, Benedick found it strange that old Hardwin, the servants and the others living here had begun to mean something to him.

Especially Noel.

Benedick watched her now as she brought out rolls of parchment. Considering that tomorrow was Epiphany, she seemed surprisingly serene, but he sensed that she was ever graceful and gracious, even in defeat. At least she was not pouring wine down his throat as she had the night before. He wondered if she had abandoned her plan to seduce him.

Too bad.

Heat flooded his loins at the thought, and Benedick shifted in his seat, frowning. He told himself that he was glad that Noel's stay was nearly ended, that he would be well rid of her and that her departure was what he wanted. But it wasn't true, and he knew it.

He wanted her.

Benedick had never believed in fate, but yesterday's strange dream disturbed him. It haunted him still, for fight it as he might, he knew a longing to be the man in the vision.

Noel's husband.

For the first time in his life, Benedick yearned for something that could not be won by might or wealth, something that would not increase his coffers or his prestige. Despite all his previous vows to the contrary, he wanted to take Noel as his wife. But his desires were tempered by uneasiness and a suspicion that he would be doing her a disservice.

Although Noel seemed convinced of his inherent goodness, Benedick was not so certain. He sought to put the

past behind him, but it was a part of him, and he couldn't
help feeling that Noel deserved better than a battle-weary
knight. And so he was determined to deny himself for her
sake and tried to feel the better for it.

So far he wasn't succeeding very well.

Startled from his somber thoughts by Noel's lilting voice,
he glanced up to find her leaning close. Too close. "Benedick, you must play, too," she said. *Oh, what he would
love to play with her....* Straightening in his seat, Benedick
dutifully took the piece of parchment she handed him as a
lively group gathered around the table to share the ink she
set out.

"Now you must pick someone in the keep and write
down his—or her—fortune," Noel instructed with a mischievous smile. "Then tie it with a ribbon when you are
done."

"Fortune?" Benedick asked dubiously.

"Yes, of course. As the new year approaches, we all
wish to know what it holds for us. And so we make predictions about upcoming events—and each other. 'Tis—"

Benedick held up his hand. "I know. I know. Tradition,"
he muttered, but he wasn't annoyed as he once would have
been by the admission. Instead, when Noel laughed gaily
at his surly response, he felt the same sort of warmth he
had known only in his dreams. It was as if he and Noel
were bound by more than a few days together. They bantered readily despite the tension that sometimes flared between them, and Benedick realized that he was at ease in
her presence as he had never been with anyone else. It felt
good. Familiar. Like the home he had never known.

Frowning at his wayward thoughts, Benedick snapped up
his parchment and predicted much hard work in the months
ahead for a certain squire who had enjoyed his holiday all
too well. Then he sat back and waited for the others to
finish. Some wrote laboriously, some lightly, and Benedick
noted Alard's cocky grin with misgivings. He hoped what
the squire had written was not too ribald for Noel's ears.

As Benedick watched, Noel gathered up the rolls and

distributed them once again. When she leaned over to present him a fat one tied with scarlet ribbon, he studied her intently. Although she appeared to hand them out randomly, he wondered warily if she had set aside a special prediction for him. Shifting uneasily, he was not so sure whether he should have joined in this particular game.

The first few fortunes were tame enough: a rich harvest, a fat purse and a handsome stranger were vague enough to please those who read them aloud. Alard scoffed at his, and Hardwin greeted the eerily soothfast prophecy of fewer duties ahead with relief. But when it was Noel's turn, Benedick glanced at her sharply. Yesterday's dream clung to him, its own predictions all too vivid for his liking, and he knew a sudden urge to rip the document from her hands and toss it into the fire.

Smiling, Noel released the ribbon, unrolled the parchment and began to recite. "You shall marry a man, brave and true, who loves no other as well as you—and present him with a healthy babe before the year is through!"

Beaming at the announcement, Noel looked directly at Benedick as if daring him to dispute it, but he could not meet her gaze. Enmeshed in jealousy and doubt, he had to be nudged twice before picking up his own roll. He finally pulled away the scarlet sash only to feel his heart betray him with a jerk when he recognized Noel's fine hand.

"'Your future is cloudy, for your path is forked,'" he read. *And so is your tongue,* Benedick was tempted to add. "'Choose wisely, and good fortune of home and hearth will be yours, the riches of the soul. But keep upon your present road and you will deny yourself all.'"

Benedick smiled in spite of himself at her feeble attempts to influence him. Did she think that he, a hardened warrior, would be swayed by a mere game? Slanting her a glance, Benedict saw blue eyes sparkling with mischief and hope, cheeks delicately flushed and lips twitching with mirth. She teased him still.

And in that moment, his heart, ever the defector, bowed

in surrender, forcing him to admit just how much he loved her.

The revelation wasn't as startling as it should have been. Benedick wasn't struck dumb, hit by lightning or visited by angels. He simply looked at his ward and, in that instant, knew what had been coming upon him gradually all along. And it seemed as if everything, from the first time that he saw her, had led up to this moment. It was love—not affection or lust or familiarity—that moved him, and the knowledge burned as brightly as her infernal Yule log.

"But you knew that already," she said.

Startled by the words that so echoed his thoughts, Benedick lifted his brows in question.

"You knew that you have but one choice to make," Noel chided gently. Aye, but dare he?

Vaguely Benedick heard Alard beg for Christmas kisses, signaling the end of the game, and the others moved on, but he remained where he was, savoring the idea that he, a bastard and a killer, could know this most tender of sensations. The elusive peace of his dreams was suddenly within reach, and he wondered if this feeling, so intangible but so strong, would be enough for her.

Should he decide her future in his favor?

"Benedick." Noel's soft voice garnered his attention, and he watched her draw her chair closer to his own. Soon she faced him, her knees nearly touching his, and she leaned forward to take his hands. Not one, this time, but both, her pale, slender fingers light upon his larger, callused digits.

"I know that you forbade me to give you any more gifts," she began, and though Benedick tried to interrupt her, she continued on, determined. "But you cannot prevent this gift, for it has already been given, without your permission—or my own."

Puzzled, Benedick eyed her curiously, noting the slight tremor in her voice and the blush in her cheeks. "Last night, I had planned..." She faltered, her lashes fluttering as she dropped her gaze to their entwined hands, and Benedick felt heat surge through him.

"But when you…" She paused and took a deep breath before beginning again. "Suffice to say that last night I thought long and hard, and I realized that I had used my wish selfishly, that what I want and what I think is best for you might not be right. In truth, I am no soothsayer, and I can not ordain the future."

Benedick lifted his brows in question, bewildered, once more, by her speech.

She looked at him unswervingly. "Even though I still desire it," she admitted with a smile, "I am rescinding my Christmas wish."

Benedick blinked. Her *Christmas wish?* Was she serious? His gaze stole over her somber features and guileless eyes, and he knew the answer. To have such faith. Once he would have mocked it, but now Benedick found it as pure and bright as a star that gave light to a darkened world. For wasn't that what faith was all about, believing in the unbelievable?

Including love.

"I know that tomorrow is Epiphany, and I will hold to our agreement, but I would have you know that you hold my heart in your keeping. 'Tis my gift to you, and you cannot return it, even if you will," she said. Her smile wavered, and Benedick felt his own heart twist in response.

She bent her head, her voice low. "I have another gift for you, perhaps not of greater value, but one which you might treasure more."

At her breathy whisper, Benedick's hands jerked in her gentle grasp. Heat flooded his body, pounding through him, as he considered just what this present might be. *Oh, Noel, you have no idea what I treasure,* he thought.

Although Benedick felt her fingers tremble, she lifted her face to gaze at him directly, her eyes bright and clear. And he knew. They both knew what she was offering. She would give him her body, without bargain or demand, at the urging of her heart, if he would accept it.

He ought to refuse her, of course. She was gently bred, and had no business crawling into his bed. He should wait until they were married, at least, Benedick told himself, but he was hard and throbbing for want of her. And he was tired of waiting. After days of watching her, desiring her, loving her, he did not have the will to refuse her.

Releasing her hands, Benedick rose shakily from his chair. "I will retire now," he said, his breath swift and shallow as he saw the blush rise in her cheeks. "Alard," he called. "Since your holiday is nearly over, I free you from your duty to attend me this night. Sleep here by the warmth of the hearth, or find some other bed, if you wish."

Alard shot him a look, fraught with significance, that Benedick ignored. Keeping a tight rein on his taut body, he turned and made his way up to the great chamber, wondering if little Noel would dare to follow.

Once there, he blessed her for turning the room into a warm, inviting, refuge worthy of her presence. The hearth burned brightly, coloring the sunny walls with a golden glow, and the expensive carpet was soft beneath his feet. Stripping swiftly, Benedick pulled the bed curtains partially open and climbed in, leaning back against the pillows as anticipation roared in his veins.

Along with misgivings.

He shouldn't let her come to him, he thought again. He should tell her to go, Benedick vowed. But when his door opened, it felt so right to have her there—as if the dreams of a lifetime were real at last—and he could not deny her or himself.

Noel said nothing, but stepped inside and bolted the portal behind her. When she moved forward, he caught his breath at the sight of her by firelight, her golden hair loose and flowing. She was wrapped in a fur cloak, and as he watched, she pushed it aside and let it drop to the floor, revealing herself to his ardent gaze.

She was naked.

Benedick choked back a groan as his body jerked in response. She stood before him proudly, her pale skin glowing, her breasts high and rose tipped, her belly flat and her slender legs delightfully curved. Then, as if she had used up all her boldness with her daring display, she hurried to the bed and slipped under the covers, pulling them clear up to her nose.

Benedick swallowed a laugh as he looked down at her visible features, shadowy in the dimness of the partially curtained bed. Her eyes were closed, and she looked as if prepared to have a tooth drawn. Apparently her heart was eager to gift him her maidenhead, but the rest of her was not so enthusiastic.

He ought to send her away and wait until they were wed, Benedick told himself again, but he had her now, in his bed, and he was not about to let her go. Slowly he lifted the edge of the blanket and pulled it downward, revealing her dainty mouth and chin, her long throat and the pale curve of her breast in the near darkness. At her tiny waist, he halted and folded back the cover. Then he lightly touched her brow with one finger. Her eyes flew open, her gaze locking with his, and whatever she saw there made her shiver.

"Be not afraid, Noel," Benedick whispered, though the words came out more roughly than he would have liked.

"I am not, really. 'Tis just that I have heard it called a messy, painful business and I—"

"Nay," he said, stopping her lips with a finger. Breathing in her fragrance, mixed with greenery and Christmas scents, he smiled. "The magic is all around us."

Benedick saw her tension ease away as her mouth curved softly, and he traced it with his finger, shuddering when her tongue reached out to touch him. Holding himself in check, he trailed his finger over her cheek, along her neck, against her racing pulse, then over one silky shoulder and lower. His eyes followed the path, up her breast, rising with her rapid breaths, and slowly, gently, to the rose-hued peak.

"Benedick." Her breathless whisper undid him, and he moved over her, reveling in the feel of her hardened nipples against his chest. Burying one hand in her silken tresses,

he took her mouth in lush, rich kisses, and she met him
with delighted gasps and delicious strokes of her tongue.
He paused for breath, savoring the touch of their bodies,
the golden length of her hair, the beauty of her face, soft
with desire, and the look in the eyes that met his own.

And then he began again, with warm, wet, wondrous
kisses of awakening and discovery. He caressed her hair,
and put his lips to her throat, sending his tongue out to
taste her skin, smooth and flawless. He tempered his
strength, putting his weight on his elbows as he laved her
breast and her nipple, careful not to draw too hard as she
responded with innocent abandon.

Finally, aching for her, Benedick nudged her knees apart
and pressed his painful hardness against the center of her.
The moist welcome nearly unmanned him, and he sucked
in a harsh breath of restraint. Kissing her again, he took
himself in hand and rubbed against her, bathing himself in
her dewy heat until he could not bear it a moment longer.
Breaking the kiss, Benedick gasped against her throat and
positioned himself. He was sweating, rigid with the knowledge that this was Noel, and he must hurt her.

''I love you, Benedick,'' she whispered, and he lifted his
head. In the shadows, he met her gaze, clear, unflinching,
and with a low groan, he buried himself inside her in one
long, slow thrust. So consumed by sensation that he could
do nothing but savor it, Benedick closed his eyes, overwhelmed by it all. Pleasure. Heat. Noel.

He was home at last.

Her hips nudged his, and Benedick blinked as awareness
returned. Although his head felt thick and groggy, he tried
to sharpen his wits when he looked down at her. Virgin no
longer, she did not rebuke him for his roughness, but wore
a dreamy smile that made her appear as dazed as he felt.

'''Tis wondrous,'' she said, arching tentatively against
him.

''Wondrous,'' he echoed, grinning at her, and then he
moved, slow, sweeping thrusts that made her sigh with
delight. He lifted himself up, pushing forward, deep and

smooth, again and again and again until she cried out, her slender fingers clutching his arms. Her release fed his own, and it swept over him in waves, urgent and fierce and wrenching.

At last, he collapsed upon her, barely summoning the strength to roll onto his sweat-slickened back. Drawing her with him and smoothing her long locks away from her face, Benedick felt totally sated, utterly content. He had lived the dream, and the reality was better beyond imagining. Holding her close, inhaling her perfume and feeling the gentle beat of her heart, he felt overcome with some strange emotion.

Happiness.

Startled by the discovery, he laughed aloud. "There must be magic," he said, shaking his head in wonder as Noel smiled in agreement. "I do not deserve it," he admitted. Although unable to stop his answering grin, he knew no reason why he, of all men, had found such joy.

"Yes, you do," she answered softly.

"I do not deserve you," he asserted, even as his grip on her tightened. It was too late now, for he would never let her go, whether she willed it or no.

"Of course, you do," she said in a voice wise beyond her years. And Benedick was struck by her prescience.

"You knew it all along, didn't you?" he asked in amazement.

"What?"

"That I would marry you." He heard her swift intake of breath and felt her searching gaze.

"Will you?"

"Yes," he said simply.

Noel, as usual, surprised him. She neither gloated nor rejoiced, but eyed him intently. "Why?"

"Because I cannot live without you," Benedick answered, truthfully. "I love you, Noel."

Her slow smile warmed him clear down to his bones, and he knew a sudden, resurging need to possess her, to claim her as his own, now and forever. Gripping his arms, she lifted herself up to kiss him, her hair flowing around them, and Benedick felt himself stiffen inside her.

"You got your Christmas wish, after all," he said as he rolled her beneath him. *And so did I, though I knew it not.*

"Oh, no," Noel said, breathless. "My wish was that you marry me. You must have fallen in love with me all on your own."

Benedick grinned at her absurd reasoning. "No more Christmas wishes, then?" he whispered. Watching her face, he began to move, slowly and surely, and reveled in her response.

"For now," she said with a gasp. "But next year..."

Epilogue

Benedick breathed in the familiar scents of the season, greenery and berries and spices, and felt his heart lighten. There was something about Christmas that never failed to cheer him. As Noel often said, it was a time when men were more charitable toward their brothers, but to Benedick, the holiday meant so much more. The years lifted away, as if he were renewed like the infernal Yule log, which seemed to grow bigger every year.

Grinning at the thought, Benedick gazed lovingly at the scene around him, his hall bedecked for the celebration, his people busily preparing for this, the second day of the twelve days, and his children, all of them healthy and fine. Benedick drew in a deep breath at the sight of his sons and daughters gathered around the high table with sweets and gifts for his wife, whose birthday they were celebrating on this Christmas evening.

And then suddenly, his vision dimmed and he felt an eerie dizziness, as if he had seen in all before: Petronella holding the baby, Godard with his back to him, and Noel seated in the shadows. His heart pounded a frantic pace he had not known since his days on the battlefields, but a vague memory to him now, and he pushed aside some of the revelers in his haste to reach his chair, for fear that someone had taken his place.

It was empty.

Foolishness, Benedick thought as he ran a hand through his hair and grinned. Or was it? Slowly the dream came back to him, a vision from long ago in which he stood outside this family circle looking in, wishing that he could be here and hold this future in his hands.

And now he did.

He owed it all to Noel's Christmas wish, Benedick thought, and then shook his head at such a nonsensical notion. Obviously some of Noel's fancies had rubbed off on him over the years, he decided as he scooped up Gabby, who was lifting her arms to him impatiently. It was only natural, he told himself, for did he not indulge his wife inordinately?

"Kiss, Papa," Gabby demanded, and he complied, giving her a loud smack on the cheek that sent her into a fit of giggles. Then again, his wife also indulged him aplenty, he thought with a grin. Had she not given him all this? And made this keep a home, filling it with life and laughter and love.

"Make a wish," Benedick urged, his voice roughened by emotion, and he saw Noel's swift glance, her tender smile and the still-mischievous sparkle in her eye.

"Why?" Gabby piped up.

"You aren't going to wish for another baby, are you?" Petronella asked suspiciously.

Benedick eyed his wife's slender body. If she knew a child was on the way, she often requested a fat, healthy infant. But her belly was as flat as a girl's, so he didn't think a baby was in the offing, though not for lack of bedding. His innocent Noel had developed into a lusty wench, as eager for a romp as he, and just as content to lie afterward in his arms, that certain warmth surrounding them.

"Why?" Gabby said.

"No baby this year," Noel said. "This Christmas, I shall wish for something entirely different." Then she paused, drawing the moment out until she had everyone's attention. "I would ask for a happy, healthy new year for us all."

"Aw, that's not different," Godard complained.

"But it's what I want," Noel said, reaching out to hug the twins, who stood on either side of her.

"Happy Birthday, Mama," they all shouted then, accepting her hugs and kisses with various degrees of enthusiasm, depending up their ages. Godard, Benedick noted, was too much a man, but someday he would come to appreciate the more tender emotions, as his father had.

Over the general clamour, Gabby's voice rose high and shrill, ringing sharply in Benedick's ear. "Why wish?" she demanded. "Why wish?" They all looked to Noel, who smiled at Benedick, deferring the question to the head of the household as often was her wont.

"'Tis tradition," he replied, with a grin.

* * * * * *

Author Note

Since Christmas is my favorite time of the year, I especially enjoyed writing *A Wish for Noel*. Like Noel, much of my pleasure in the season comes from memories of my mother, who made the holiday so very special. Although the world seems to move faster now, I try to keep as many of her traditions as I can for my own children in the hope that they, too, will carry these memories with them always.

In transferring my love of Christmas to my characters, I was hampered by the discovery that many treasured customs were not around during the late thirteenth century, but medieval revelers still found many ways to celebrate—for a whopping twelve days. And some of our observances, such as kissing under the mistletoe, were just as popular in the time of knights and their ladies.

I am fascinated by those years, as well as the Regency, and enjoy using both periods as settings for my romances. Although the Regency lends itself more easily to romps like *The Vicar's Daughter*, I have fun with all of my books, including the upcoming *The de Burgh Bride*, due out in February. My eleventh historical, it is a sequel to my 1995 title *Taming The Wolf*, which was nominated for Best Medieval in *Romantic Times'* Reviewers' Choice Awards.

Taming The Wolf introduced the seven de Burgh brothers and left one of them with the onerous duty of marrying The

Fitzhugh, the daughter of their enemy and infamous in her own right. I hope those who have been waiting to find out which brother weds the notorious heiress will be pleased with *The de Burgh Bride.*

As always, I'm happy to hear from readers at the following address. An SASE for reply is appreciated: Deborah Simmons, P.O. Box 274, Ontario, Ohio, 44862.

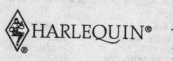

Harlequin® Historical!

Coming in December
from Harlequin Historical

A Warrior's Bride

**Award-winning author Margaret Moore
creates another exciting story
set in medieval times!**

A WARRIOR'S BRIDE (ISBN 28995-2)
available wherever Harlequin Historicals are sold.

Can the scholarly
Geoffrey de Burgh tame
the "wicked" Lady Elene,
who must become his wife?

Find out in Deborah Simmons's
terrific new medieval novel

Coming in January
to your favorite paperback book outlet.

The deBurgh Bride

THE deBURGH BRIDE (ISBN 28999-5)

Indiscreet

Camilla Ferrand wants everyone, especially her dying grandfather, to stop worrying about her. So she tells them that she is engaged to be married. But with no future husband in sight, it's going to be difficult to keep up the pretense. Then she meets the very handsome and mysterious Benedict Ellsworth who generously offers to accompany Camilla to her family's estate—as her most devoted fiancé.

But at what cost does this *generosity* come?

From the bestselling author of *Impulse*

Available in November 1997
at your favorite retail outlet.

Candace Camp also writes for Silhouette® as Kristen James

 MIRA The brightest star in women's fiction

MCCIND